Nether Regions

NAT BURNS

Bella
BOOKS
2015

Bella Books, Inc.
P.O. Box 10543
Tallahassee, FL 32302

First Bella Books Edition 2015

Editor: Medora MacDougall
Cover Designer: Linda Callaghan

ISBN: 978-1-59493-434-6

Other Bella Books by Nat Burns

Two Weeks in August
House of Cards
The Quality of Blue
Identity
The Book of Eleanor
Poison Flowers

Acknowledgements

I offer many thanks to my editor, Medora MacDougall. She enjoys my work almost as much as I do and makes the alterations a joy.

I need, also, to acknowledge the southern half of the United States. Your magic and mystery speak to me. Your hidden beauty and amazing people have inspired this book.

About the Author

Author Nat Burns is a writer and editor who now lives in Albuquerque, NM after retiring from a medical publishing career in Virginia. She is primarily a romance novelist but has been known to pen some sci-fi and horror from time to time under several pseudonyms. Nine novels have been published in the past three years and her work has appeared in numerous anthologies. Complete information and samples of her work can be found at www.natburns.com.

Dedication

This work is dedicated to my family, friends and faithful readers—those who always love me and support me as I travel absently through my fictional worlds.

CHAPTER ONE

Summer in Redstar, Alabama, usually settled in for a long, unwelcome stay. The people of the town regarded summer as an intruding mother-in-law dragging suitcases packed with heat and suffocating humidity. And though the sin of rudeness was employed by mid-July, there was no relief until her departure in mid-October.

Delora November was already harboring her own rude thoughts about the weather, even though by early May it had yet to sear the tiny leaves of the willow tree into brown ash. The thought of another long, humid summer of work and more work was almost more than she could tolerate. She wished she could leave, could shake the dust of this town off her discount store-brand athletic shoes. And she would, really, if only Louie would let go of her life.

The thought of Louie made nausea steal over her and she moved quickly from the back door into the relative gloom of Blossom's Diner. Ancient Johnny Pellen was telling the story about the black bear again and the comforting cadence of it soothed Delora's roiling stomach. She fetched herself a short glass of unsweetened iced tea from the urn and downed it fast, no sugar.

"Well, it weighed in at might near six hundred pounds and they say bears in that part of 'Bama never get that big," Johnny summed up.

The tourist who was listening to Johnny ramble merely shook the *USA Today* he was perusing and made polite noises of interest.

Delora wiped an already gleaming counter and let her eyes roam the diner. The Jacksons were still okay over in the smoking section. Marina had given them the bill and they were lingering over a meal-ending cigarette. They were regulars and would let Marina or Delora know if they needed anything else.

She was most concerned about the family of five that was occupying booth eight. The booth abutted one of the huge panes of glass that made up the front wall and she was worried about young Jimmy's airplane. It was a giant plastic jet airliner, and she was just waiting for one of the wings to take out the window. Jimmy was piloting in earnest too, even climbing onto the seat next to his bedraggled mother and banking the jet over her head and the head of his little sister as well.

The father, a quiet older man, was trying to study the menu while dealing with Jimmy's younger brother who was about eighteen months old and experiencing everything on the table. The father would read one sentence of the menu, grab little brother's hand, pry something from his clenched fingertips, then intone, "Jimmy, son, will you please sit down!" before returning to try the menu again.

"Want me to get them?" Marina asked, coming up close behind her.

"No, I already got them coffee. My table, I'll do it."

Concern sparked in Marina's dark eyes. "You don't look so good. Are you sick today?" Her accent was a pleasant blend of America and her native Mexico.

Delora took a minute to admire Marina's inky black hair and finely defined features. "Nope, I went outside for a minute and the heat got to me. I'm fine."

She fetched the tattered order book from her pocket, checked to make sure she had a pen, then moved with expert grace across the floor.

"So, have y'all had a chance to decide?" she asked, reaching to right the saltshaker the baby had tumbled. She absently tossed some of the spilled salt over her left shoulder and caught Jimmy's eye, giving him such a look that he parked the airliner and sat next to his sister, pretending to peer at the menu.

"I'll have two Bright-Eyes for the kids, with milk, and I'll have the Hearty Breakfast platter." The mother had probably been up since dawn. Traveling with a family this young couldn't be easy.

"And the baby?" She made a face at the toddler and he giggled and squirmed on his father's lap.

"The baby can just eat off my plate, if that's okay?"

"Sure. And you, sir?"

"I think I'll have the Hearty as well, but can I have sausage instead of the bacon?"

"Absolutely," Delora said as she gathered up the menus. "You'll like our sausage. It's local and fresh ground. Good and spicy."

Interpreting her comment as interest, the man transformed before her eyes, changing from a tired, beaten-down father into the young rapscallion he must have been before settling down and raising a trio of children.

"I do like it spicy. Just how spicy is this local grind?" he asked, his voice light and flirtatious.

Delora sighed. There was something too compelling about conquering new territory for most men. She had no doubt that Mr. Tired Face would step out on Mrs. Tired Face the first real opportunity offered him. She glanced at Mrs. Tired Face and saw her shuttered disgust at her husband's behavior. The kids all sensed the change in Daddy as well, for they had stilled to watch the exchange.

"Not too spicy, don't worry," she said as she left the table.

She tore off the middle copy of their order and placed it on the carousel for Tommy Jay, then started a run of fresh coffee. The Jacksons left, still talking animatedly, and Delora wondered how their marriage had lasted so long. Maybe it was because they had so much in common. Tyrone Jackson was a professor at the University of South Alabama over in Fairhope, and his wife, Sharell, was a librarian. It seemed they always had something interesting to talk about.

The fragrance of newly brewed coffee washed across her and she felt strangely at peace. Her marriage to Louie was over, in fact, if not in the Alabama legal system, and she felt good not having to analyze why it wasn't working anymore.

"It's done, honey," Marina said as she slid by carrying a new order of eggs for Johnny.

Surprised, Delora looked down and realized she'd stood idle while the whole carafe of coffee filled. She glanced to the kitchen access and saw the steaming plates awaiting her. Lifting the coffeepot, she hurried back to the Tired Face parents and refilled their cups, assuring them that their food would be right out. Her left hand deposited more plastic containers of creamer even as she hurried away. With speed born from years of practice, she filled small glasses with milk from the cooler and, with the glasses balanced in one hand and the two children's pancakes and sausage links in the other, raced them back to the booth. One more trip and she had the parents served and made sure they were settled with plenty of ketchup and warm syrup.

As she turned to return to the kitchen she heard a loud expletive and whirled to find that young Jimmy's jet airliner, in the hands of his sister, had veered and dumped milk across the table. Since the father was trying to rise to help the mother mop up the table, Delora automatically leaned to take the baby even as she murmured assurances that there was no harm done. The baby watched his parents clean up the milk, his hands sticky and clasped around a mottled mess of pancake. He continued to chew as Delora leaned with her free hand to pile the milk-soaked napkins into an empty coffee cup.

"It's okay," she assured the apologetic parents. "Accidents happen. Don't worry yourself about it."

The young girl huddled, as if ashamed, against the pocked vinyl of the booth seat. "It's all right, honey," Delora said directly to her. "We know you didn't mean to do it."

Delora shifted the baby against her hip and smiled when he presented a gap-toothed, pancake-filled grin. "You're a cutie, aren't you?" she teased, poking a finger into the baby's round tummy.

"Oh, here, I'll take him," the mother said, brushing her disarrayed hair from her forehead. "You're good with kids. How many do you have?"

Delora stiffened and quickly returned the child to his mother. "None. Nope. Just helped my mom with foster kids is all," she explained as she removed the overflowing coffee cup and emptied milk glass. "I'll get you a new cup of coffee."

Feeling their curious stares heating her back, Delora faced the concerned eyes of Marina in front of her. It was too much. She dumped the dishes into the cavernous kitchen sinks, waved apologetically to Marina and went out the back door still wearing her apron. She just needed a minute—just a minute or two—alone. With dismay she saw Hinchey Barlowe getting out of his pickup.

"Hey, hold up, slick." Hinchey caught up with Delora as she stepped into the late morning sunlight. "What's the matter?"

Delora wasn't crying, would not cry no matter what, but she was shook hard by what the woman had asked her. She was good with children, by golly, always had been, but now all that was over with. It was a fact best not thought about too much.

"Nothing. Nothing to worry about. How are you, Hinchey?"

Hinchey's pink face pinched with worry as he studied her. Delora knew how much Hinchey cared for her, and pangs of guilt nagged at her every time they were together. He was always a comfort, however, and she considered him a dear friend. His face relaxed and he took a deep breath before speaking.

"Okay. I'm okay, but there must have been something going on for you to have come out that way. What happened?"

"Nothing really. This family in there just got to be too much for me."

She chewed a thumbnail, her eyes looking along the long slope of I-65 leading out of town. "I just needed a minute."

He watched her a long while, until Delora started worrying about him noting the shadows beneath her eyes and her disgracefully chewed nails.

"I sure do worry about you sometimes, Delora."

She smiled and raised her eyes to look at him. "I worry about me too, Hinchey. I do. Seems like the good Lord has a whole different plan for me than what I had set aside for myself."

"How do you mean?" He cocked his head to one side.

"I mean," she straightened her apron and smoothed her hair, "I got a living to earn. Come on in and I'll get you some breakfast. Do you know what you want?"

He grinned, his gaze going all befuddled. "Yeah, but I'm not so sure the state of Alabama would look kindly on me having my way with a married woman."

Delora laughed hollowly, envisioning Mr. Tired Face in her mind, and moved through the door he held open for her. "How you do go on, Hinchey Barlowe."

She fetched more milk, poured a new cup of coffee for Mrs. Tired Face and motioned for Hinchey to sit at the counter. The Tired Face Family was just as she left them—as if she'd never left their side.

CHAPTER TWO

Sometimes at night, especially on dark nights unlit by the light of the moon and stars, Sophie swore the bayou gave off its own glow from deep within the watery depths. The bayou was a living creature, breathing with each inhalation and exhalation of the tide, and the glow, like bright eyes, seemed to follow this tide. Perhaps the bayou was female, for it was brightest once a month, just after the new moon.

Sophie, watching the water from a slatted rocking chair on the porch, rocked and lazily wondered if the swamp water was like a rechargeable battery, storing so much moon and sun energy over time that it glowed when there was no other light source.

She pushed a bundle of thick blond curls from her cheek and studied the emanated light. Perhaps there was a whole world down there with its own photoelectric infrastructure. A fairyland. A marine fairy glen.

Smiling at her flight of fancy, Sophie lifted slim arms above her head and jutted her chest to give her back a good stretch. She'd spent most of the afternoon mixing potions and that always made her back feel twisted in knots. The potions were good though—especially a powerful tincture for Anna Michael's cramps. Anna had fibroids and, to date, had refused surgery. Sophie didn't blame her; surgery was expensive. Most of the people in Bayou Lisse lived paycheck to paycheck, and health insurance was a true luxury. Anna was far too busy looking after four children anyway. Her man was pretty much useless, so everything fell back on her.

"'Your sons and daughters shall prophesy, your old men shall dream dreams and your young shall see visions,'" Sophie's grandmother said as she settled into the chair next to her.

Beulah Cofe, called Grandam by the members of her family, was a small woman with an abundance of long braided hair, black striped with silver, and deep-set brown eyes that surprised with their occult keenness. She'd been troubled by a series of mild strokes during the past few years so she often had a hard time getting around. Some days she felt stronger than others, and this Sunday had been a good one for her. She'd gone to church, then, after coming home, had helped with dinner. Here it was nigh on ten o'clock and she was still going strong.

"What's that from? I like that one." Sophie studied her grandmother.

Beulah pulled her worn house sweater close about her neck with sun-spotted hands. "The Bible."

"'And your young shall see visions.'" Sophie liked the sound of the words as much as she liked the sentiment the phrase conveyed.

Beulah looked out across the bayou with serene eyes. The water slapped gently against the pilings below their feet. The sound was a comfort to both of them, always had been. "Who were you working this evening?"

"A couple folks." Sophie paused to chew at a hangnail on her right thumb. "Anna's fibroids mostly. I sent a little shift to Righteous and Stephen too. I think they're having trouble again."

"What's going on with them?" Beulah waved to one of the otter babies as it slid by below them, moving as if on wheels. In the twilight Sophie couldn't make out which one it was; there were five that lived below the house.

Sophie sighed. Grandam knew as well as she did how Righteous's unfaithfulness troubled Stephen.

"You best be working on Clary. Sal's done gone off and left her with the girls again."

"No." Sophie angered immediately upon hearing the news. Clary, their housekeeper, had taken up with Salty Davis about a year ago, and he made a habit of going off from time to time and staying gone for two or three days at a stretch. "That son-of-a-bitch. What does he think he's doing?"

Beulah screwed up her already wizened features. "I can't get too riled up, for some reason. The sense on this one won't go where I want it to. Maybe just a little shift to keep him straight is all that's needed."

"Hmmph." Sophie wasn't convinced. "You or me?"

Beulah sighed and was quiet a long minute. The swamp filled the silence with insect whir and frog splash. "I'll get this one. You're closer to her than I am and have a might bit more attitude."

Sophie smiled and a small chuckle rose from her. "Nothing wrong with bein' against injustice, Grandam. I just don't want nobody doing our Clary wrong."

"What are you two cooking up out here?" Clary asked as she stepped quietly onto the decking of the porch. "Whenever I hear my name spoken by you two, I start to worry."

Sophie wondered how much she'd heard. Sometimes Clary moved like a wraith through their small house. "We're talking about Salty. He doing right by you?"

Clary, wearing cut-off jeans and a pale blue button-down shirt, looked good tonight. She stepped into the sparse light from the bayou, and Sophie could feel Clary's brown eyes boring into her even though night shadows prevented her from seeing them clearly. Clary moved to the railing and, lifting a leg, rested one side of her bottom on it.

"Only him and the good Lord know the answer to that one. He doesn't *act* triflin', I'll give him that. Good to me as the day is long. He just…disappears…from time to time. Damned if I know why." She turned and seemed to peer at something on the water.

The three women stayed that way a long time, allowing the spell of the bayou to wrap them in its peace.

Clary was as much a child of Bayou Lisse as Beulah and Sophie. Born on the water in a houseboat owned by her father, she was part of the close-knit family of the Manu Lisse, which is how outsiders referred to them. No one could posit much on how the Manu Lisse came to be. Some said, predictably, that they were clearly a branch of the Cajun peoples who settled southern Louisiana. Grandam had told Sophie that this was what the Manu allowed the outsiders to think, with a mind leaning toward the less they know the better. The true origin of the Manu was far more intriguing. It was admitted, in hushed whispers, that it was Roma blood that flowed in their veins. They were Gypsies hailing from ancient Egypt and had been brought to Europe as slaves to build the great cities spawning in the cradle of civilization.

How they came to Bayou Lisse had been lost, but Sophie liked to imagine it was settled by a group of friends escaping the religious persecution of Europe. The beauty of life on the bayou would be a fitting peace after such horrible suffering.

Whatever their origin, the families of the Lisse knew one another by legend if not by sight. Clary's mother was not unknown to Beulah twenty years ago even though they'd never met. When Beulah was summoned to heal the infected leg of Waverly Evans, she worked diligently to heal the bacterial suppuration left by the suckers of diseased leeches, and the two women discovered an unspoken kinship. Later, when Waverly was on her feet again, her daughter Clary knocked on the door of Salamander House and offered herself to the Cofe family. The Evans family was poor but had many children. Clary was a type of gift, an offering of gratitude. Allowed to freely come and go as she pleased, over the years she had become an indelible part of the Cofe family as well as the Evans, serving as a bridge of kinship between the two clans. Twenty years later, it was as if that barefoot girl in curly ninny tails and buckteeth had never lived apart from the Cofe women.

"There has to be a reason," offered Beulah. "Just doesn't make sense. Is he off with his ex-wife?"

"No, Ruth died, remember? Sophie told the girls about it."

"Right." Sophie remembered, with a painful lurch of emotion, the day she'd made herself tell Salty's daughters Sissy, then eleven, and Macy, a baby at three, about their mother's death from pancreatic cancer. She would never truly forget, no matter how hard she tried, the feel of Macy's hand, sweltering in disbelief, tugging in her own as she asked Sophie to take her to her mama. Sophie knew she meant the mama she remembered, the plump and sassy woman now wasted and taken by disease. Sophie's powerlessness had been complete and disturbing.

"I think he's off doing man things." Clary sighed as she tilted her head and leaned it against a porch upright.

"Like Kith, you mean?" Sophie watched Clary and noted her nod.

"Maybe. I can't think what else it would be."

"It's not another woman," Grandam interjected. "I can feel that. He has goodness there."

"Did you get the potions finished?" Clary allowed one arm to slither along the porch piling. Sophie couldn't answer because she was busy watching the gracefulness of the movement. "I can run them around for you if you have a heavy day tomorrow."

Sophie leaned her head against the back of the rocking chair. "You're a fine woman, Clary Evans, you know that?"

Clary and Beulah broke into low laughter.

Sophie tilted her head to see Grandam's profile. "What?"

"Fine woman, get me a smoke, will you?" Grandam said to Clary, ignoring Sophie.

Clary, with a smirk of amusement, disappeared inside. She reappeared seconds later reverently carrying one of Beulah's carefully rationed cigarettes. She handed it to Beulah and leaned to tease at it with a lighter.

"Speaking of cheating men, I saw Larry Hawking's Avalon parked over at the Quality Inn in Goshen," she said.

Sophie leaned forward. "No! Was Fritzie's car there too?" Fritzie Ramsey and Larry had been carrying on for years.

"Of course. Parked around the corner, though."

"I can't blame him," Sophie said quietly.

"Why?" Beulah asked.

"Cancer. Lung. I thought you knew."

Beulah looked at the cigarette glowing between her fingers. "No. No one told me. How far's he gone?" She took one more pull, then flicked the cigarette into the water.

"About two months in. I saw him last week."

"Does Fritzie know, you reckon?" Clary asked. She had remained by the doorway, one hand resting on the jamb.

"Hell, he won't even talk to Alice about it."

"He won't tell his wife? I can't believe that. They have a lot of business to take care of before he passes." Beulah moved to rise from her chair and Clary stepped to help her. "You need to talk with him, Sophia."

"That's too much meddling for me, Grandam. Let the man die in peace."

Beulah eyed her granddaughter. "You know there's no peace after if you don't leave your family in order. I'm tucking in for the night. You comin'?"

Sophie nodded. "After a swim."

Grandam blew her a kiss, using her mouth alone. "Mind the gators. Lord mind you," she said as she and Clary moved into the house.

Sophie felt the reverberation of the slapping screen door as much as heard it. The soft murmur of the two women's voices carried to her as she stood and absently removed her jeans, T-shirt and underclothing. Naked, her arms and legs glowing ghostlike in the dusk, she made her way along the plank steps and down to the lower landing. Her favorite otter, Astute, chattered to her as he floated by on her left. It was a good thing he was there; it meant no gators were close. It wasn't likely one would bother her anyway. The bayou fed them well and it wasn't her bleeding time.

The shock of the cold water after the heat of the day almost took her breath as she slipped into the shallows by the landing. Moving deeper in, she encountered random warm pockets that comforted her. Tucking her head under, she looked for the fairy villages, trying to follow the light trails as they descended. Though she was diligent, the trails dispersed as she closed in on them and she found only sand and muck. Surfacing, she felt Astute's hand-like claw against her shoulder, so she turned and made cooing noises at the adolescent creature. He backed off, his prattle giggling at her and she laughed and turned to float on her back. The stars seemed to mock her as they danced in the night sky. She wondered suddenly where the bayou ended and the sky began.

CHAPTER THREE

Delora stirred restlessly. She turned and curled onto her side, her right palm automatically coming to rest protectively against the blanket of scar tissue that covered her body from waist to thigh.

She could feel a cool trickle of fluid sledding against the outer lips of her vagina and falling to pool on the sheet under her thighs. It felt pleasant at first, with the same pleasurable release felt when she'd wet the bed as a child. But this wetness was too cold, too foreign so she stirred toward wakefulness, sighing in irritation. She tried to orient herself: naked, in bed, the musty scent of Louie on her. Where was he? Another odor penetrated her dream state, this one harsh and oily, and she felt a stinging sensation as the cool wetness penetrated deep into the tender tissues folded against her groin.

The headache brought about by last night's case of beer throbbed as she opened her eyes to dawn's encroachment. Her husband Louie was there, above her, smiling down as if knowing he was finally going to have the last word. His eyes were sorrowful as he watched her, as if he regretted that he was victor. As if he felt sorry for her defeat.

The stick match bloomed in his right hand as his thumb strummed it. He pressed his other hand against her forehead—a benediction crafted to hold her to the bed because he knew that in seconds she would realize the origin of the petroleum smell that was compounding the aching inside her skull. She realized then that it was lighter fluid and knew there was no escape.

The match descended and the final shreds of her hard-won complacency streamed heavenward in an inferno of yellow and blue. At first there was no pain, only amazement that the years of fighting and violence would end in this one act. But as the fire moved inside, discomfort grew into a frenzied pain that snatched her breath away. She knew she would never feel this agony again, and as she thought this thought, the river of fire worked its way deeper inside her body.

Remembered pain seared through Delora's body, fierce and real. She awakened with a jolt and leapt from the narrow bed, breath rasping harshly from her lungs. She stood in the center of the room, arms hanging loosely at her sides, her hands shaking as she tried to breathe. After a short time, after she had calmed and the sweat had begun evaporating and cooling her body, she made her way into the bathroom. She opened the cabinet under the basin and reached way into the back. There, nestled against the cold water intake, she found a half-full bottle of vodka. She held it pressed to the front of her T-shirt for a few seconds. Without taking her eyes off her reflection in the shadowed mirror, she lifted the bottle of cool vodka to her lips and took a deep pull. She stared into her own eyes for a moment longer thinking how very much like a shark's eyes they were, dim and lifeless and focused on survival.

* * *

He answered on the first ring. Delora was glad. It meant he was awake and she wasn't disturbing him. The hoarse whisper of his voice comforted her immediately, irrationally.

She tucked the top sheet tightly around her body and settled onto the bed, the cell phone held delicately in her right hand. "Hey, Bucky."

"Hey, doll, what's new?"

"I'm having a bad night," she said, trying to keep her voice steady.

"Can't sleep?" His words were slurred, the letters half-pronounced, but Delora could understand him easier than most. In the beginning, she'd had a hard time listening to the distorted words rambling from a mouth that could no longer contain its saliva. There'd been time enough to get used to Bucky Clyde Thorpe's speech during the months of healing at the Wallace Burn Unit in Mobile, however. They'd become close very quickly and within a few days she could discern his meaning. After just a few weeks she looked forward to hearing his words of comfort and encouragement.

She often wondered what it was about Bucky that drew her. Did his one bright blue eye mesmerize her, peering hawk-like from his pink, shiny face, guessing her every thought even as she thought it? His face was gruesome, actually, with tiny suture scars scattered amid patches of red, raw skin. The eye, though blue and quizzical, always appeared bloodshot, the edges of the eyelid inflamed. His other eye was gone, burned away by the fiery car crash that had taken just about everything else from him. An oval patch of skin sutured over the eye socket tried to provide a type of cosmetic protection but actually imparted an evil asymmetry to his features.

No, there was nothing beautiful about Bucky Clyde, yet she was held spellbound by him, captured by his labored existence and his no-nonsense reality checks. The spell was inescapable, even after two years back at home. She called him almost every day. He was psychologist, mentor and friend. Perhaps the amazing pain he had suffered during his two-year recovery, so much more extreme than her own, had catapulted him into a place both godlike and hellish, a place of supreme knowledge in a mind held captive by a crippled, half-functioning body.

"Sleep? Now, what's that?" She pulled at short tufts of blond hair with fretful fingers. "Sometimes I still have bad dreams when I sleep."

"Dreams. Me too."

She could hear the rasp of his breath as they collectively mulled over the mutual horrors that had changed their lives in just a few short moments. She leaned and pushed a finger against the toenail of her left big toe.

"Is Louie acting up again?"

"No, he's been pretty calm lately." She sighed and shifted on the bed. "Rosalie and I had a fight though."

"You and Rosalie? What about?"

"Stupid shit. The groceries. I hate her so much."

"I don't know why you stay there, Del. You need to get away from her. She's only a foster mom to you." Anger crept into his voice, making his speech even harsher.

"Yeah. I know." There was nothing more to say about this. They'd gone over this ground a hundred times. He knew of her Southern Baptist sense of duty. He knew she was still afraid of what Louie might do to her. In fact, Bucky Clyde was the only one she'd told the truth about the fire. How it had been Louie who'd started it by pouring lighter fluid on her.

They calmed again into a companionable silence. An owl called somewhere outside her window and was answered by a low mating warble from deeper inland.

"How are you, Bucky? Did that last surgery give you much relief?"

"Umhmm. They lengthened some of the skin behind my knee. It had drawn up right tight." He paused. "You know…"

"What?" She drew her palm across the smooth surface of the sheet. It was soothing.

"I still feel my other leg sometimes. They said all the nerves were gone. I think they grew back."

"How can you feel something that isn't there? That's kind of weird, isn't it?"

"No, I read that it's possible. Phantom pain. I really think I have that."

"So what's it feel like?"

"Like throbbing. Like blood going through it."

"I wonder if I could feel my womb," she mused. "I don't feel much of anything there anymore."

"Yeah, all my stuff is gone too." He laughed ruefully, and Delora blushed, sorry she had brought the subject up.

"I'm sorry, Buck."

"Me too. I used to like sex."

"It was okay. I just wish I had the choice again, that's all."

"How's everything at the Blossom?"

Delora thought of the diner where she worked. She thought first about the bright linoleum floor, then about the coffee smell. The fresh-brewed smell, not that sour, old coffee smell. She didn't much care for that. Or for the bleach smell of the kitchen.

Her co-worker Marina's face appeared in her mind's eye. Marina. She was beautiful, exotic, with soft Latin features and a lithe, tanned body.

"Delora?"

"It's fine. I'm fine." She spent some time telling him about how the sun rose in iridescent stages that morning as she watched it through the eastern-facing kitchen windows. She didn't mention Marina.

"That sounds good," he said. "I wish I could have seen it."

"Me too. I really miss you."

"I'm sure you don't miss seeing me every day."

She heard him rise and hop, carrying his cell phone. "It's true, you're not very pretty, but then neither am I."

"Don't say that. Hey, Bonnie came to see me today. She brought me chocolates."

"Sounds like things are getting serious."

Bucky laughed. "Nah, she ate most of them."

"You said she was a healthy girl." Delora lifted one of her own slim legs and stared at it.

"She is. Fleshy."

"What?" She couldn't understand this word as it wasn't one he used often.

"Fleshy. To make up for what I lost."

"Oh, flesh. I get it." She yawned and tried to muffle it. "I guess I better get some sleep if I can. I have Blossom's in the morning and the club tomorrow night."

"How late?"

"You mean the French Club? Usually about two in the morning."

"Then you get up again?"

She laughed. "Yep. Opening Blossom's at six."

"I don't get it, Delora. You could move away from there and do something sane."

"Sane?"

"Yeah, sane. Like work one job. Like finding someone who really cares about you."

"I know."

The silence grew and Delora began to feel like she could breathe again.

"You know the door here is always open."

She thought of the little two-room apartment in Myrtle Beach that he'd described to her and the sudden love she felt for him made her heart pound. "Thank you, honey. I'll remember that."

"Goodnight, Delora. Love you bunches."

"You too. Sleep. I'll call you tomorrow."

Peeper frogs called loudly to one another and the sound seemed to swell and fill the room when his voice no longer sounded in Delora's ear. Reaching up, she switched off the light and let their arrhythmic song lull her to sleep.

CHAPTER FOUR

Father Snake slithered off like mercury spills, and Sophie sat down hard, one cheek of her denim-covered bottom sliding into the wet marsh surrounding Bayou Lisse. She swore a host of colorful invectives and, using a nearby sapling, pulled herself to her feet. She swiped at her jeans with both hands and swore again when she saw the amount of duckweed and silt that muddied her hands. Irritated at her bad luck, she wiped the back of one hand across her forehead and swung her thick blond braid behind one shoulder. Stepping carefully, she bent and dipped her hands into a calm pool, spreading sawgrass and duckweed until she had created a small water-filled basin for herself. Rinsing her hands repeatedly, she scooped the odorous muck from her jeans. Then, relatively clean, she rinsed her hands one final time and stamped her foot at the contrary snake, surely long gone by now.

"I only wanted some of your juice, you blasted fool," she said. "I don't know why you got to be so selfish with it."

Satisfied to have spoken her piece, she retrieved the worn gathering basket that always accompanied her on these jaunts and proceeded along the bank toward home. On the way she paused to dig spicy cattail roots and to pull a couple strips of pine bark, thanking each plant for the gift as she accepted it.

The bayou was unusually noisy today. Sophie paused a moment to listen to the insistent message. Nothing much was conveyed beyond the usual getting-on-with-life messages. She moved onward.

The water stretched lazily to her left. There was a sluggish current dead center, but the edges today were as still and smelly as a sickroom. New summer green framed the water on both sides, and the verdant growth extended down along the riverbank, the nodding heads of the plants sipping daintily at the water.

Tired, Sophie plopped onto a low bank backed by riotous willow trees and placed her basket in the middle of her folded legs. She peered into it, mentally checking off a grocery list of herbs—slippery elm for Carol's sore throat, burdock for the Kiel boy's skin tumor, balm to strew outside on the deck at the house and white willow to replenish her store. She still needed thyme and plantain, but she continued to sit. Just for a while. Being quiet and empty was a true indulgence, and wandering the bayou gathering supplies served as camouflage for an occasional bit of woolgathering. Not a lot—she was far too busy usually. But once in a while it was nice to sit and study the water by daylight, recharging her batteries.

A splash to her left caught her attention, and she saw the swirl of a catfish tail as the fish worked his way back to the bottom after a quick snack of leggy water gliders.

A tuft of sinewy plantain leaves snared her interest, and she leaned to one side, clippers extended, and snipped off a few, leaving thanks behind.

She sighed and fingered the thick plantain leaves. She thought of her mother and wondered what she was doing. They had managed to forge a strong relationship despite Faye's penchant for men, cigarettes and booze, in that order, none of which factored into Sophie's life. During her time as a healer, she'd seen too many times what addiction did to people and she'd healed a lot of black eyes dealt to women by their men. Not to mention the fact that she just wasn't wired that way.

She realized, while still young, that she was different from other people and not only because she belonged to the Manu Lisse. An excursion with Cousin Rudee's erection in a canoe on Lamplighter Tributary had proven to her that she did not even possess that longing for the pant and quick heave of the heterosexual tussle. It never confused her, she was too well-balanced in nature for any real trouble to grow, but when her eyes met the warm brown gaze of Kinsey Phelps in the cafeteria area of Stafford High School, it had all made sense. She was pulled toward women. Sophie had accepted this fact as easily as the knowledge that the sun rises each morning, and she set about making the lesbian world her own.

She piled the plantain leaves neatly into the basket, her thoughts drifting to Stephen and Righteous and their troubles. Herbs and care just wouldn't heal some things. All she could offer was a sympathetic ear and whatever limited advice she could about maintaining a relationship. She sighed. What did she know about gay men? Or relationships, for that matter? She knew love when she saw it, however, and those two loved one another. Could love win out over unfaithfulness? She nodded to the bayou as if understanding some great secret. Sure it could. She saw evidence of that almost every day. Why else would Panda Cross's husband, Mikie, allow her to come back home after a weeklong man and drinking binge. Mysteries. Life was full of them.

More plantain beckoned a few feet away, so she stood, grimacing when the wet seams of her jeans scraped against the tender flesh of her thighs. Back to work.

"There you are," Clary said some time later as Sophie stepped out of the thicket into the yard behind Salamander House. The yard, sloped and surprisingly green, lay behind the cabin that had been in Sophie's family since Great-Granda Wassel Fox Cofe had built it in the late 1940s. It was ramshackle, true, with tin and tar paper along the bottom and screen that was frayed around the outer edges, but it was home and hers and she loved it dearly.

The woman she loved just as dearly sat outside, on the border of the slope of well-tended lawn. It was a wheelchair day, so Sophie knew Grandam had not slept well after leaving her on the porch last night.

"Ida just called, said Karen's water broke. She early?" Beulah's voice, coming from the frail wheelchair-bound form, was surprisingly forceful. Her slim hands never slowed as she twisted cattail talismans with expertise born from years of practice and she felt no need to look up at her granddaughter.

Sophie nodded and ran to press her lips to Beulah's soft, rosemary-scented cheek. "Just let me change pants. Damned moccasin dumped me."

She handed the laden basket to Clary and walked into the house. Clary laughed as she followed. "You know they're not partial to being milked. How many times you been bit?"

"Yeah, well." Sophie stepped out of her jeans and handed them to Clary.

A stack of clean, folded laundry rested just inside the bedroom door atop the bureau. Sophie riffled through it until she found denim shorts and slipped into them, zipping them closed. Checking her T-shirt, she determined it was clean enough and grabbed up her canvas pack from the coat hook next to the door.

"You comin'?" She looked at Clary expectantly.

"Can't. Promised Ella Jane I'd keep the girls. Beulah's going to nap," she said. She shook out Sophie's jeans with a moue of disgust. "You and the damn swamp, I swear."

Sophie was allowing her forward momentum to lead her out the door as she snatched her keys from a small table. "You'd best tell your sister to stay home with those kids before she ends up with another ulcer. She works way too much."

Sophie did not wait to hear Clary's possible response; she had already brought the engine of her small silver Toyota to life.

CHAPTER FIVE

Falling into autopilot, Hinchey rolled his polished Tacoma into the parking area in front of his house. He sat a moment, watching the house. Soft light spilled from the living room windows.

"It's eight o'clock, do you know where your mother is?" he asked himself gently, chuckling at his own sense of the absurd.

Emma Barlowe had a passion for TV sitcoms and tonight was Thursday, her big night. *Friends*, *Will and Grace*. No, no one would see Mom Barlowe for a while. Later it would be *Nick at Nite* to get all the golden oldies.

Once when he had been thinking particularly deeply about the issue, he decided his mother, whose life perimeters never made it past the pet store on Harlequin Street where she worked, got a taste of a much bigger, better life by watching these television fantasies. No matter that it was as unreal as a Warner Bros. cartoon. It seemed real during those half-hour episodes and that's what mattered.

"It's me, Mama," he called absently as he entered the kitchen door.

His dinner waited on the range top. His mother, in her usual orderly manner, had separated hot and cold foods and covered each plate securely with aluminum foil. He opened the freezer, took out a frosted glass full of ice and filled it from the pitcher of fresh sweet tea resting on the counter. After transporting everything to his precisely set place at the table, he took a seat and unwrapped the hot plate. Meat loaf, mashed potatoes and stewed okra. The cold plate held sliced tomatoes and Waldorf salad, a favorite.

"Ross just fell off a sofa and they think he has a broken arm," his mother said as she entered the large kitchen.

"Ross?" Hinchey queried around a bite of meat loaf. Then he remembered. Ross was a character on the *Friends* television show. "Oh, I hope not."

"Me too. How's that meat loaf?" She poured herself a glass of tea.

"It's good, Mama. Good." He chewed without looking at her. He knew she would disappear as soon as the commercials ended.

"I used oatmeal instead of cracker crumbs this time." She sipped tea as she watched him, awaiting a response.

Hinchey swallowed and looked at his mother. She looked the same as always: faded housedress and slippers this time of day, short curly hair the color of tarnished silver, eyes a washed-out blue, mouth slack and surrounded by pronounced frown lines. Mama.

"I like this better," he said at last. "Has a better texture."

"Good. Listen, I've got a hankering for a cherry pie and I picked up a nice one today. Save some room for it."

"I will, Mama."

She shuffled from the room. Hinchey wolfed down the rest of his dinner, placed the dishes in the sink and took the back stairway two steps at a time.

"Hello, Country Stud, this is your little Keychain. How's life treating you there?"

Hinchey grinned and pressed his index fingers tip to tip. He pushed them together hard, until it hurt, as if preparing himself for a grueling race. Leaning forward, he applied these fingertips to the keys as he typed a reply.

Chain, good to see you. Life is good. Can't complain. What's happening in your neck of the woods?

Hinchey loved the little notebook computer he'd bought on sale at the Circuit City store in Goshen. It was the one possession in life he valued. It was one of his precious few personal possessions as he still lived at home with his mother. He glanced around the room and saw little of himself there—the furniture was a light pine and tan set his mother had chosen. He would have preferred individual pieces of darker maple or cherry, with plaid upholstery maybe.

He still slept in the single bed he'd slept in as a schoolboy more than fifteen years ago. Where had those years gone? He sat back and allowed his mind to wander, documenting his life to this point, his gaze lazily wandering the room. There had been two years of college at 'Bama State and then he'd gone to drinking with his buddy Larry and ended up selling cars for a living. For five years now. He'd just received his anniversary cupcake and complimentary dinner coupon May fifth. Where had his life gone?

A tinkling signal let him know that Keychain had replied. She told him about her cat, Gretchen. That she'd had to have her put down. Hinchey wrote back that it had been the right decision. At sixteen years Gretchen had lived a good long life.

They talked about other things then, about how a dust storm had settled for two days in Alliance, New Mexico, and shut down the building where Keychain worked. She said it was a nice change from her demanding schedule as an editor for a medical publishing company.

Hinchey had a sudden urge to have been there with her. Just hanging out, sipping cold beer in front of a plate glass window as the world swirled red around them. He wondered again what she was really like. How did she smell? What kind of perfume? Did she have annoying habits? Was she one of those whining, endlessly complaining women, like the ones who drove him crazy at his mom's church?

Well, that was something he'd never know. Restlessly he rose and walked to the bedroom door. He could hear his mom downstairs. She was in the kitchen, probably cooking the frozen cherry pie she'd promised earlier.

Emma Barlowe had been quite a catch in her youth. Married early, she'd popped out three children in three years. Then her plumbing had gone awry and there'd been no more. Hinchey, the youngest child, had heard this story hundreds of times in his twenty-five years. She told it regularly at church socials and at least once to every new acquaintance—along with the story of how hard she'd worked keeping the books for her husband's carpet store. They had slaved together for thirty years until he'd dropped dead one morning in between the shag and the berber.

Hinchey returned to his desk and stared at the pulsing screen. He was remembering his father's waxy face in the satin-lined, polished wood casket. He hadn't looked peaceful. Thirty years of Emma may have been the reason.

Keychain's response was blinking insistently, so Hinchey wrote her about his father's death mask. He also told her about the smell of new carpet, how the odors made him retch.

She knew immediately what he was talking about, knew it was the dyes with their fixatives and the formaldehyde used as a preservative. It turned out she had an uncle with a carpet business in New Jersey. She'd spent a few summers with his family while still in high school.

"Wow," Hinchey mouthed. He thought of Delora suddenly and felt guilty. If only she would leave Louie and be with him, he'd be complete and there'd be no need for Keychain in his life. He'd drop her without thought or regret. If Delora would come to him.

Keychain wrote that she wanted him to call her. She gave him her cell phone number and wrote that he'd better not be some type of pervert or ax murderer. Did he want to call?

Hinchey paused and dialed up her profile once again. Keychain was twenty-two years old and had a post office box in Alliance, New Mexico. There was no phone listed and he felt honored that two months of nightly conversation had engendered this much trust in him.

Sure, he wrote back. *I'll call. How about Saturday night at nine, my time?* They set the date and signed off.

Hinchey rose and unbuttoned his oxford shirt. His tie rested on the desktop so he retrieved it and hung it precisely in its empty slot in the tie holder on his closet door. He removed his shirt, folded it haphazardly, and placed it atop the other folded clothes in his dirty clothes hamper. His trousers and white cotton briefs followed the same path, and he stood naked in socks next to his bathroom door. He realized then that the bedroom door was still ajar and with a lurch of horror realized his mother could have come in while he stood naked in the room. After rushing to close the door, he pulled baggy shorts from a bureau drawer and slipped into them. Fetching his robe from the back of the bathroom door he slipped into it and made his way downstairs. The pie should be about ready.

CHAPTER SIX

Karen Witter's moans echoed loud against the close walls of the trailer. They'd been at it for hours, and the baby had dropped only slightly. Sophie could feel the tightness in her shoulders and neck; she'd been arched over Karen's heated, heaving body for too long. With a deep sigh, she pulled herself upright and stretched as she pondered what to do for the girl. Karen was exhausted. She was too damn young to be trying to give birth. The thought of that slim, childlike body being split by this incoming baby made her rage inside. Her eyes flew to Andy and she hated him for just a second. It was that boy thing, that push of nature that got so many girls in trouble. And what about the girls? Giggly fools, believing that the boy will eventually *be* the boy they see through starry eyes. That he will be the protector, the provider, the loving father of children.

She pulled her eyes away from the nibble of fear in his eyes. He was trying to be brave for his father, but Sophie could see.

She moved to the window to look out at the fog-cloaked dusk. She could see how it would be. A month or so of pride, or at least of proud parading, then the smelly diapers would get to him. The constant tang of sour milk on his wife would put him off. He'd storm from the house, a forbidden cigarette trailing smoke, and he'd find other interests. The part of himself that looked so good to Karen yesterday would be left somewhere else—at work, the diner, the bar, with another woman. Only the shell of him would come home and that only because he had to. His baby had to have someone to call daddy.

Sophie straightened her T-shirt and walked to Karen's side. She took the hot cloth from the girl's forehead and dipped it in the bowl of iced water resting on the cluttered nightstand. She stroked the cooled cloth across Karen's forehead.

"It shouldn't be too much longer," she whispered to the frightened girl. Karen's big, Gypsy eyes were wide and rolling as she tried to deal with this insult to her body. Sophie wondered briefly if she remembered any pleasure from the act that had brought about this new life kindled inside her. Had it been good for her? Or a mechanical process to keep Andy interested? Perhaps she had been just that curious to see what it was her friends were talking about. Either way, it had brought her here to this place and changed her life forever.

So... Sophie sat back in the hard, ladderback chair. Hospital in Goshen? She knew Karen had no money. Neither did her family, or Andy's, for that matter. There'd be the bill to reckon with. She always took payment in barter and gladly. Hospitals were not so accommodating.

Her hands went to Karen's abdomen, and she gauged the baby's position. Lower finally. Focusing energy on the baby, she massaged the clenching muscles enveloping it. They moved under her hands, gently pushing against the baby. Rhythm and timing consumed her completely as she pushed in tandem with each muscle contraction. The ministrations worked this time. With a gentle heave, the baby turned and moved lower into the birth canal.

Moving to sit between Karen's thighs, Sophie leaned forward on the stool. The head was crowning fast and there was a surprising amount of dark hair. Sophie combed the matted strands with her fingers, then moved the fingers wide to stretch the silky vaginal lips around the opening. The head protruded more, the underlying skin blue—a color that worried Sophie. Karen emitted loud grunting sounds of effort as she followed her body's lead and panted and pushed.

Andy stood at Karen's side, his hand going white beneath her hard, panicked grip. He watched her pain with awe and some fear. He knew the comfort expected from him but couldn't get there. Not yet. Maybe not ever.

"It's coming," Sophie said loud enough for Karen to hear. "Keep with it, Karen-girl. It'll all be over soon."

"Thank the good Lord," muttered Andy's father. "We've had about enough of that caterwaulin'."

He sat in the living room, around one corner and within spitting distance from the sagging rope cot that Andy and Karen called their bed. Neglect shouted from every room in this trailer, from the dirty garage-sale sofa to the missing curtains at the kitchen windows. Poverty is a burden, but the defeat it spawns in those affected is something else again. The unwashed smell of old food was starting to get to Sophie. She'd been here too long.

But the baby was coming. Sophie pressed against Karen's flesh until the baby's nose was freed, then carefully twisted the head up until the shoulders began working through. Then it was finished and Sophie was holding the surprisingly heavy infant, a girl. Realizing right away that something was wrong, she tipped the head down and patted the feet. A trickle of blood welled in the small nostrils. The baby moved, seemed to breathe once but did not breathe again. Sophie cleared the airway with a suction bulb, noting the blood there, slapped the feet, hung the baby upside down by her ankles and tapped the small buttocks. There was no response and the dusky color began to spread. She clamped and cut the cord and hurried from the bedroom. She laid the newborn on the cleared kitchen table, where she had prepared a small pallet. She checked the airway but saw no blockage, only a welling pool of blood deep in the baby's throat. Sophie roughly massaged the small chest, watching helplessly as the spirit rose and moved away.

"No," she whispered and turned the baby facedown, cradling the small cooling face in her palm. She tapped the back with her fingers and a stream of fluid warmed her flesh. It was blood.

"What's wrong?" Karen asked. She had risen on her elbows and was trying to watch Sophie through the doorway.

"I'm not sure," Sophie said grimly. "The labor was long and she was trapped against your pelvic bone..." She turned the babe and stared down into the small, still face. The eyes were half-closed and the tiny rosebud mouth lay still and slack. Sophie used a cloth to wipe away the blood from the small lips and nose. She pressed her ear to the chest, then her stethoscope. There were no sounds at all, only Karen's harsh breathing echoing around them. Andy's father laid down his newspaper and looked over.

The quiet form told Sophie all the secrets of death and irresistible light and nothing more. She pressed her forehead to the dead child's face. The little girl had gone away. If, indeed, she'd been there at all.

Karen wailed long and low, and grief swelled in the small rooms. Andy's mother, Ida, left the sink, the dishtowel she'd been holding floating—an ineffective parachute—to the floor where she'd stood. She stumbled to the bedroom and draped her body across the grieving girl. They sobbed together.

After slowly wrapping the tiny body in its yellow baby blanket, Sophie carried her to Karen. "This little soul wasn't meant to be," she said quietly. "Do you want to say goodbye?"

Karen extended one hand but drew it back before it connected with the heavy bundle. "Why, Sophie?" she asked, eyes spilling tears.

Sophie wanted to cry too, to sob long and hard, but she knew she needed to be the one in control.

"It wasn't anything you did, sweetness, always remember that. Maybe your body is too young. Maybe it just wasn't meant to be."

Karen looked at the bundle.

"Touch your first child, Karen. Tell her goodbye."

Karen pressed her fingers, nails dirty and covered in chipped glitter-fleck nail polish, to the baby's arm. She patted it once, then drew back. "Her name is Gloria."

Sophie straightened. "That's a beautiful name for a beautiful girl."

She laid Gloria in the cradle that had been prepared for her, then set about delivering a clean afterbirth and making Karen comfortable. There had been no episiotomy—Karen and Sophie had worked diligently to prepare—so there were no sutures. This was good. The memory and pain of the birth would fade more quickly.

When finished, she drew Andy close to Karen's side. "We'll make funeral arrangements for Gloria and we'll have a ceremony for her." She paused and drew a deep shaking breath.

"Brother Kinder will see to that, so don't worry about it. The cost will be taken care of. What you need to worry about is getting well and back on your feet. I want you to stay in bed tonight and tomorrow, except for the bathroom. And be careful. Eat only some soup for the first couple days. Remember all we talked about. Tomorrow afternoon you get up and move around some, but rest when you feel tired. Do get up and move around, though."

Andy spoke, his voice ridiculously proud. "Don't worry, Miss Sophie, won't nothing keep her down. We'll probably have to tie her down just to get her to rest at all."

Sophie nodded indulgently. "Well, don't let her do too much. Her body needs time to heal. When she hurts give her two of those pills from the bottle I left on the counter. Call me right away if her legs start hurting or her chest hitches up, okay?"

Karen appeared subdued, a small child who had fallen ill. Her mother was on the road, working tomatoes on the eastern shore of

Virginia. Karen needed her mama, now especially, and Sophie was sorry the woman wasn't here to offer comfort. Andy's mother was a poor substitute, usually finding too much fault in her young daughter-in-law. "I'll check in on y'all tomorrow. Sleep now, okay?"

After using the phone to call the funeral home, Sophie carried Gloria outside to the front stoop and waited for the undertaker's car to come. Thoughts of her own mortality surfaced to trouble her as she rocked the cooling infant in her arms. She had been a healer for more than twenty years now and had dealt with her share of death and new life. Always before she had managed to keep her equilibrium about it. Her acceptance had been Zen-like, understanding the vagaries of life and death—decisions beyond her control. This, though—this rankled. She looked at the baby's swaddled, still form, safe in its brand-new baby blanket, probably bought from the Walmart in Goshen.

Karen, only fourteen, didn't need a baby, true, yet why hadn't the powers that be taken the baby earlier, before she had to suffer the pain of labor and birth, then the death of a fully formed child. Then, to add insult to injury, Gloria had appeared healthy, a viable infant. She just hadn't been able to awaken to this life. The ways of the universe are unknowable and often cruel. Pondering the fine line between life and death, Sophie suddenly felt very alone.

CHAPTER SEVEN

Two-five-six Royal Court was quiet when Delora arrived home about ten that evening. She unlocked the door with a practiced stealth that anyone watching would have marveled at. Inside, she pressed the door closed and slipped the shoes from her feet. Luckily her bedroom was nearest the door so she could usually sneak in without too much noise.

After removing her work clothes, she wrapped herself in a towel and crept along the hall to sponge off at the bathroom sink. Though she longed for a hot shower, running the shower this time of night with these old pipes would surely wake everyone. She'd made that mistake before. She brushed her teeth and returned to her room as silently as she'd left it.

The window beckoned and, dropping her towel, she walked across to it. A weary twig of sweet gardenia struggled to bloom just outside, and she breathed in the wafting fragrance as she pressed her forehead against the cool pane of glass stretching across the top of the half-open window.

Sometimes at night, naked like this, with just the ratcheting night bugs and her own imagination, she could be whole again. One hand reached down and stretched across the injured part and she felt the rough numbness of the skin there. She remembered times, before the fire, when she had displayed that part of herself to Louie, silently wanting his hand to caress there, to smooth that plane of softness. She turned from the window. There'd be no more of that. Wearily she opened the closet door and moved several boxes until she could access the cooler in the back left corner. Reaching inside, she lifted out a small hip flask of vodka.

As she turned away, something caught her eye. A creased and tattered backpack had shifted to one side during her foray into the cooler. It resembled a ruptured stomach, its contents spilling out onto the closet floor. She moved into the tiny space, tugging a T-shirt from the top shelf and shrugging into it. Thus clothed, she knelt and neatened the pack enough so that she could pull it from the closet.

Back on the bed, she sat tailor-style and systematically unloaded the bag's contents. Tucked down one side was her father's wooden cigar box. She carefully pulled it loose and rested it on the blanket, then retrieved a small silk bag. Peach-colored, it was gathered into a purse shape by a single satin cord. She hefted its loosely constructed weight thoughtfully back and forth on her widespread fingers before placing it on the bed. Beneath the purse lay an eight-inch by five-inch manila envelope. She pulled this free, revealing a tapestry lipstick case and three books below it.

She reverently smoothed one hand across the sleek, though water-stained, cover of *Tales from Shakespeare*. Her mother had delighted in reading this to her every evening. As a young girl, Delora never understood the specific words, but the stories conveyed well. The cadence of the phrases had touched her, that and her mother's obvious love for the work. Opening the book, she touched pages her mother had fondled and felt unreasonably close to her and comforted overall.

The second book was a clothbound edition of *Aesop's Fables*, a favorite of her father's, and the third was an old copy of *'Twas the Night Before Christmas*. This last was the first book she had learned to read all by herself. Reading it aloud had been a holiday ritual, usually at Christmas Eve dinner. She set the book aside. She hadn't read it since the Christmas before her parents' death.

The backpack was now empty except for a small stuffed dog her father had won at a carnival when Delora was about four. One ear had been heavily chewed, and Delora remembered acutely the pleasure she had derived from the feel of the coated vinyl in her mouth. Bearing stains and cuts from the storm that had taken her parents' lives, it had been through a lot.

Delora placed it back in the bag and turned her attention to the humidor. Constructed of polished cherry, it was dark and mysterious, reminding Delora of faraway lands with unpronounceable names. The top opened with a slow creak and inside rested another part of Delora's old life. She lifted out the small bottle of perfume and gently wiggled the stopper loose. The scent of her mother filled her nostrils and permeated the room. She took a deep breath and a familiar longing stirred in her.

There was nothing left of the comfortable ranch-style home she and her parents had occupied. Her mother and father's bedroom, which always bore this smell, was gone. The storm had stolen that as well as her parents.

She looked down at the box and stoppered the Chanel. This bag contained what little had been found amid the rubble of her home. Her Aunt Freda had given her a few things as well.

She opened the envelope next and peered inside. Photos, dozens of them. They were dog-eared from too much handling. In the beginning she had played a game by holding each photo in turn and, by trying very hard, to remember even the smallest detail from whatever event the photo depicted. She would sit for hours remembering or perhaps dreaming, inventing. She could never be sure.

That was a long time ago, however, so today she merely pressed the envelope closed and pushed it into the pack.

Reverently, taking time to finger each piece with tender, respectful nostalgia, Delora repacked the contents. She approached it as one would a puzzle, fitting each box or parcel into its exact nesting space. She sighed as she pulled the covering taut across the fullness. This was her real life. The life she led day to day now was someone else's life that she had stumbled into.

She touched the cold bottle of vodka nestled into the triangle created by her folded legs and lit her last cigarette of the day. Who was this scarred woman who drank straight vodka from the bottle late at night, reveling in her loneliness as if doing penance? This was not Delora Marrs Clark—the pampered only child of two loving parents. No, this was Delora Marrs Clark November, an entirely different person. Delora sincerely hoped the windows of heaven were shuttered when it came to her life. It was appalling to believe her parents could see who their daughter had become.

Dispirited and ashamed, she rose and placed the sack on the floor of the closet, behind her beaten-up sneakers. She closed the door and stood indecisively in the middle of the room.

She was only twenty-four. A babe still and her life was done. Yet she would not give up everything. The quiet magic of the night stole across her and, crushing out the cigarette, she relaxed against the pillows of her bed. Her fingers idly caressed one satiny pillow and teased a protruding corner. She'd bought these pillows herself, with her own money, from the discount store in Goshen. The overabundance of pillows on the bed pleased her and she felt almost guilty for pampering herself. Her eyes snared on her partially exposed abdomen and she flipped a corner of the comforter across it. Not that guilty. With her next run of big tips she planned to buy a smiley face throw rug for the center of the room.

Lord knows, she'd better not buy any more maps. Her eyes grew fond as she studied the wall opposite her bed. About eighteen months ago, while foraging in Raymond's used book store, she had discovered a huge fold-out map of the world. Bearing the National Geographic logo on the bottom left corner, the map was awe-inspiring, taking up the better part of the wall and dragging Delora in headfirst. The deep sky blue of the oceans soothed her as the outlined, colorful countries excited her. Strangely enough, it was the continent of North America that captured her interest more than any other. Colorful pushpins bristled in intriguing locales such as San Francisco, Corpus Christi, Key West, Fargo, Spokane. She said the names to herself, allowing the words to roll off her tongue like diamonds, with hard edges and dazzling facets. The other continents just couldn't match up. Turkey and Algeria, China and Kazakhstan. They didn't fall as well. Too harsh maybe.

She cracked the seal on the bottle and lifted the moist neck to her lips. Delaying the first sip, she teased her full bottom lip with the wetness of the rim, allowing the fresh, cool smell of the vodka to waft across her senses. The first sip was always the best. This was why she seldom overindulged. The taste got old quickly. A certain amount helped her sleep, however, and she welcomed that.

Other maps decorated other walls. To her left stretched the great state of Alabama. The tourism bureau in Goshen gave those away free. She'd had to pay for the now-faded road maps, however, and the dog-eared atlas from Walmart that lay on the floor next to her bed. That was okay. Maps were a necessity. How else would she find her way away from Redstar when it was time?

She took a deep sip and let her eyes roam the small bedroom. Having her own room again was one of the best things to happen to her in a long time. Not having Louie's obnoxious presence next to her was a delightful freedom. She'd hated the way he dominated any room he entered. She still hated the sour sweet beer smell of him.

Turning on her side, she slid her right hand along her thigh and up her side feeling the point of numb sensitivity that was almost a pain when her fingers strayed into the area of burned skin. If he ever touched her again she would die, absolutely drop like a bludgeoned cow.

According to the doctors in Mobile, her repaired flesh could not take the thrust of a lover. They had made a point of telling Louie this. Blind and crippled by a repaired, rigid ankle broken while running from the fire, Louie was not likely to hurt her physically again. His words still hurt, however, and he knew just how to use them as weapons. These hours, though, from work until morning were hers alone and she cherished each one of them. No Louie, no Rosalie, just Delora and the image of who she used to be before she knew them.

CHAPTER EIGHT

Bayou water slapped with gentle insistence against the south side of Salamander House. Sophie listened intently for a few minutes to see if there was a message there. She determined the slapping was just a friendly hello and turned her attention back to Stephen Combs' words.

"I don't know, Clary," he was saying as his teeth and tongue worried a stringy piece of celery. "I could probably take it a little better if he was honest. It's the lying that gets to me."

"No, you couldn't," Sophie interjected. She was separating leaf lettuce from its stalk and did not look at him as she spoke. "And it's the cheating that is getting to you too. That and the fact he is choosing someone else over you time and again."

"But that's just it, he's still with me." He leaned toward her with avid curiosity, still chewing. "What's that about?"

Clary, carefully washing watercress at the sink, answered. "It's just not something we can understand. Some people are plain born unfaithful. I think your Righteous is one of them."

"You've known him longer than me. Have you ever known him to be with just one person?" Stephen asked quietly.

Sophie snorted before Clary could answer and Clary gave her a sour look.

"Hell, the only person he's ever settled with is you, Stephen. I remember when you came to town driving that beat-up Chevy pickup. He thought the sun rose and set in you. Didn't he, Sophie?"

"Umhm," Sophie agreed halfheartedly. "I remember how it was when they first saw one another. All of a sudden it was like the rest of us weren't there anymore."

Stephen laughed hollowly. "Lord, he was impressive. I remember remarking on how wide his cheekbones were and wondering about his ancestry."

"You mean like having Eskimo or Indian blood?" Clary placed a stack of plates on the table.

"Right." Stephen moved lazily to spread them across the table. "You don't see black people with that wide a face. He has to have something else mixed in."

"What does he say?" Sophie asked as she studied Clary's wide cheekbones.

Stephen shrugged and lifted a handful of forks. "Says he doesn't know. His grandparents died when he was a boy so what little bit of knowledge they had was lost."

"Shame," said Beulah, laying her hand over her heart in a gesture of remembrance for those who had passed on.

Stephen's face hardened. "What I want to know is why he feels like it's okay to have sex with all the little chickies he runs with."

"It's an easy thing," explained Sophie. "Get someone new to rub the rod a little, to relieve the pressure. I don't think there's love involved. Sensuality and passion of a sort, yes, but it's not like what you two have."

"I know," Stephen sighed. "It doesn't make it right, though."

"No, but sometimes it's not up to us to know why someone does what he does. Maybe our job is just to love who we love."

"There's no way to tell you how I feel," Stephen said abruptly. His fingers began fretting a bowl of Washington State apples that Clary had put out that morning.

"You're going to bruise them," Sophie chided softly, never taking her eyes from her task.

"I know how you feel," Beulah said quietly.

Early June in the Alabama swamp means bugs and lots of them. Beulah sat at the kitchen door, thoughtfully twisting a thread pulled from her sweater and watching the poetry as the insect tribes spiraled around one another in a joyful frenzy of procreation. "You think no man ever cheated on me? I can tell you plenty about how you feel.

Why do you think I've been hitched so many times? I didn't get tired of that many men; they just found new pussy more appealing."

"Miss Cofe," Clary scolded. She turned from the sink, eyes wide. "You know better than to say such."

"But it's true," Beulah protested.

"True or not, there's no need for vulgarity."

Beulah smiled, her mouth filled with stars in the sudden light of the kitchen as she turned her head and radiance caught her golden tooth. Though she was old, almost ninety by the last guess, her grin revealed the dimpled energy of a young, budding woman. "What's the matter Clary? Ain't you got no pussy?"

"She does, I can vouch for it," Sophie chimed in, getting into the spirit of play.

Clary shot Sophie a glance full of ill will. "I leave my pussy at home and that's where I'll keep her, thank you."

"I'm gonna tell Salty you said that. He'll think he's the luckiest man."

"What did I say?" Clary spread her wet hands in a gesture of innocence, her round, brown features childlike.

"Y'all stop," Stephen said. "I come here for advice and y'all act like fools."

"Just calm yourself, honey," Beulah said, her voice gentle. "No need to fret. What's the boy up to now?"

Stephen squirmed. "There's this new boy, just a baby. Chili Bowling saw them together and told me about it, and I swear Righteous is gonna leave me for him.

"Now, Stephen, you said that about the last one, that black boy from Minion."

"Yes," Stephen agreed, as if the point he was making was the most sensible thing. "And he almost did."

Tears welled in his eyes and he lifted his hands to hide the emotion. "I just don't know what's wrong with me. Why can't he stay in our bed?"

"There's nothing wrong with you, boy. He's only working through his own purpose. What's up to you is whether you tolerate it or not." Beulah rolled her chair closer and patted his arm with hands that had birthed and buried a large portion of Redstar. "If you love him enough, you'll wait for him to come around."

"It's not that simple," he replied with an annoyed twist of his shoulders.

Sophie turned from the salad she was combining and studied him. There was a shift in energy, and it disturbed her normal complacency. She too wondered why Righteous, a tall, skinny, not particularly attractive black man, wouldn't stay at home. Stephen with his blond hair, tanned, even features and muscular build was certainly as good as or better than the bar trash he strayed with. Stephen always appeared perfectly attired as well. Even today, knocking around with friends, he wore a polo shirt and pressed khaki shorts. Brown leather loafers, gently worn, covered his sockless feet.

"Of course it's that simple, Stephen," she said gently. "First you need to talk to him honestly and tell him exactly how you feel about what he's doing to your life. Then, if he won't stop, knowing how you feel about it, then you have to decide whether you leave or stay. It is that simple."

Stephen stared at Sophie. She saw his face change as he realized the truth of her words. He had no defense and merely tucked his head.

Clary turned in time to see the exchange. "How is Righteous doing overall, Stephen? Is he still working steady?"

"Yeah, at Thirsty's."

"He's still there at the Thirsty Rogue. That's good." Clary smiled and nodded at him.

"But that's the thing. Why won't he look for another job? One that doesn't have all those young boys around? He obviously can't resist them."

"Have you told him that? About the job and what it's doing to y'all's relationship?" Clary turned back to the sink before he could answer.

"Oh yeah. We argue about it every few days it seems. It ain't doing a bit of good. He likes the job."

"He is a good bartender, I hear," Beulah offered. "Amos Willis told me Righteous never lets a customer go dry."

"I'm sure," Stephen agreed bitterly.

Clary turned off the faucet with an angry snap. "Give the boy some credit if you do love him. The way you say you do. What he's doing to you is all wrong, we all know, but it's like being hooked on booze. Something he fell into and can't help."

"And we'd like to say that if he just didn't drink, everything would be okay, like not working at Thirsty's would fix it all," Sophie added.

Silence fell, populated only by the whine of the insects and whisper of the water outside. Beulah sighed once and Clary moved to sit next to them at the table. She lifted a glass of iced tea to her lips.

Stephen sat sullen, studying the watered texture of the sweet tea in his own glass. Sophie watched him, knowing that his dignity was slipping away and that he felt powerless to prevent it.

"Stephen?" Sophie asked.

"Yeah." He sighed and sat back in his chair. "I just don't like being made a fool of, that's all."

"I know," Sophie agreed. "It's in your power to change that. You can't change him, you know."

"I know. I also know I can't take much more. I won't take much more."

Beulah turned to look at him and rolled her chair away from his side and closer to the table. She began laying silverware out next to the plates. "Whatever you decide, it'll be all right. We'll still feed you. That'll never change."

It took a few minutes for the gravity to lift but when it did, Sophie let go a sigh of relief. Clary brought the tuna salad, the potato salad and the watermelon from the refrigerator, balancing the platters precariously until Stephen leaped to take the melon and place it on the table. Sophie brought the pitcher of mint tea and arranged the tossed salad next to the selection of dressings.

"I'll get the ice," Clary muttered as she opened the freezer.

"Nothing hot?" Stephen asked.

"Fried chicken from Albert's. Here, want a leg?" Beulah handed him the bowl.

"You know I don't like dark meat, Grandam. How long I been coming here? You should know that by now."

Sophie was the first to laugh, puzzling everyone. Gradually the other women got it and laughed as they settled themselves at the table. Stephen watched them, bewildered until he got the joke and blushed, stuffing bread into his mouth.

"Dark meat. I get it," he said, his wry expression setting the women laughing helplessly.

Sophie leaned back in her chair and studied them. Stephen, as usual, was eating with single-minded purpose, heaping potato salad onto his plate. Grandam was picking at a golden chicken thigh, but Sophie could tell she was far away. She'd been slipping away lately and Sophie knew it was almost time for her to pass on. Her body was the only thing anchoring her here and even that was getting smaller and lighter. It was probably a matter of months and it saddened her. She'd be mighty lonely without this old woman who knew her inside and out. It would take years before someone else could catch on to all that Sophie was. Most people these days plain weren't interested; they were moving to a faster beat that she wasn't sure she wanted to share.

"Can I get you anything, Sophie, honey?" Clary asked, leaning across the table and touching her hand.

"No, no, I'm fine. You go ahead." Sophie smiled to put the other woman at ease.

Clary. There'd always be Clary. Though Grandam had saved Clary's mother's leg more than thirty years ago, Clary had worked for them since and that would never change. She wouldn't accept money, either, a good thing as sometimes there just wasn't enough of that to go around, but she got at least two meals there every day and sometimes stayed over in the room attached out back. These days she was more interested in going home to the small waterborne house left by her mother who had died peacefully in her sleep last year.

Clary met Salty Davis while shopping at Biggen's Grocery in Goshen. Clary went there every month, when Grandam's check came, or in between if they had a real run on amulets, to buy the staples not provided by the bayou families they helped. Clary had once told Sophie, in an embarrassed whisper, that she and Salty felt drawn to one another as soon as they met.

Salty, a shy, widowed, handsome man of color, worked at Biggen's as a cashier, and Clary found herself more often than not checking out in his line, even if it was longer than the others. Salty always had an inviting smile coupled with friendly conversation and eventually he'd gotten up the nerve to ask Clary out for a drink. They'd gone to a little bar owned by Sophie's friend, Angie Bibb. Angie later told Sophie that Salty and Clary were a match made in heaven. Sophie tended to feel the same way. Salty's two girls, Sissy, now thirteen, and Macy, five, had become family almost overnight and fit as if they'd been there forever.

Sophie sighed. She was truly blessed. She'd never gone hungry. Never had any real hardship. And her life was filled with people who cared for her and, even better, allowed her to care for them.

Leaning forward, she took a spoonful of everything. The potatoes in the salad had come from the Paisley family. She had lanced Timmy's boils and left with a sack of last year's shed potatoes. The watercress had come from Dame Ada far over to the east side of the bayou. She had called Sophie out for the recurring ringworm that no amount of treatment seemed to help. Sophie believed it was the piglets she let roam about her cabin. She was messing with them all the time, but no matter how Sophie warned her to leave them alone, she just wouldn't.

The watermelon had come from Franklin Colby, whose wife Diane had been delivered of a healthy boy last week, and the leaf lettuce and tomatoes had been left at the door, no doubt a gift from one of the many people they'd helped during the years.

Yes, life was good. Sophie realized this but she couldn't help the longing that filled her heart. It seemed that, although she dealt with people all day every day, she walked alone. There didn't seem to be anyone who was hers and hers alone.

CHAPTER NINE

Righteous strolled along Garth Street, his right hand twitching as he remembered the incredibly soft touch of the boy. The boy. Righteous could not even remember his name. He paused on the asphalt as a shiny Ford and a rusted-out pickup slid by. He thrust his hips gently. Righteous felt the boy all over him. Sweet little white boy with eyelashes out to there.

He thought of Stephen, who had eyelashes just as long and his demeanor changed. Guilt gnawed at his stomach, churning the liquor inside. He sighed sadly and moved on. Rounding the corner, he fished keys from his pocket and plopped into his cold Ford. Sitting silently still in the early morning coolness, he allowed Stephen's sweetness to fill his mind. He saw Stephen's face but oddly enough it wasn't wearing the frown of disapproval that he saw so often these days, but rather the gentle, sweet smile from the days when they'd honeymooned in Bali two years ago.

Stephen had to be the handsomest, most loving man Righteous had ever met, and he could not understand why he chased the boys when he had Stephen at home. It made no sense. To keep hurting his lover this way was akin to abuse. Righteous set his lips in a grim line, vowing to behave. And to make sure Stephen never found out for sure. What he did not know wouldn't hurt him.

He sighed, filled with self-loathing. He pulled his car onto Garth and headed slowly south along Route 46 toward Redstar. Soon Goshen's lights faded behind him. His mind wove a kind of poetry as he thought of the sexual exploits of the past week. If truth be told, Righteous was bored with the easy access to sex that working at Thirsty's gave him. Still, he had been doing this a long time and he knew the chickie would go on to someone else, someone who held the power of the moment. Righteous would fade away and there would be someone new for both of them. It was like a game of musical chairs. The only constant in his life was Stephen, and yet he seemed hell-bent on ruining that.

He thought of his parents, his mother killing his father with the hoodoo and drinking herself into a dead liver from the guilt of it all. They'd gone before he was twelve, and what he'd learned about relationships from them could fit in his grandmother's thimble. His grandma and grandpa had done all right, together forty years before the big storm had washed them away. By then he was on his own and sleeping with the uncle of one of his friends from school. Then he'd met Stephen. Although the attraction had been fast and fierce, their relationship had grown slow, with Righteous stepping back periodically into his old comfortable life with the uncle. He'd never been faithful to Stephen, really faithful, even though they had been together almost three years.

The lights of Redstar appeared out of the country blackness, and Righteous straightened himself in the seat. He quieted his feelings of guilt and inadequacy and pulled up in front of the trailer that he and Stephen rented from Old Man Beard.

Stephen had left the little lamp in the living room switched on for him. He always offered such kind gestures.

Righteous entered quietly and stepped into the bathroom to strip and wash up. Moments later he slid into the warm bed next to Stephen. Stephen turned and pressed a sleepy kiss to Righteous's forehead then turned back to cuddle into his pillow. Righteous held him close, spoon-fashion, and wanted to cry from the beautiful way they felt together.

CHAPTER TEN

Morning came too soon. Delora heard Rosalie clattering dishes in the kitchen and quickly pulled herself from the bed and into an old chenille robe.

Rosalie James was still pretty even though her weight was pushing four hundred pounds. Her face was cherubic in its frame of jowl; this face was the one thing that allowed Delora to continue to harbor some feeling of affection for her foster mother. Rosalie had been a harsh mother, not easy to please and making no bones about the fact she'd only taken in Delora and the other children for the monthly stipends provided by the state. Her tone, when she said it, often made Delora wish she had been two children left orphaned instead of only one.

Rosalie's lips writhed around a piece of cold bagel as she eyed Delora with judging eyes. "Best get him up now. You know I can't be helping him with my back the way it is."

"Yes, Mama," Delora said, gulping the orange juice she'd poured while standing at the refrigerator. The cold acid threatened to crawl back up her esophagus as she moved along the hallway. Dark and dim, with peeling wallpaper that smelled of old smoke, the hallway reminded Delora of pounding fights with her foster sisters, sisters who had grown to lanky womanhood and gone off with greasy men with names like Chuck and Billy Ray. These sisters came back periodically, with black eyes and broken teeth. Mama Rosalie, as she had done with Delora, would take them back into the fold and charge them high rent until they found a new man and a new home. It was her duty, after all.

Pausing outside Louie's door, the voices came back to her. "At least he didn't burn your beautiful face" had been the hushed confidence from her friend, Nita May Ginter. "You could have ended up like him."

Delora had gotten god-weary sick and tired of hearing that. She wished Louie had burned her face. Then at least she would have no excuses. Her life really would be over. Actual scars hidden, she could move among regular people with little trouble. They didn't know what lay beneath her clothing. They didn't know she was disfigured, dysfunctional, less than a woman. If it had been her face burned in the fire, they would know right away, would have no doubt. She wouldn't have to say with body language and voice, no, you can't come near me. I'm not whole.

The healing had been bad—weeks lying flat on her back, a gel-coated pessary preventing her vagina walls from falling inward and healing together. She would never be able to have children now, they'd told her sadly. The delicate tissues there would never be able to take the stress. Then there had been the infection and the hysterectomy and it was a done deal. It was okay by her; she didn't need children now anyway. How could half a person give the whole love a child required? She had enough to take care of as it was.

Louie was awake. He had his face turned toward the slanting, early morning sunlight, and the weak glow from behind gave his shiny, scarred face the topography of coal. She paused, hand on the doorknob, to study the almost appealing landscape.

"Well, ain't you gonna say anything?" he asked after a few long minutes of silence. He turned his ravaged face toward her and was no longer beautiful. "It's gotta be you, Delora. Ain't nobody else in the state of Alabama can stand still as a retard like you can."

Delora moved into the room and touched his arm. Grasping and pulling on her arm, he pivoted his large frame on the bed until his feet touched the floor. He sat there a long time, a hacking cough shaking his shoulders, while Delora moved to the bureau and lit a cigarette for him. Back at his side, she pressed it between his fingers and heaved him to his feet, his wooden walking stick pinching the flesh of her forearm.

They made their way out into the hall and to the bathroom where Louie pissed long and hard. He lifted the cigarette to his lips as he leaned over the toilet and took a deep drag of the tobacco smoke. Delora let her gaze roam across his back, now hidden beneath the white cotton of his T-shirt and had a hard time imagining her hands gripping that back as he pounded his flesh into hers. She had a hard time imagining that she had even sought his company at every break and lunch period at Tyson County High School. Those days seemed a long time ago, especially as each of the two years they'd spent healing from the fire had seemed like it lasted ten.

Lost in reverie, Delora squeaked in surprise when Louie's hand fumbled hard on her shoulder. She lifted his cane from the rim of the washbasin, and they lumbered along the hall together toward the bright light of the kitchen.

"Mornin', Louie," Rosalie said. She stood at the stove frying a large pan of bacon and sausage. Eggs in their little nests on the counter patiently awaited their turn in the pan.

"Smells good, Rose," Louie said as he felt his way into his chair. He fixed sightless eyes on the window and Delora knew he could feel the heat on his skin.

She fetched plates and silverware and set the table, folding napkins into neat triangles next to each setting. She moved to the toaster as Rosalie broke more eggs into the sizzling frying pan. They moved together in a well-rehearsed routine as Louie sat at the table smoking, lost in thought. Some mornings he would talk about the job he had had before, driving a tractor-trailer for Ebbler Trucking. His cross-country time had been the best in eight years they'd told him. He also acquired fewer tickets in three years than any of the other drivers.

Delora knew these stories line by line and was able to tune them out easily. It was the quiet days that troubled her. They were like storms brewing. He always came out of the quiet times angry. Often they could placate him with beer, but this was unpredictable; his anger sometimes stalked them for days.

Delora kept her eyes averted from Louie as they ate and guilt gnawed at her. Why couldn't she be more compassionate? The sight of Louie eating never failed to spoil her appetite. It wasn't so much the messy way he ate, more the avid way he ate—face almost in his plate as he loaded his mouth and chewed with bovine persistence. She hated him, that was all. Hated him for stealing her life.

Thief, she mouthed silently as she chewed her toast.

Soon her simple meal was finished, and she stood thankfully to leave the table.

"And where do you think you're going?" Louie's voice arrested her.

Delora paused in the act of rinsing her plate in the sink.

"To work, Louie," she answered quietly.

"I don't think so. I'm seeing Franklin at the park this morning and I'll be needing you for my bath."

"Louie, I can't. I have to be at work by eight thirty on greenhouse days. You know that."

Louie slammed his fork next to his plate, the clanking sound as it glanced off the plate making Delora cringe. "I've spoken, Delora. And I don't want to hear backtalk."

Delora chewed her bottom lip and clutched her robe more tightly about her neck. Rosalie had paused in eating her breakfast and was watching Delora with jaundiced eyes.

"So what, you want me to lose this job? Who'll buy the groceries then? Do you want us to be living in the streets?" Delora spoke without thinking.

Louie sat back in his chair, heels of his palms pressed against the table edge. "You're skating on thin ice, Delora."

Delora turned to Rosalie, her mouth working helplessly.

Rosalie sighed as if the weight of the world rested on her shoulders. "Stop it, you two. Yes, Delora, I'll get him ready and to the park. Just get your ass on out of here."

Delora glanced doubtfully at Louie. He sat immobile, but she could tell the battle was over. She muttered a grateful thanks to Rosalie and hurried to her room.

CHAPTER ELEVEN

Salamander House was unusually quiet Tuesday morning. Sophie rolled over in bed and stretched, feeling blood move into her feet and hands. She wiggled her fingers and toes, marveling at the wonderful rightness of the Universe's creation.

She paused to gauge her mood. She felt alone again today. These days it seemed her mind realized too often that there was no one out there for Sophie. She was a partner to the Bayou Lisse and that was all. The bayou was a jealous mistress and would let no one else aboard.

"Pshaw," Sophie muttered aloud as she turned onto her stomach. She ground her hips into the mattress slowly, enjoying the push and pull against her pubis. She sighed and stilled, cupping her chin with a closed fist, allowing mind to rule body. Who could love a thirty-year-old swamp witch anyway?

She thought of saucy Massie Styles, rebel child and scandal of Tyson County. She would welcome Sophie, and their coupling would be fun, accompanied by laughter and a good bit of rough-and-tumble desire. She could smell the tangy yarrow-like smell of Massie's hair and feel her coarse, deeply-tanned skin under her right hand. She clenched that hand, alone in her bed, and realized that wasn't what she wanted. Not really. Being with Massie satiated that need for woman-flesh for a while, but it didn't go very deep, didn't touch the places Sophie needed to have touched.

Sophie rolled onto her back and stared at the rippled texture of the ceiling. She spied her favorite gnome peeking at her, revealed by a curve of plaster that defined his hat and one chubby cheek. He'd been there for years, conversing with her since she was a small child.

"Too alone's not good, Mankin," she told him with a knowledgeable air. "I know the work is important, but what about me?"

Mankin looked at her with fixed, twinkling eyes.

"Life's a joy," he said in her mother's voice. "Stop feeling sorry and get up and do something useful."

Sophie stuck out her bottom lip. "No," she said stubbornly. "I'm just gonna lay here and let everyone get on with things as best they can."

Mankin shook his small head, mouth in a somber line. "It just doesn't work that way, Sophie."

"I know," she interrupted. "I was put here in the bayou for a reason. I know. I'm just...I'm tired, I guess."

"Heal thyself," he said with infuriating smugness.

She pulled her eyes away, letting her head fall to one side. "Bastard."

She rose and moved to the bathroom. She could hear Clary working in the kitchen. The sound was comforting.

Clary had both doors open so a slow draft of healthy air moved through the entire house. Sophie inhaled and found growing herb smell mixed in with the cooking smells of roast chicken and stuffing.

"Working on lunch, I see," Sophie said as she entered the brightness of the kitchen. She rubbed eyes not quite ready for morning sun.

Clary looked up from the onions she was chopping and smiled at Sophie. "Good morning, sleepyhead. I needed to cook this chicken Henry Collins sent. What'd you do for him?"

"Healed Cicely's abscessed tooth." Sophie yawned and opened the refrigerator.

Clary stared at Sophie as if ciphering a difficult equation. "That was two years ago."

Sophie shrugged and nabbed milk from the icebox. "Guess he got in a habit," she replied.

"Habit, hell. I didn't know they were still coming from him. That's a chicken a week for two years..."

Sophie laughed. "Don't even try," she said as she moved to the table, milk in one hand, a box of bran flakes in the other.

Clary laughed and resumed her task. "Damn," she muttered.

"Where's Grandam?"

"Church day," Clary answered as she reached to close the refrigerator door that Sophie had left ajar. She favored Sophie with a sour look of reprimand.

Sophie grinned at her as she chewed cereal. She had forgotten that Tuesdays were Grandam's day to quilt for the homeless. During the past six years the ladies auxiliary of the Light of Holiness Church had made nine quilts for the homeless shelter in Goshen. Making the quilts was also an important social outlet and know-it-all Irma Geneva Haws usually picked Grandam up on the way, no doubt giving her an earful of local gossip as they drove the sixteen miles to the church.

The kitchen fell silent again as the bayou morning intruded. Water lapped the shore outside, and a river otter, probably the small troublemaker Astute, scraped a piece of food against the tin underpinning of the house. The local family of otters had discovered the protective tin to be a great tool for cutting open crayfish and other river delicacies.

"What are you up to today?" Clary asked as she opened the oven to check on the cooking bird.

"Only one visit for a change, checking on Myria's leg."

She lifted the bowl and drank the last swallows of cereal-flavored milk. "Need to make some workings this afternoon, though."

"For who?" Clary wiped her hands and sat at the table across from Sophie.

"I ain't telling you squat...unless you give me a kiss." Sophie leaned forward, exuding a charm Clary had always found irresistible.

"Behave yourself," she admonished. "For who?"

"Salty sure has you whipped," Sophie stated with some amusement.

"You know I don't swing thataway," Clary reminded her.

Sophie smiled wickedly. She so loved to give Clary a hard time.

"You're just horny. You need to go out more, find you someone," Clary said finally.

"Go where?"

"Go over to Thirsty's."

"Too many guys," Sophie sighed. "And the women there out-butch me."

Clary laughed. "I'm going to go get mint for this afternoon's tea. You'd best get on with what you've got to do before you get yourself in trouble."

Clary rose and strode out the kitchen door. Sophie leaned back in her chair and laughed ruefully.

* * *

"We sure are glad you're sticking to the old ways, Miss Sophie. Your grandma saved my daddy's arm with nothing but a bandage and some root herbs. And this after Doc Franklin had given up on it."

Myria Pulet's smile was big and infectious, and her dark eyes gleamed with joy even when she was sick or in pain. Sophie had seen her through many highs and lows during the past twenty years.

"I'm glad too, Myria," she replied, packing up unopened gauze packages and surgical tape and taking a seat at the kitchen table. "There's a whole lot more to healing than just doling out medicine. You've got to work with nature."

Myria leaned to push gently at the bandage newly fastened to her right calf. It was a stark white against the dark chocolate of her skin. "How long you reckon it'll take for this to heal?"

"Now, Myria. What do we always say?" Sophie chided gently.

Myria smiled again and laughed, embarrassed. "Seven days. Don't ask until seven days."

"That's right. The good Lord made the world in seven days according to the Bible. It's foolish for us to expect any more than that." Myria's grandchildren, playing in the cabin doorway, attracted Sophie's attention. Poor as dirt, they were nevertheless happier than anyone would have a right to request.

Kinsie, the youngest girl, was playing with a cricket that had wandered inside. Clearly understanding that a cricket in the house means good luck, she was endeavoring, squatting on chubby toddler legs, to coax the departing cricket back inside.

"Let it go on, Kinsie baby. More will come."

Kinsie swiveled to look at Sophie. The other children stilled and studied her as well.

"More crickets?" Kinsie spoke well for her age, although a pronounced lisp accented her S sounds.

"Ummhmm. You can't force him to stay. It stops the magic, you know."

Raleigh, six years old and unusually affectionate for a boy his age, crawled into Sophie's lap and wrapped one skinny arm about her neck. With breath scented from morning cereal, he addressed her in a very adult voice. "You mean the crickets won't come back, right?"

"Yep, they won't come visit if you take away their free will. We all like that free will, don't we?"

"Free will," agreed Kinsie, rising and watching the cricket crawl outside into the morning sunlight.

"Why do you have Raleigh today, Myria?" Sophie asked, cupping the boy's chin with one hand and examining his face. "He's not sick is he?"

Myria rose and walked carefully into the kitchen. "No. Just a triflin' mama. She wouldn't get outta the bed in time to get him ready for school." She lit the gas fire under one of the stove burners and blew out the match with an emphatic grunt.

Sophie looked at Raleigh, somnolent on her lap and thought of his mother. Floray, Myria's daughter, was as good-natured as her mother, but depression and hopelessness attacked her often. Divorced from a common-law marriage, with four children and a job at the local CVS pharmacy, Floray had a solid foundation for her feelings.

"What about the other girls? Did they get there?"

"They got up and ready all right, but no one wanted to fool with him or the baby."

"Did Floray ever get up?"

Myria nodded as she separated tea bags into two mugs. "She brung them over. That Sterling was here again. He come with her. I just don't like that boy." She sighed and leaned one ample hip against the counter, folding her arms into a protective pretzel across her body. She gazed out the kitchen screen door into the bare dirt front yard. A few pale petunias bloomed raggedly in urns just off the leaning front porch. She seemed to be studying them.

"Is that Fletch and Mary's boy?"

Raleigh, intrigued by Myria's elderly golden retriever, Sam, squirmed from Sophie's lap and moved to see what the dog was stalking under an abandoned truck tire at the edge of the yard.

"He is."

"I thought he was a good fella."

Myria brought over the full mugs of brewing tea and set one on the table in front of Sophie. "They're all hoodlums, you know. All them young boys with their dicks in their hands. They only want one thing and they think my girl is gonna give it to them."

Sophie nodded at the truth of Myria's words. "Is she using protection?"

Myria sighed and settled her motherly body into the chair opposite Sophie. "Far as I know. She goes over to the free clinic and gets pills. They give her them rubbers too, so I guess she's all right."

She turned her attention to her grandson. "Raleigh! You get away from there. Mister Water Snake might be out there looking for you."

Raleigh, typically obedient, lured Sam from the tire and into the clearing where he promptly sprawled his body across the dog's tawny back. Sophie smiled.

"I'll take him over to the school for you," she said. "I think I'll stop in and see to the Tom kids and it's on my way."

"Ain't you the sweetest thing? One of these days I'm gonna have to get Carlton to teach me how to drive."

Sophie took a deep pull on her hot tea as she stood. "Don't do that. Then y'all have to get another car. It's not worth it."

"Raleigh! Get your shoes, boy. You're going with Miss Sophie."

Kinsie crawled into Myria's lap and slipped her thumb into her mouth. Raleigh stuck his head around the door. "Going where?"

"To school. Your shoes are over there next to the bed."

Myria shook Kinsie into a more comfortable position before snuggling her as only a grandmother can. "Ain't you just the prettiest little baby? Sophie, you see this beautiful baby girl I got?"

Kinsie laughed and Sophie shook her head. "You do spoil them babies, Myria."

Sophie moved into the bedroom of the small four-room cabin. A thin mattress rested atop the wire supports on a rickety double bed against the east wall. It was probably the bed where Myria had been born. A faded quilt, frayed on one corner, no doubt by a puppy long gone, covered the mattress and extended a good six inches all the way around. The room held little more, only a scarred bureau and a darkly stained chest at the foot of the bed. Clothes on wire hangers hung from pegs fixed along two walls and a pile of dirty clothes spilled from a basket near the head of the bed. The air smelled of old cooking oil.

Raleigh sat on the chest pulling on battered sneakers. He saw Sophie and favored her with his grandmother's smile. "You takin' me to school?"

"Yep. Thought I would. You need help with that shoe?" She knelt to tie his sneakers.

"What if I don't want to go?"

She let her eyes roam across his face as she tied. "I'd say what's the reason? I thought you liked school, bucko."

"It's all right. Cousin Tam's boy don't go to school, though."

"Well, he should, but he's a lot older than you are."

"He says he don't need no school 'cause he can make more money selling for Cheetah Race. Maybe I can do that when I get older."

Sophie tried to keep anger from racing a billiard ball path through her body. She wanted to snatch up Raleigh and shake sense into him.

She'd seen so many kids like him, stepping off the cliff of innocence into the chasm of dead eyes and departed spirit. She snared herself into a corset of iron and willed herself to speak calmly and rationally.

"That's exactly what you don't want to do, Raleigh. Cheetah is a gangster, pure and simple, and Tam's boy is going to be dead within three years. He took that path of his own choosing. If you make that same choice you'll end up there too. It all looks fine and mighty now, big bucks and better times, but you mark my words and pay attention. You're six now. By the time you hit nine—no, Tam's boy is smart—let's say by the time you're twelve, he'll be gone. I want you to come to me on that day and tell me that you understand what I'm telling you now. Will you do that one favor for me?"

Raleigh eyed her with some fear but still defiance. "That ain't so. What if you're wrong?"

She cupped both his knees between her palms, skinny, bone-sharp knees, and looked him square in the eyes. "Then you come to me and I'll tell you I'm wrong. In the meantime, you do what I say, you go to school and stay on that other path that your grandma and me believe in. Will you do that? Have we got a deal?"

His gaze was skeptical, but he nodded, sealing the deal.

"Let's get you to class then." She stroked his head, the coarse, densely curled hair rough against her palm. He left the room, and Sophie heard him slip out the kitchen door.

Back in the kitchen, Myria and Kinsie hadn't moved; it looked as though both were dozing in a warm shaft of sunlight. Reluctantly Sophie spoke, her voice soft so as not to disturb the sleeping child.

"Myria, watch that leg now. Cuts that low on the leg need more care. Walk it every day, but not more than a quarter mile and take it real slow. I'll be back the day after tomorrow to check on it and change the bandage. Keep it dry till then too, okay?"

Myria nodded. "Thank you for taking the boy. There's two jars of green beans on the counter there. You take them on. I know how Miss Beulah loves my green beans."

Sophie didn't argue but only took one of the jars off the counter as she followed Raleigh into the growing early summer sun.

CHAPTER TWELVE

After showering, Delora pulled on shorts and a T-shirt, ran a brush through her wet hair and headed her car west along Bentley Walk Road toward Spinner's Fen, the greenhouse where she worked three mornings each week. It was a pleasant drive. Trees, still bearing their translucent spring greenery, interlaced branches across the smoothly paved highway as she rounded a bend. Front Street was mostly residential, like the area where she, Louie and Rosalie lived, but these houses were old, maintained by descendants striving desperately to keep antebellum glory alive and kicking. They were doing a good job too. These houses were dressed in their Sunday finery every day of the week with hanging plants placed perfectly above crisp white gingerbread railings. Serene colors of house paint—pale yellows, blues, peaches—butted against lawns verdant and weed free. Expensive boxwoods, harmoniously trimmed, bordered most yards.

Spinners Fen fell at the end of Front Street where it intersected State Route 116. There the houses were less numerous. Turning left onto Carelton, she passed the little high-dollar strip mall on her left. The centerpiece, Mannings Grocery, carried mysterious items such as almond paste, lemon curd and canned shark meat. Spinner's Fen sprawled just behind the mall area with a large graveled parking area and two greenhouses that hid the fallow storage field behind.

Annie Meeks was there already. Morning dew still lay heavily upon all the Spinner Fen greenery, yet she was there plucking yellowed leaves off the new stock of small marigolds that had been delivered by a wholesaler late the day before.

"I heard you drive up," she said, more to the marigold than to Delora. "Muffler's still leaking. Didn't you take it to Jerry like I told you?"

Delora moved to hook the chain that would hold the lightweight greenhouse doors open during the business day. "Couldn't take me," she answered. "He doesn't have any free time until Wednesday."

"Hmmm." Annie nodded her understanding. "He has been busy."

They worked in silence for some time, Delora opening the doors for business and Annie arranging the new, spruced-up plants on the showroom displays. When the shop was ready to greet the public, Delora moved outside and started watering the larger stock. This was the part of the work she enjoyed most. Although she'd probably helped a thousand customers in the year she'd worked at Spinner's Fen, she much preferred the time alone with the plants. They were old friends and she treated them as such. They might have been her children the way she nurtured them, tending their torn leaves, nourishing them daily, even speaking to them as if she expected an answer.

Plants, kids and animals. She'd always had a way with them. She certainly preferred them to the adult humans she dealt with each day. It had to be a character flaw, she was sure, but she decided long ago that it had to do with her own lack of self-esteem. She felt less capable than others and presumed everyone knew. Plants, kids and animals never judged and plain didn't care.

The greenhouse remained quiet; that was unusual for a Tuesday morning this time of year. Typically, the customers were out early because gardeners, as a rule, rose with the dawn and had most of their outside labor done before the sun rose too high. Southern Alabama's climate could be brutal, but most natives knew how to work around it.

Delora liked the solitude. Annie was on the other side of the property, checking on the special-order boxwood imports that had come in last week, so Delora was able to let her mind wander freely as she tended the coleus. The little pinkish leaves were perky and danced for her; she felt honored by their display.

Delora was thinking about her parents again today. She did this one or two days a month. She called them "Storm Days" in her mind and expected a rough twenty-four hours. The 1982 hurricane that had taken half the town had stolen her life as well. The damage had been severe, but Delora, safe at her Aunt Freda's house in Jackson,

Mississippi, had endured the storm secondhand, although she had been deeply frightened by the keening and wailing of her aunt when the storm's potent aftermath became known.

Her parents, Sherman and Rita Clark, had been active in the small community of Redstar and were well-respected by the people there. Her father, a political figure serving on the administrative board, had supported beautification and cleanup programs during his terms. Her mother promoted school programs and had been an ever-present figure in the schools Delora had attended. Until her fourth grade year...when suddenly she was no longer there.

Sometimes Delora thought the people of the town missed Sherman and Rita more than she did. Numbness was the emotion most encountered when she thought of them. She remembered their beauty.

Her mother had been petite and energetic, always impeccably groomed from hair to clothing to toenails. There was never a hair out of place or a collar upturned. To this day, this fact amazed Delora and gave her mother something of a supernatural aura.

Her father had been a true politician, hardly ever seen without his dark blue business suit and tie. Even in the evenings, he dressed for dinner in chinos and a polo shirt. Nights found him fully clothed in broadcloth pajamas, usually a dark blue, although holidays often brought out green or red versions of the same style.

An image persisted in Delora's mind, so perfect that it seemed to be something she'd seen on television...or in an old movie. She saw her parents together at the foot of her bed. One sat on each side of the bed, bookending her feet. Her father was on the left, wearing his dark blue pajamas, his closely cropped hair mussed in the back. Her mother sat to her right, in a boat neck gown of pale beige. Her long blond hair was still, even this late in the day, styled in a sleek twist along the back of her head, but wispy escaping bangs framed her face along the top. Her eyes had been beautiful, large and blue in color. Delora had inherited these eyes along with her father's strong brow and chin. Her mother's face had been a perfect oval with a small nose and sweetly arced lips. The two of them had been laughing at their only daughter, at something witty she had said. Delora didn't remember what had caused the laughter—that had faded over time—but she did remember the feelings of warmth and camaraderie she had felt, cocooned in her bed with a loving parent on either side.

Delora, picking slugs off the variegated coleus, smiled just a little. She'd been a happy child. She was spoiled, the only grandchild on her father's side, as he was an only child, his mother having died from typhus when he was young. His father had never remarried after her death, preferring to live quietly in his polished townhouse attended by his secretary, Claude. Although Grandpa Cecil had been reserved and very polite, Claude was a silly man who delighted in surprising Delora with balloons and music boxes. During Grandpa Cecil's funeral, Claude held her hand and cried. He also cried at her parents' funeral two months later. Then he had disappeared, leaving behind for her a snow globe containing a tiny replica of the Swiss Alps.

Her mother's father, Langston Marrs, died in a farming accident when Freda and Rita were still very young. After the settlement of the generous life insurance policy, Nettie Marrs had lived in seclusion, her girls attending the best private boarding schools money could buy. The visits Delora and her family made to Grandmother Marrs's farmhouse had been tense and unsatisfying. Yet they went dutifully twice a year, at Thanksgiving and Christmas, until, at the age of fifty-four, Grandmother Marrs had endured a stroke that left her partially paralyzed. She now lived in a nursing home outside Chattanooga, Tennessee. Delora did not visit.

Delora sighed and rubbed at her back as she stretched. Hunching over while picking at the plants made her back ache if she did it too long.

She thought of Aunt Freda, plagued by every minor illness known to man. Her back ached; she had migraines, painful teeth and sweaty palms. It was always something new. Her weekly phone calls to Delora were endless litanies of new complaints. She had never had children due to mysterious, unspecified "female trouble" and Delora knew this was a good thing. The poor child would have been neurotic as hell.

Freda's long-suffering husband, Chute Myers, had to be the kindest, most sympathetic man Delora had ever met. He commiserated with his wife as if he meant it. Delora, as she got older, began to note extended absences and finally figured out that Chute had a little drinking problem and was a skilled closet nipper.

Delora pictured his thin beatific face and smiled at the memory. Everyone has his own way of coping, and Uncle Chute found his by passing through life in a vodka-induced fog. Delora didn't blame him. Dealing with Aunt Freda on a daily basis would be tough for anyone.

It saddened her that Aunt Freda hadn't wanted her. Freda put it differently, saying to the judge in Goshen that her poor health just wouldn't allow her to take on a young, spirited girl. The judge, grandfather to her friend Nita May, had seen Freda's state of mind and given Delora to the state. He realized, no doubt, that Delora wouldn't do so well in Freda's care. Unfortunately, he hadn't known that the state child services roulette wheel had come back around to Rosalie James.

Freda, of course, cried guiltily that day and looked at Delora with sad, pleading eyes. Delora, still numb and not sure how she should feel, had watched Freda and Chute hurry from the courtroom.

Later, when she realized what Freda's denial was going to mean in her life, she'd felt great bitterness. Living with Rosalie had never been easy but, as one embattled day followed the next, Delora forgot the days of fragrant, busy mothers and tall, smiling fathers. Her life structured itself into caring for the other foster children in Rosalie's home, attending church and excelling in all her classes at school. She liked school. It challenged her and her powerful mind grew to engulf knowledge and claim it as her own.

Delora met Louie November during her third year of high school. Louie came in late in the year, his family fresh from the Washington, D.C., area. His father was a long-haul truck driver who had been lured to Redstar by the call of the gulf waters. Louie's mother worked at the dime store in Redstar until she was killed in a botched robbery. The sudden loss of both of their mothers was a point of commonality they shared, pulling the two of them together.

Louie. He found in her a willing victim to accompany him on his journey to mediocrity. Delora, who excelled in schoolwork, did not always excel in people, so she was drawn easily into his codependent games.

Urged on by school counselors in her senior year, Delora decided to go to a four-year college. She wasn't sure what she wanted to major in, but she liked the idea of continuing her school days. Rosalie was appalled by the idea, however, saying good girls had no need of college. They married. They settled down and tried to make their husbands and children happy. Colleges were places of sin and debauchery. Girls who attended did so to find a wild lifestyle, too far from church and other things of the Lord. Rosalie would not have one of her girls throwing her life away in such a manner.

Rosalie's friend, Geraldine Pacer, operated the Grant Business School, and Rosalie arranged for Delora to enroll in the secretarial program there after graduation. The secretarial classes bored Delora into a state of further numbness. During this time, she and Louie became more of an item and she became involved in his partying lifestyle. Together they learned to drink well, falling into careless sex and a heavy marijuana habit.

The wedding was inevitable, the road all downhill. It was a small church ceremony and Delora's life was sealed.

Her parents' death, when that tree bisected their home during the hurricane, had left a hole in Delora, and in the family, that could never be filled. Freda mentioned the loss each time she called, and Delora remained empty year after year. Being taken in by Rosalie hadn't done much to fill that void; she was not a loving person and Delora had never been able to form any real connection with her. If she could have, maybe some of the numbness would have eased.

Delora tried again, by creating a family of sorts with Louie, but it too was a black hole that never seemed to get smaller. Louie November made her feel something once, although the feelings had soured quickly into tolerance and now a type of cloudy hatred. Delora wished she could hate him outright, with a clean sparkling knife-edge of hatred. She couldn't. The feelings she had for him went beyond that. Hate is the antithesis of love, and she didn't love him enough to gain that other side. She felt indifferent toward him, only wishing he could be removed from her life, surgically detached and flushed away.

Thinking of Louie disturbed the peace of her morning, and she pushed thoughts of him away as her hands expertly ferreted slugs out from leaf bottoms and stem crevices. She had opened the Mason jar of alcohol she habitually carried with her while at work and was dropping the pests into the jar as she removed them. Annie had a real problem with slugs, and Delora spent a lot of time manually removing them. They especially liked the coleus, so Delora made sure she checked them daily. Her effort was paying off; the young populations had diminished noticeably.

Rosalie did all right. Delora couldn't fault her. She was as self-obsessed and greedy as a person could be, but she had provided Delora with three hot meals and a room of her own. The mothering, the involved guidance, had been scarce, replaced by an admonition of responsibility—to the household and to God.

What doesn't kill us makes us stronger, Delora thought just as the toe of her sneaker caught on a supple branch that was held taut and unyielding by two oversized pots of shrubbery. She went down like an unexpected sneeze. She managed to salvage the three small coleus pots that fell with her but nicked the soft skin of her abdomen on the vertical side of one of the large pots, right through the thin shorts she wore. A damp, alarming warmth spread immediately.

"Oh, shit," she muttered as she righted the coleus pots. The harsh scent of alcohol and slug corpses stung her nostrils as a stinging pain spread across her lower belly.

CHAPTER THIRTEEN

Eleven thirty and here they were just getting started. Sophie sighed as she surreptitiously checked her wristwatch. Damn. She was going to be tired in the morning.

"Look, Al," she said, her voice cajoling, "we've got to sew that up or you're going to bleed all over the place."

Alvin Borrow had pulled from Sophie's grasp and now stood dancing in the middle of the living room. His wife Doris had switched off Frank Sinatra some time ago, so Al danced to a tune only he could hear. Doris stood by the stereo cabinet, arms folded across her chest. She looked forbidding.

"Alvin, I'm not kidding. Now, come on over here and let's get this done," Sophie demanded.

"I don't much care if it bleeds everywhere," he answered. "I paid two hundred eighty-nine dollars for this here rug." He indicated the beautiful red and gold Oriental carpet on which he swayed.

"Yeah, but I picked it out, you damn fool," Doris said. "An' I'm not partial to having it ruined."

"Well, if you hadn't stabbed me, I wouldn't be bleeding!" he said, his tone oddly dismissive. "If I want to mess up the rug, I will, and I don't want to hear any more about it."

He closed his eyes and moved his feet in a perfect waltz step. Fresh blood darkened his white undershirt.

Sophie heard Doris make small clucking sighs of disapproval.

Sophie was a tall woman and healthy, but she wasn't sure she could take Al down. He worked at the bottling plant lifting pallets of soda off the line and onto trucks. He was a big, burly man. Yet with his eyes closed and swaying gently to the silent music, he appeared as innocent as a small child. If Sophie wasn't aware of his history of domestic abuse, she might have felt sorry for him.

Maybe it was time to try threats.

"Alvin, I swear on the Almighty, I'm going to take your ass straight to MedCentral in Goshen if you don't come here and let me see to that stab wound. You're losing a lot of blood."

Alvin paused and looked down at his shirt, now saturated with a darkening pool. Perhaps the alcohol was wearing off and he was coming to his senses. He glared at Doris. "See what the bitch done done to me, Miss Sophie. You know that ain't right."

"I hear you, Al, but you can't be going after her the way you do time and again. That builds up in a person, you know? Then one day that person snaps." She shrugged. "Today was her day."

Blood from Alvin's wound had inundated the lower front of his T-shirt and the saturated parts were turning an intriguing shade of purple. He moved toward the kitchen table. Sophie pushed him into a chair.

"Was it a clean knife? Or had you used it?" she asked Doris.

Doris took a seat at Alvin's side and crossed her arms over her ample chest. She seemed disinclined to answer even though half an hour ago she had made a frantic phone call summoning Sophie to her husband's side.

"Doris? I need to know this."

Sophie gently pulled the T-shirt over Alvin's head. Although he sat upright at the kitchen table, the alcohol he'd consumed had turned his body loose and pliant and his form wobbled under her hands.

"Doris? Which knife was it?"

"Bitch done stabbed me. Stabbed me!" He lowered his head and looked at the blood on his fingers. He stood unsteadily and moved from the table.

"It was a butter knife is all," Doris said finally. "It was clean. Out of the rack there."

Alvin seemed truly perplexed. "What in the hell did I do to her?" he asked, right hand pressed to the wound, blocking Sophie's view of it. No doubt he was starting to feel some pain.

"Don't give me that crap," Doris said. "No matter what I do, how hard I work, nothing's ever good enough for you. I listen to your complaining from morning 'til night."

Sophie sighed, certain the argument she'd interrupted upon her arrival was gaining fresh steam. She moved around the table and grabbed Alvin by the arm. He resisted, and she snapped a hand up to grab and twist his earlobe. Pain doubled him and she was able to pull him back down into the kitchen chair.

"I didn't do nothing to the bitch," he exclaimed, panting. "She knows I like my hamburgers rare, but does she even care? No, ever' damn thing has to be her way."

"Hush now, and let me look at this."

Grabbing surgical scissors from the counter behind her, Sophie knelt and expertly started trimming belly hair from the wound.

"Doris, look what you done," he whined, looking down at the ragged wound.

"Shut up, Al," she snapped in reply. She moved close to see what Sophie was doing. "I'm real sorry he's such a pain, Miss Sophie. We sure hate getting you out here this time of night and all," she continued.

"That's okay, Doris. I know it was something that couldn't be helped." She glanced up and her gaze met the other woman's, a tacit understanding passing between them.

Alvin, whether from the pints of beer he'd consumed or the pint of blood wetting his shirt, was finally getting sleepy and had calmed somewhat.

The gash was pretty deep, through the heavy layer of fat and almost into the underlying muscle. Doris must have slashed deep, or perhaps Alvin had fallen onto her in the fight, but Sophie had handled worse. Luckily, Doris had gone to the side and low instead of deep into Alvin's barrel chest. She poured saline solution into the gash, catching the overrun with his balled-up T-shirt.

Fetching Novocain gel from her backpack, she donned rubber gloves and smeared the gel heavily around the wound and a little way inside the gaping edges.

"What's that?" Doris asked, bending over Alvin and studying it.

"It numbs it, so I can sew it up."

His chest was broad and convex, with a heavy covering of dark blond hair, curly like the thick patch covering his head. Closing the wound was going to be tough, and she debated whether she should try shaving the hair around the gash, instead of just trimming it. Using two fingers she pressed the edges of the wound together. The gel hindered her by trapping the hair into a congealed mass. She continued trimming close until the area was a gory mix of blood, gel and clipped hair.

"Hand me some paper towels, will you, Doris?"

Doris, looking just a little queasy, pulled the roll off the holder and handed it to the healer.

Alvin, rallying, twisted under her hands. "Hey, hey there, what's this you're doing?" he asked, his voice slurring. "That hurts."

He saw the scissors and tried to push her hands away. "Don't be cuttin' on me. Look like a damned poodle, you get through with me."

"Alvin, you are plucking my last nerve," Sophie said, her voice hard as nails. "Better a poodle cut than dead, you ass. Sit back there and shut up. I mean it."

Seeing the steel in her gaze, Alvin backed down and let his hands fall to his sides.

Continuing to hold the wound closed with one hand, Sophie mopped at the area using a good number of the paper towels. She saw a few clumps of hair she'd missed and clipped them away, then used the towels to wipe the hair clippings off his skin. The wound gaped open again as soon as she removed her pinching grip. Fresh blood welled and trickled into the thin coating of gel still covering his skin.

Alvin must have felt the release for he looked down at the wound. "Goddamn," he said. "Look at that."

"Yeah," Sophie agreed, "look at that. This is a pretty big cut. Not deep but wide." She turned to squint up at Doris. "You sure you don't want to go to Goshen on this one? Y'all have good insurance."

Doris blushed. "No, Miss Sophie. You tend it, if you don't mind. It's…well, it's embarrassing and I just don't want everyone knowing our business."

Sophie took a deep breath and turned back to Alvin.

"What're you going to do?" he whispered with a drunken, conspiratorial air.

Sophie twisted her hand to one side and came up with a sterile package. Breaking it open, she used surgical forceps to remove the curved needle attached to a precut length of suturing thread. "I'm gonna sew it up real nice."

Alvin suddenly transformed into a small boy. "Will it hurt?"

Sophie studied him a long time. "I've numbed the area. You'll feel some stinging and some pressure, but it shouldn't be bad. You let me know if it hurts too bad, okay?"

"Maybe I should have another beer?"

Sophie pondered the idea, deciding to hold off on pain medication until tomorrow. "Sure. Doris, get him one more, but that's all for tonight."

After cleaning the gash with saline and a peroxide solution, she determined that the knife hadn't been sharp enough to pierce the muscle more than a minor surface scratch. It was taking a chance, but she figured she wouldn't need to suture the muscle at all, just a few runs through the white fascia covering it. Pus pockets could develop in the overlying fat, but the knife had been clean, she had thoroughly cleaned the wound and Alvin was healthy and a clean fellow. She'd take a chance on it.

Expertly plying the curved needle through his flesh, she went one layer deep and sewed the ragged edges of lightly slashed fascia together with absorbable sutures before opening a new suture packet and tackling the skin. An hour later she sat back on her haunches and studied the seamed line across his abdomen. It was a good job.

"That looks real pretty, Miss Sophie," Doris whispered at her ear.

Embarrassed, Sophie busied herself with cleaning up the mess. "I've only been doing it since I was knee-high to a grasshopper. Grandam started me out on dead chickens when I was about five."

"You healer witches ain't quite right, I swear," Alvin mumbled. He had finished his beer and was mellowly observing the two women.

"Hush, Al," Doris hissed, pressing her lips together in a disapproving line.

Sophie bandaged the wound and working together, the two women helped Alvin to the bed. Passing the guest bedroom, Sophie noted that a lot of Doris's things were scattered about the room. Things that were conspicuously absent from the room Al now occupied.

"Sleeping in the guest room, Doris?" she asked as they made their way through the end of the long hallway that bisected the Borrows' ranch-style home.

"Yeah. He's mean as a bear. Moving in the guest room only makes it worse, but sometimes I just can't stand to be in the same room with him."

"If you need the shelter, you know you can call Clary anytime and she'll come right out to get you."

"Thank you, Miss Sophie. I do appreciate it." She smiled wanly. "I guess I'll stay on with the old bastard. He'd go to hell in a handbasket if I wasn't here to ride him about stuff."

Sophie nodded. "I understand."

As they stepped into the kitchen, Doris paused. "Listen, I got to thank you for not calling the law and all, Miss Sophie. That'd be a whole lot more trouble than either Al or me are worth."

"Well, I know you didn't mean him any harm. Things get out of control sometimes."

"You're right about that. It's the drink that makes him so hard to get on with. He's a different person when he's sober."

"Does he still drink every day?"

"No, only about three times a week. Not as bad as he used to. He's getting older, I guess."

"Good." Sophie wrapped her dirty utensils in paper towels for sterilization at home. "He'll be hurting in the morning. I left a bottle of pills on the counter. Two every six hours and take his temperature each time. Call me if it's up. And no drinking. Make sure, okay?"

"I want to give you this."

Sophie looked at the money lying in Doris's hand. It was a sizeable wad. "That's too much, Doris. You know I take barter. It doesn't have to be cash."

Even as she said it, she thought about the electric bill, the phone bill and the pharmacy bill, all requiring money.

"We're doing good, lately. Alvin moved up and got an increase. I wish you'd take this." She pushed the money toward Sophie. "It's a couple hundred and I know you need it to help you go on with the good you do. We can spare it."

Sophie studied Doris's kind face. She had put on a little weight during the past few years but still was an attractive woman. She looked like pictures of Mrs. Santa Claus. She wore heavy gold jewelry at her ears, neck and fingers.

"All right," Sophie sighed. "If you're sure. It'll help a lot."

Doris smiled and turned to help Sophie pack her backpack. They talked about Alvin's follow-up care and Sophie promised to return in two days. They would decide then when he could return to work. Doris promised she'd keep Al down until Sophie saw him again.

"He'll just have to use up some of his vacation time. It's what he gets for going on about the damn hamburgers. Doesn't he realize eating raw hamburger can make him sick?"

Sophie smiled. "Looks like eating well-cooked hamburgers isn't doing him too much good either."

Doris laughed as she saw Sophie to the door. "Well, most of the time the burgers don't come with a stabbing. Tonight was dinner and theater."

The two women laughed together, and Sophie paused on the front stoop, shivering slightly in the coolish early morning air. "Next time, don't take matters into your own hands, Doris. If Al had died you'd be shed of one set of problems but troubled by a whole new set."

Doris pursed her lips and nodded, letting Sophie know it was a point well taken. "I'll remember. Thank you again, Miss Sophie. Tell Miss Beulah hello for us, okay?"

Sophie nodded and slid into her car, shutting the door carefully so she wouldn't disturb the neighbors.

CHAPTER FOURTEEN

"Hey, lover boy." The voice on the phone was low and husky and undeniably desirable. Stephen felt ridiculously happy to hear from his partner.

"Right? Is that you?" Stephen hated the chirpy sound of his voice. "Where are you?"

"Just getting up. How's your day going?" He yawned as if presenting evidence of sleeping in.

Stephen glanced about the littered office of Backslant Publishing and wondered how his day *was* going. Kind of pointless, really. "It's all right, honey. Going on as usual. Are you getting ready for work?"

"No, not yet. I still have a couple hours. Listen, I was thinking. What would you say to us moving? Going somewhere else to live?"

Stephen sat up straighter in his chair, his eyes fixating on a washed-out print of the Rhine River in Germany. "What do you mean?"

"You and me. Moving. I was thinking I would love to go on down to Key West like we used to talk about. Didn't you love it there when we visited?"

"Yeah, I did." Stephen swallowed and surprising tears blurred his gaze. He thought of his job, leaving it and looking for a new one. He thought about changing insurance, taking lower pay and losing seniority.

"Yes, let's do it," he answered firmly.

Righteous was silent a long time. "You mean it, Stephen?"

"Home is where you are, Righteous." Stephen had buried his face in his free hand.

Righteous sighed as if he'd been holding his breath a long time. "I'll put my notice in today. Do we have enough in the bank to do this? Put money down on a new place and all?"

Stephen laughed gently. It was so like Righteous not to know. "We'll be okay. Things may be tight for a while, but it'll be okay. At least we'll be together."

"I love you, Stephen, you know I do."

"I know." Stephen was going to cry outright. He glanced around the office to see who would see even as tears escaped and moistened his cheeks.

"Okay." Righteous seemed to sense Stephen's emotional fragility and seemed at a loss for words himself. "I guess I'll see you tonight then. I'll come home as early as I can."

"Yes, tonight," Stephen said softly.

"All right. Be safe."

Stephen replaced the handset into the cradle of the telephone and cupped his face in both hands as a silent sob slipped from him. He was touched because he knew that Righteous was trying. He did want to be with Stephen and was making his choice. Leaving Redstar and Goshen would get him away from the profligate life he'd fallen into. Maybe if he could escape that life he could find his way back to faithfulness with Stephen and that was all Stephen wanted.

Filled with a new joy and a feeling of new perspective, Stephen mopped his cheek with his shirtsleeve and straightened his desk.

"So, how's the Whitley piece coming?"

Conrad Ramsey stood in the doorway, his body spread wide, a palm pressed to each doorjamb. The body beneath his oxford shirt and tight khakis appeared to be a work of Michelangelo perfection.

"Done," Stephen responded, looking away. "It's in your queue."

Conrad moved into the room and lifted a letter opener that was resting on Stephen's desk. He moved it back and forth slowly, from one hand to the next. "Are you okay? You look like you might be upset."

Stephen knew Conrad wanted him to meet his gaze, but his emotions were too raw. "I'm fine, Conrad. Thanks."

"We're moving," he finally said. "Away. Down south."

Conrad drew back to study Stephen's face. "What do you mean?"

"He just called me. As soon as we can get everything set up, we're out of here."

"Damn." Conrad stood and moved to the door. "Well, what do you know."

He moved through the door into the hallway, then turned back to give Stephen an encouraging smile. "Good. That's good, Stephen. Good."

CHAPTER FIFTEEN

Morning brought routine into Sophie's day. She preferred this to the restless nights that had been bothering her lately. Usually her sleep was beneficial, but lately the grinding loneliness she'd been feeling had crept into the netherworld of her slumber.

She rose from her tangled bed and drank coffee at the kitchen door as the sun meandered slowly into Bayou Lisse. Swarms of insects greeted the sun's warmth by busying themselves with their own daily chores. Papa Gator growled about a half mile away. It was late in the season for him to be looking for a girlfriend so he was probably warning off a trespassing male.

Sophie sighed and stepped outside. Her bare feet recoiled from the roughness of the wooden floorboards of the porch, but she moved on, coffee mug warming her cupped palms. Just off the porch, on the right, stretched the ancient herb garden Grandam had nurtured since Sophie's mother was a child. One of Sophie's greatest pleasures was the garden, and she walked toward it through the dry, prickly grass. She loved to stroll through the herbs, her hands caressing the various plants and releasing each unique fragrance. Even after all these years, it never failed to delight her.

Today she noted the seven-year love was coming along, almost a foot high, just now showing the growth of the heavy head that would bob at her in the late summer weeks. There was five-finger grass, low and lush green, garderobe, filling the air with spice, and a huge bush of herba Louisa already scenting her hands with lemon oil. The elf leaf encircled the entire garden, truly the only formal touch, but Sophie never trimmed them into shrub shape, just letting the little purple flowers trail where they may. She liked it better that way, portraying nature more precisely.

Her eyes took in the enormous bayou on her left and the endless flow of the Root River on her right. Root River was known as Cofe Creek by most of the locals because her family had lived here on this water as long as anyone could remember. Mints, lady, brandy and catmint grew along the banks there, and several large, old willows, called trees of enchantment by Grandam, shaded it.

Sophie liked living here. She liked the call of the swamp and the slow pace of life, as slow as the Root River in deep summer. Some of the friends she'd gone to school with had talked about moving to Goshen or Mobile, some even as far north as New York. And they had. She still got the occasional postcard from Kinsey, who had moved to Atlanta. She said there were gay women everywhere there, and she was planning to have a commitment ceremony with her girlfriend, Gerri. In a church and everything. Sophie had to shake her head over that one. The idea wasn't even thinkable here in Redstar. Lesbianism, gayness, was okay as long as you didn't talk openly about it. Sophie knew a handful of gay couples in Redstar and they were well tolerated. If one of them acted differently, however, or tried to be acknowledged publicly as gay, Sophie knew that would change.

Being a lesbian in a small southern town wasn't the best situation, Sophie realized, but leaving Redstar and Bayou Lisse never even entered into the equation. Everything that really meant anything to her was here—here in the three hundred square miles that was her life.

She walked toward the bayou, empty coffee mug trailing from one hand. A nettle stabbed at one foot, and she hopped, cursing, then limped onward. Sometimes she wondered why she stayed, really. She knew it was a sense of loyalty to Grandam and to her family. Sophie's mother, Faye, had moved away to Port Saint Joe, Florida, when Sophie was young. She had left Sophie with Grandam when it became evident how strongly the girl felt about leaving the bayou.

"You two are of a kind," Faye told them, her new man sitting outside in his shiny Chevrolet pickup truck. Her hug had been fierce and long, and Sophie would always remember the smell of her— White Shoulders perfume combined with Juicy Fruit gum.

There had been only five visits during Sophie's trek toward womanhood, visits filled with presents and tales of life among Florida's elite. Sophie had her mother's wild, tawny hair, though, and her mother's mother and that was just about enough. And the swamp. All gifts she was grateful for.

The water of the bayou was still this morning, lush with duckweed. A frog scurried at her approach and overhanging wild roses bobbed a slow good morning. The stillness was palpable, stealing across her and immersing her in another language. This was why she stayed. The bayou talked to her, made her one of its own.

The family told her she was a sensitive, that she had the gift of the wild. All the Cofe women had it, or so it was told. Grandam certainly did. Sophie knew Faye possessed the gift but hated it. Some did turn away; Sophie had always known she could if she wanted to. If she wanted to move off the water, move farther into Redstar, no one would hold her to task. Life would go on.

In her heart, though, Sophie knew that the gift was not to be ignored. There was a rightness to it. To turn away and not do what she was able to do was a sacrilege, a wrong turn in the universal order. Faye had gone against it and her life was fine. On the surface. Sophie knew, as did Grandam, that it could come back around, and they were prepared to be nearby if Faye needed them. The gift was a simple thing really. Sophie could heal. She could use the way of the wild to bring anything back to wholeness.

She looked off into the bayou, her blond eyelashes and brows glowing golden in the morning sunlight. The light was penetrating into the water as well, bringing a teeming life-force to the surface. Sophie watched the Lisse waken as she paced gently back and forth along the shoreline. She thought about her day, listing patients in her mind, planning the best routes to each house, chaining them together in the most efficient way.

Her mind settled and refreshed, Sophie walked up the slope toward the house, absently sidestepping the nettle. The air had heated while she'd been at the water, and the sun was now heavy on her face and shoulders as she moved toward the porch.

Humming from the kitchen alerted her to Clary's presence. As did the harsh smell of grits.

"Hey, baby," Clary called as the screen door slapped shut behind Sophie. "Isn't it a beautiful day?"

"Sure is," admitted Sophie. She studied Clary, gauging her mood and found her to be particularly blissful. "So, Salty give you a little last night?"

Clary blushed and tucked her head. "Get on in that shower and leave me be, Sophia Cofe. What's my business is my business."

Sophie laughed and moved on toward Beulah's room. "Hey, Grandam, get up. Clary got a little piece of that good thing last night."

Beulah, curled on her side, laughed even before she was fully awake. "No kidding. Good for her."

Sophie moved into the bathroom and switched on the shower. "I wonder who's smiling the biggest, her or Salty," she called loud enough for Clary to hear.

"Y'all just stop now," Clary said, slamming the spoon against the edge of the pan to shake off the grits clinging to it. The sound reverberated through the house like a gunshot.

"Sheesh. I didn't mean nothing," Sophie muttered to herself as she stripped and slipped into the shower stall.

Grandam moved clumsily into the bathroom, her slippers shuffling against the tiles. "You got a lot of stops today?"

"Yeah, six. You gettin' on okay?" She peeked around the curtain, watching as Grandam carefully lowered herself onto the toilet.

"Feeling strong," she replied as she emptied her bladder.

Sophie decided against washing her hair because she was running late, so she stepped out almost as soon as Grandam hobbled from the bathroom.

"You need a shower, Grandam?"

"No, not yet. I'll get Clary to help me later."

Sophie turned off the water and dried off, imagining a lover's hands moving across her flesh. She missed having a lover; the occurrences had been too few and too far apart. She sighed and brought her thoughts back to reality. She had work to do.

After dressing and sharing buttery garlic grits and more coffee with Grandam, Sophie traveled north on Route 46.

The Larsens, Samell and Pyree, lived on Root River in the shadow of a defunct fish factory. Their five kids were always getting into something and Pyree had called yesterday to say that her youngest had developed a rash on his bottom. It was probably poison ivy, but Pyree seemed to think it was something else. Pulling into the bare dirt parking area in front of the small clapboard house, Sophie laughed as two children and three dogs crowded around to greet her.

"You here to see Nab?" asked seven-year-old Ada, her braided hair poking out in all directions and framing two huge brown eyes in a tan face.

"Yes, and why aren't you ready for school, young lady? It's not summer yet," Sophie said as she fetched her bag from the car.

"Going in late, all of us are," she answered, running alongside Sophie as she walked to the porch. "Teachers day, or something like that. Bus is gonna be two hours late."

"Well, that's nice," Sophie said. "I hope you're using the time to help your mama with the babies."

"We are," said Mary, the quiet nine-year-old. "But Nab's been crying all night. Says it itches him something fierce."

Pyree looked as though she'd had little sleep. Puffy skin surrounded her large brown eyes and her smile was fragile. She still wore her faded nightgown. The baby, two-year-old Nab, was standing in the playpen, rubbing his own eyes. He wore nothing but a diaper.

"Hey, Pyree. Hear you had a rough night."

"He's been crying," she explained. "I think it must hurt him."

Sophie nodded and moved to lift the child. He clung to her neck and allowed Sophie to carry him to the kitchen table. "Any idea what he got into?"

"No, maybe something outside but nothing I saw." She shrugged her shoulders and scratched at her mussed, home-straightened hair.

"You girls clean this off," Sophie directed, indicating the table laden with breakfast dishes. Ada and Mary began clearing and Sophie, with her one free hand, rinsed a paper towel in hot water and wiped the surface clean. "Get me a clean towel, will you?" she asked Mary.

After spreading the towel, she carefully placed Nab on the table and looked into his eyes. "You got a boo-boo, honey? Show Sophie where it hurts."

Nab looked doubtfully at his mother, and Sophie thought for a moment that he would cry. With Pyree's encouragement, however, he moved one plump thigh toward Sophie. She spoke soothing words as she examined the patch of skin where his buttocks met his leg. The skin there was inflamed, but not cracked like a fungal infection. She sweet-talked Nab into laying on his stomach using an orange lollipop as incentive and, peering closely, saw that the inflammation had been made worse by repeated scratching with dirty fingernails. Stretching the dark skin, she noted that the pale risings had substance and her diagnosis was confirmed.

"He's got a patch of chiggers," she said. "You need to keep the kids away from wherever he was playing yesterday or the day before."

"Chiggers?"

"They're little bugs. Your mama must have told you about them. Hell, you've probably had them a time or two yourself."

"Yeah, I think so. But they never looked like that," she protested, pointing to Nab's skin.

"Well, he's two. They ganged up on him. You got a cucumber?"

Pyree looked puzzled. "A cuke?"

"Yeah, I need one, best fresh out of the garden."

"But it's early in the season. They're not ripe yet."

"Where they growin'?" She handed Nab back to his mother.

"Out back. Mary, show Miss Sophie the garden."

Mary looked up from the library book she was reading. "Yes, ma'am."

She led Sophie around the front of the house to a long strip of cultivated land between the river and the back of the house. There were eight cucumber hills. Sophie chose the nearest one and knelt down. She found a baby cucumber, barely free from its blossom and covered in bristles. She picked it, careful not to disturb any of the sister cucumbers on the vine and, after brushing it off, popped it into her mouth. She chewed it thoroughly, not swallowing, allowing saliva and cucumber juice to mingle in her mouth. She spit it into her palm and led the way back into the house.

"What's that for, Miss Sophie," Mary asked, her voice a serious whisper.

"Nab," Sophie whispered back just as seriously.

"I mean, what does it do?"

Sophie laughed. "I'm just picking on you. It'll help his sore place feel better. We'll put that on for a while, then we'll put another medicine on to smother out those old chiggers."

"Will it work?" Mary asked.

"It better. It has before."

Inside, Nab was riding his mother's hip as she packed lunches for the other children. Fifteen-year-old Kylie had come out of the bedroom and was helping. Ada and her brother Tim, twelve, were finally dressed and filling their bookbags beside the front door.

"Mary, get yourself ready now. The bus'll be here in just a little bit."

"I'm ready. I just gotta get my bag."

"I'll take him," Sophie said, shifting Nab from Pyree's hip to her own. She stood him on the table and pulled apart his diaper. She checked him for other chigger signs, awkwardly holding him with one hand. She would have asked for help with the wiggling, fretful child but knew Pyree was plenty busy getting the older kids off to school. Sophie would manage Nab.

There were no other chigger sites, and Sophie smoothed the cucumber paste across the four-inch by four-inch patch on his upper thigh. Reaching into her bag, she pulled out a large gauze patch and surgical tape.

"Can you stand real still?" she asked Nab as she found his gaze with hers. "I want to put a picture on you."

He watched her warily, so she tore open the gauze and showed him the white square. "You know what this picture is?"

He sniffled, unwilling to be pulled in completely, but she could tell he was curious. "Let me put it on and I'll tell you."

She quickly pressed the patch on his skin and showed him the tape. "Now I've gotta put the frame around it. It may tickle, but don't you laugh, okay?"

A smile touched the corner of his plump lips, and his dark eyes twinkled.

"This here is a picture of a white rabbit in a cotton field. See how white it is?" She taped the gauze on with a loose taping, then refastened his diaper. "Later on, we'll see if we can find his eyes."

She stood him on the floor and he ran to Pyree, grabbing hold of her leg and babbling about rabbits.

The bus pulled up outside, brakes squeaking. The annoying tick of its safety lights sounded loud inside the kitchen. Moments later there was only Pyree, Nab and Sophie in the house.

"You done already?" Pyree used a paper towel to swab at her perspiring face.

"For now. I've got to hang around for twenty minutes or so."

Pyree smiled for the first time that morning. "Good. Let's have something cold."

Chiding Nab, who'd become fretful again, Pyree poured two glasses of sweet iced tea from a cracked ceramic pitcher and handed one to Sophie. With a sigh, Sophie settled herself at the table and took a long pull off the tea. "Ahh, that's good."

"I like it strong," Pyree said as she sat and pulled Nab onto her lap. "So tell me how Miss Beulah is feelin' these days."

"Vinegary as ever. You know nothing will keep her down for long. The stroke weakened her some, but she can get around on her own."

"Good to know, that is. You tell her Pyree said hello."

"Has he eaten?" Sophie watched the boy as he pressed and studied what he could see of the bandage. She knew she'd have to tape the next one on better if it was going to last any time.

"Yeah. He had breakfast early. Had to do something to quiet him down."

They talked about mundane things for a while—new babies that Sophie had delivered, the death of the Witter baby, problems with

Pyree's oldest girl who had recently become sexual with her young boyfriend. They also talked about Pyree's birth control shots, delivered at the health department in Redstar every six months. She was happy to report no side effects other than feeling sick to her stomach some mornings.

"And that's a small price to pay. This one is more than enough to keep me busy for a while," Pyree said as she tickled Nab until he squealed. His flailing loosened the bandage, and Sophie moved to get more gauze and tape from her bag. She also brought over a tube of zinc oxide.

"Okay, Nab. Time to put on a new rabbit picture. You ready?"

Nab hid his head in his mother's chest, but Sophie, with Pyree's help, soon had the chigger inflammation smeared with zinc and tightly rebandaged. The cucumber paste had eased the irritation somewhat and the zinc further soothed the area. He was a much happier baby.

"Leave this on all day," Sophie directed as she washed her hands at the sink. "We want to keep that white stuff on to smother any larvae and the bandage on to keep it all clean. He could get a nasty infection if we're not careful, okay?"

Pyree nodded. "I can't thank you enough, Miss Sophie. He's acting better already."

"Good." Sophie smiled at Nab and rubbed his rough, tightly curled hair. "I'll leave the rest of this tube with you. You'll need to put some more on tomorrow evening after you give him a bath. He can just stay dirty till then. He'll probably get the bandage dirty when he messes and wets his diapers. Just clean it off the best you can. I'll be by tomorrow to check on it."

She tidied the kitchen area where she had worked and gathered her supplies, preparing to leave. Pyree let Nab slide to the floor, and she walked to the refrigerator. "Listen, I have some good leaf lettuce Samell picked yesterday evening. It's still sweet as sugar, though it's getting late for lettuce. I'm gonna give you a good mess of that and a bottle of my icebox pickle."

"Why, thank you kindly, Pyree. Are you sure y'all can spare it? You got a good group to feed here."

"Naw, Samell's good in the garden, always has been. There's plenty to spare."

Sophie looked around at the small frame house, built years ago by Habitat for Humanity. It was clean, well-maintained and cluttered, of course, with the debris of five active children. The Larsens were doing okay. They had a good supply of groceries scattered around the kitchen. Sometimes Sophie felt as though she took the last bite of food from some tables, and she often refused offerings if she felt accepting them would cause hardship on a family. Today she accepted the full grocery bag graciously.

"Well, you've made Grandam's day. There's nothing she likes better than fresh leaf lettuce," Sophie said as she approached the kitchen door. "I'll be on then. You tell Mary I said to draw some rabbit eyes on that bandage. Nab will be expecting it."

She walked out into the brilliant day, already planning her next visit.

CHAPTER SIXTEEN

They were getting embarrassingly loud. She was a big girl with that compact, dense fat some girls harbor. Her face was round, red now with anger, and Delora found herself waiting for the girl to bust loose and knock her husband's head off. It wouldn't be an easy feat, however, for he looked as shriveled and tough as beef jerky and just as ugly. Especially with his face twisted in rage as it was now. He made Delora feel as though she was staring into a pot of boiling water. She was not a bit surprised when the pot boiled over.

With a blurred snap, his hand was in his wife's hair, jerking her head back and pulling her toward him, almost out of her chair. The girl's fury brought her right fist around in a roundhouse punch and connected solidly with the side of his head. He blinked his eyes, probably seeing stars, and shook her until her heavy arms flopped loosely on the wooden tabletop. She glared up at him through a mass of disordered hair. Hatred radiated from her entire body.

"I told you to shut up. I've had just about enough of you today. The boy is going fishing with me Tuesday and that's all, you hear me?" He grabbed her chin in his free hand and made sure she heard him by talking with his face only three inches from hers.

Delora was glad the club was mostly empty although the few rummies at the bar were enjoying the show.

She looked away. Once when she and Louie had been fighting about how to cook a Thanksgiving turkey, he had grabbed her hair just like this husband. Only Louie had used the fistful of hair to drag her down the hall and into the bathroom. He'd then stuck her face against the cold, clammy porcelain inside the toilet, making sure she got a good mouthful. He said it was to wash out her mouth for the way she was smart-mouthing him.

She realized now that was when she had stopped talking to him. Beyond the normal daily requirements, she did not seek him out. She lost interest. Gone was the fantasy that he would be the man she wanted him to be. A man who would treat her in such a way could never be what she expected.

Seeing the man and his wife made her heart thump in her chest. The man had let go, but a swirling air of humiliation and anger hung above both of them. He was pretending he was cool, only doing his husbandly duty. She was wishing him dead and gone from her life, the wish written on every molecule of her body. Delora felt sad for her. Had been her. Was her.

Maybe being burned the way she had been burned was a good thing overall. Louie seldom had anything to do with her now and this was a blessing. She no longer had to feel that way about anyone. These days it was a gentler emotion, a "when my ship comes in" type of longing for his disappearance instead of the harsh craving she'd once had.

"Shame, isn't it?" Esther said.

Delora turned, caught off guard by the heavy woman's quiet approach.

"Sure is. And you just don't know who to blame."

Esther pushed back her sandy, graying curls with one hand as she straightened liquor bottles with the other. "When it gets to this point, everyone is involved," she replied.

"She needs to get away from him," Delora added.

"Nope." Esther looked squarely at Delora. "She likes it. I mean subconsciously, of course. Egging him on gives her a sense of power. She knows just what to do to push his buttons and that's power. Of a sick sort."

"But look what he did to her."

"Look what she did to him. He's wrong, dead wrong, but so is she. He needs to learn to mind his temper, and she needs to back off. It's a no-win situation."

"That's for sure."

Had she egged Louie on? Had she provoked him? She felt sure she had, but it was easy to do with Louie. He was a quick trigger and her very existence seemed to irk him.

They watched the grumbling duo. Watched them lift their drinks and converse in a stilted manner.

"So what do they do?" Delora asked finally.

Esther checked the ice bin and found it lacking.

"They get on. Day after day. Until one gets hurt beyond repair, whether physical or emotional. Then they divorce. Those two have a baby—a one-year-old. She's the one that'll pay. Her and her brother. Either way they'll pay, whether they stay together like this or separate."

"And the sad thing is, both of them will probably grow up thinking this is the way people should live."

"Right."

Esther disappeared through the kitchen doorway. Delora reached into the fridge below the bar and pulled out a jar of maraschino cherries. She filled the cherry section of the garnish tray. There'd been a run on Manhattans earlier.

"You know what'll happen. Kristen, that's the baby, will grow up thinking that it's okay to let a man beat on you, to disrespect you. Then she'll marry a man just like dear old dad." Esther dumped the bucket of ice into the bin hard as if punctuating her prediction.

Hinchey entered and paused just inside the door to allow his eyes to adjust to the dimness. He saw Delora and his face brightened.

"Your boyfriend's here," Esther muttered.

"Hey, Delora. Esther," Hinchey said with a nod of welcome as he took a seat at the bar.

"Hinchey, how you doing?" Esther asked with fondness. She'd once babysat him while his mom played bingo.

"I'm good, Ess. You all right today?"

"Good. Can't complain. Jeb finally got that vinyl siding on the house. You need to come on over and see it."

He grinned boyishly and rubbed his hands together. "Is that a dinner invitation? If so, I'm there."

Esther laughed and said, "Then consider yourself invited. You come over Sunday afternoon and you'll get the best pot roast you've ever set your teeth into. It'll make your tongue slap your brains out trying to get to it."

Delora smiled at the phrase. "You want a beer, Hinchey?"

At his nod, she fetched a Michelob from the cooler, popped the cap and set it on the bar in front of him. She leaned back and lit a cigarette, glad that the French Club still allowed smoking at the bar.

"Thanks, sweetness."

"You hungry, Hinchey?" Esther asked. "Mike just whipped up some fries and cheeseburgers back there."

"Yeah. I'll take one of each," he answered, lifting the beer to his lips.

He turned to Delora. "So, are you okay?"

"Not much. Just watched a fight between that couple over by the window."

Hinchey craned his neck as he took a long swig of beer. "Them? Fighting? Who are they?"

"Imports, looks like. Esther knows them."

"Did I hear my name?" Esther entered from the back having given Mike Hinchey's order in person.

"That couple?" Delora inclined her head. "Hinchey wants to know who they are."

Esther peered at Hinchey. "No one you'd know. They moved here from Virginia a couple years back. He works over at Bryson's, moving rock every day."

"What were they fighting about?"

Before Esther could get wound up into speculation, Delora excused herself and walked along the back of the bar and down the cluttered hall to the employee washroom. There was a company phone there and she paused beside it. Hesitating only a brief moment, she pulled her cell phone from her pocket and pushed a button.

"Bucky? Are you busy?"

"Never too busy for you."

"Did you have a good day?"

"Good enough. Therapy in the morning. Phone conference in the afternoon."

"Conference about what?"

"A new job. Horse racing game."

"Which company?"

"Still TechGaming."

"They're coming out with a lot of new stuff. Asian Knight must have done well for them." Not being a gamer herself, she often wondered how the first game Bucky designed had sold.

"Did well for me. Gave me more money than I can use. Need a loan?"

Delora laughed. Bucky always cheered her. "No. Don't think so."

"How's things with you?"

"Not great. I'm really scared."

"Why? What's Louie doing?" Bucky's breathing became more labored.

"Nothing really." She rushed to reassure him. "It's just indirect things. The other day I found a can of lighter fluid under his bed. I was changing the sheets and knocked it over."

"Oh no."

"Yeah. Right there under the bed."

"Did you tell him you found it?"

"No way. I talk to him as little as possible."

"I thought he couldn't…the trial…"

"That was a part of his release because I didn't press charges, that he couldn't have it in his possession. We're supposed to light his cigarettes, for Pete's sake."

"Turn the bastard in," he advised impatiently.

"No."

"So, wonder what he was going to do with it."

"What I want to know is, who the hell bought it for him? Rosalie? She knows better."

"She should know better." The sarcasm in his voice surprised Delora. "She probably did know better."

"She is a bitch."

"Yeah, and I know she has it in for you somehow."

"Why would you think that?"

"The way she treats you. Making you work like a dog. Three jobs so you can pay that ridiculous rent for living in her house." He was breathing hard from the exertion of speaking such long sentences.

"There's nowhere else I can go," Delora said quietly.

"Why do you say that?"

"You know why. Rosalie's all the family I have."

"Bullshit. She's not your family, just someone the state gave you to."

"There's no way I could take care of Louie by myself. Rosalie's bigger than I am and she can steady him. I can't do it; I dropped him once."

"You're making excuses. You've got no business lifting anything. You were hurt too when your house burned."

"I know." Delora realized some time ago that she was taking the path of least resistance. The easy way. Though shamed by this fact, she felt powerless to change her life.

"Are you going to stay there forever?"

"No, of course not. I really do hate it."

"No one can change that but you."

"I know that," she replied petulantly.

"Good."

"Louie hid the remote the other day."

"Why?"

"So he could give me grief. I looked for the damned thing for forty-five minutes and then suddenly he had it. I was so pissed."

"He's stupid. A brute."

"Mmhm. All men are."

"Are you sure?"

"Well, other than you, there's one guy I know, nice as the day is long. You remember me telling you about Hinchey?"

"Sure. You sweet on him?"

"Oh no, he still is on me, though, wants me to marry him. Leave Louie."

"You could do that. Divorce Louie and go with Hinchey."

"You know I can't do that. It wouldn't be right."

"If he loves you though, he would accept it."

"He's a young man. Deserves children and a wife who can be all he expects. You know what I mean."

Bucky sighed. "I do."

Delora answered with a hollow sigh of her own. "I'm going to go home now. I have to go in early tomorrow."

"You be careful, now. I mean it. You watch that bastard Louie."

"I will. Love you, Bucky."

"Love you. Sleep, okay? Wait. Todd died. Did I tell you?"

"No, when?" Pain clutched at Delora's chest. Todd Mays had been a patient with them at the burn center. Trapped in a house fire, he had been victim to a number of postevent infections that caused him to be a constant patient more than a year after the fire.

"Yesterday. His mom called me. They couldn't get that last infection under control, then he got pneumonia."

"I guess he just let go," Delora whispered, one hand pressed against her lower belly as if confirming the life-force there.

"I'm sad," Bucky Clyde said. "I wish I could talk to him again."

"He called you as much as I do, didn't he?"

"Yeah," Bucky Clyde agreed softly.

"Are we gonna be all right, Bucky? Ever? It's been two years and I don't feel all right."

Bucky Clyde didn't reply right away, and Delora could picture him, indulging in his nervous-thinking gesture, fingering the bill of his ever-present baseball cap with his stubby three-fingered right hand. When he spoke, his voice was very clear, very strong.

"We're forever changed, Delora. There's no way we can forget that."

Delora knew this to be true, but hearing him verify it grounded her anew. "I know, Bucky, I know." She sighed deeply. "What are you going to do tomorrow?"

There was no need to talk about Todd's funeral. Neither of them would go.

"Therapy, of course, then I get to play a new paintball game."

"New game, cool."

Bucky Clyde was hopelessly addicted to computer games, playing and designing. Paintball games, in which you had to outmaneuver and outstrategize your opponent, were his particular favorites.

"My mom sent it."

"Oh, no way," Delora exclaimed. "She contacted you? Why didn't you tell me?"

"Hopes. Don't want to get them up—yours or mine."

"But that's great. How did she know you liked the paintball games?" Bucky Clyde's mother was an alcoholic who really went off the deep end after Bucky Clyde's car accident.

"Ron told her."

"So she's back talking to your brother too? What brought about her change of heart?"

"I guess getting older. Realizing how mortal we all are."

"Has she stopped?"

"Drinking? No. I'm not sure she ever will. She sounded good the last couple times she called, though."

"That's a good sign." She looked up and saw Esther studying the plates resting under the warmers. "Listen, Bucky, gotta run. I love you. I'm so, so sorry about Todd."

"Me too. Love you. Take care of yourself. Watch him."

Delora hung up and pressed her forehead to the phone's hard plastic coolness. A hand that had crept low pressed against the gauze square covering the gash from her morning fall at the greenhouse. The pressure made the cut sting just a little more.

CHAPTER SEVENTEEN

The knock, when it sounded, was later than expected, yet Beulah nodded her head. She'd been expecting someone all day but hadn't figured it would come this late in the evening. Hell, it felt like it was almost tomorrow.

She knew the person would change all their lives and she was a little surprised when Sophie finally opened the door. What kind of special presence was this? A little old bedraggled girl, thin as a pipe stem. Yet she seemed powerful—as if she had a wildcat coiled inside waiting to expand at the least prompting. Beulah looked her up and down, trying to know something. She saw the woman was afraid, but fear had been mastered, pushed down, and the only thing left to shine was an attitude of "fuck you and the horse you rode in on."

Sophie was barring the door, staring at the little woman as if dumbstruck. The little woman was staring back. Peering intently, Beulah could see the energy pulsing between them and smiled. *So this was the way of it.*

"Sophie, move yourself and let our visitor in."

Sophie, chastened, stepped aside and dropped her eyes finally. "Please, come in," she said, her voice subdued.

The woman moved inside slowly, eyes roaming the main room of the house. She didn't seem afraid, just curious. Weren't they all? Beulah thought tiredly.

"So what can we help you with?" she asked the little powerhouse.

"I hear you're good with medicine and I got a problem." The voice was strong, not meek, yet seemed tired as if she'd lived life and come out the other side.

Sophie stepped farther aside and stood by the bedroom door, her dark eyes studying the woman. Beulah noted her restlessness but ignored it. "You'd best tell us your name."

"I'm Delora November. My homeplace was over on Cox's Creek. You probably knew my daddy, Sherman Clark. He and my mama died in the big squall of '82 when I was a kid." She sighed, the litany finished.

Beulah nodded, the information digested. The girl was older than she'd thought, probably married.

"Sure, I knew of Sherman. My last husband said he was a good supervisor; best on the board. He left early because he didn't like the way things were being handled by the other supervisors, it was said. Tried to make his own way," Beulah responded.

Silence fell. In another world, the one of verandas, mint juleps and pretense, Beulah and Sophie would have listed their own pedigree but here, in the seething energy of the Alabama bayou, no trade was needed.

"So what is it? What does the house of Cofe need to do for you?"

Delora reminded Sophie of a rabbit transferring from one cage to another. She looked at the healer's things scattered throughout the house—curiosity overcoming trepidation.

She's got vinegar, Sophie thought, hands coming up to tuck in errant strands of blond hair, then down to straighten her shirt.

Delora stopped when she reached the center of the front room. Hands hanging limp at her sides, she remained perfectly still, not exactly a convicted felon awaiting execution, but close enough to make Beulah seem uncomfortable. And, as was Beulah's wont, she manifested her discomfort in petulant anger.

"Well, what is it?" she barked.

Delora jumped slightly, but her eyes, cold blue fire, fastened hard on Beulah.

"They say you know all about medicine, those women in town."

Sophie pulled her loose collar closer about her neck, feeling a chill sweep through her cotton shirt.

"We know enough," Beulah said. "Just tell us what you need and I'll tell you whether it's enough for you."

The girl mulled it over for a long time, her gaze studying the yarbs and parts in jars along the walls.

Sophie tried to see the shelves with new eyes. She had built the shelves herself all in one afternoon. It had been the week the black-checkered loon had visited. He'd stayed three days, floating on the water just outside the door of Salamander House. He'd watched Sophie with his red, mocking eyes, head feathers high with death's victory over life.

His low, mournful cry each evening had told them three times again about the death of Sophie's daddy while he was working in Canton, Mississippi. Each shelf on the front room wall bore part of her daddy in it. The horizontal grain of the pale green locust told of his love for the railroad. The widely spaced knots were the cars of the toy trains he used to run every evening before going to bed. Each bracket was a harsh thought she'd brought to him when he punished her. The satiny finish of the boards, rubbed there by Sophie's patience and spit, were the hopes and dreams he'd harbored for his Sophie.

"See, I had this accident a few years ago and was in the hospital for a while. It was all healed up, then this week I fell and it busted open again."

Sophie moved across the room to set fire to a handful of candles. They had electric, but she preferred candlelight.

"Show me," Beulah demanded.

Delora glanced briefly at Sophie, then loosened her blue jeans. She dropped them, then stepped aside and fetched them from the floor looking around for a ready spot to store them. She quickly chose Sophie's easy chair, draping the garment across the padded arm. Then, surprising her hosts, she slid from her panties as well. She stood waiting, her face flushed with embarrassment yet her demeanor defensive.

No, thought Sophie with dismay. *This gal's had it done and done good. Was it just for the healing you sent her to us, Lord?* Selfish thoughts rattled inside her head, but she tried to shake them off before they became full-blown. Loneliness had a way of eating at a person until need instinctively ground out charitable thought.

Delora was waiting, stirring uncomfortably.

"Was it rape, child?" Beulah asked gently.

Delora shook her head.

Taking a deep breath, Sophie pulled one of the worn dining chairs closer to Beulah's chair, then beckoned the woman to them. Delora moved forward reluctantly, her thin sandals scuffing against the floorboards.

Beulah lifted the T-shirt, and her hands began to tremble. Only steel will prevented the loud cry of anguish that threatened to escape Sophie. Delora had been burned. The entire lower half of her abdomen was puckered and ribbed, satiny in some places, coarse in others. The surgeons had tried to repair it—laying on flaps of skin taken from her outer thighs—but the mess reminded Sophie of pig stomach she'd seen lying under plastic at Biggen's Grocery in Goshen. The immediate problem was a laceration at the edge of one of the grafts. The red rim was broken and festered, angry-looking.

"You musta done too much, child. You need to take it easy still. It may be healed, but this here skin is thin as your eyelid." Beulah's voice was steady but low.

"Yeah, I know. I fell, though," Delora muttered, her face averted from the examination. Sophie stood and moved to the center of the room.

Sophie's mind whirled with curiosity. This was no old burn—no toddler pulling hot water off the stove. This was recent. A car accident perhaps? What had the girl said—"I had an accident?" House fire? Delora was plain lucky she hadn't been burned this way all over; it would have taken her life.

Shaking her head, Beulah motioned for Delora to sit. She seemed impressed when the young woman placed her jeans on the seat so her bare bottom wouldn't rest on Sophie's old chair. Not many would have been polite enough to care.

Beulah picked up her work from the end table and resumed spinning the fine threads, each count of nine working into the amulet and increasing the vibratory power.

Standing at a tall worktable, a wooden surface worn to a friendly patina, Sophie studied Delora as she mixed thyme and comfrey with a little calendula and some honey.

Delora was delicate and small, but her compact body appeared sturdy. Her face was agreeable: large eyes and mouth above a pointed chin. Long blond bangs shadowed the blue of her eyes, battling her eyelashes with every blink. The ends of her hair looked as if they'd been damaged and the top bleached naturally pale by the sun. The head of hair as a whole, though cut short and blunt, appeared stressed, as if it had been growing a long time.

"What's the tattoo?" Sophie asked suddenly, her eyes fetching up on the ink staining Delora's knee.

Delora turned in subdued surprise as if wondering if Sophie could be talking to her. "Tattoo?"

She followed Sophie's gaze and looked at her knee, poking it gently. "Just a reminder."

She fell silent again, her attention drifting.

Beulah grunted, and Sophie knew not to pry too deeply. Yet. There'd be time enough.

Sophie stirred, heating the pot on the orange spiral of the electric ring. The spicy tang of thyme and heating honey permeated the room. She wondered what she could mix in to build the girl's tissues. Alum? Too temporary. The jars on the shelves glinted at her like beckoning children. She moved toward them through candlelight. Dried cherries caught her eye first so she cradled the jar in her palm. Walnut bark, tree of evil, signaled it was another good choice so she lifted that one down as well.

Returning to the worktable, she opened the jars, pausing to acknowledge the unique scent wafting from each. She crumbled a handful of stringy tree bark, then tossed cherries into the brew. The cherries looked up at her, their little faces nestled in a pillow of hairy tree fiber. She cooed at them a little, her imagination conjuring them in little sickbeds. Soon they would rise and move on into a life far from this mist of healing steam.

Sophie's eyes found the girl and she sent her the healing force from the cauldron. Delora sat silent and still, unaware of the energy flowing across her. She was so still she might have been dead, but Sophie chased that thought away before it could root and grow.

"It's almost ready," she stated softly just to see if the girl would respond.

Delora didn't lift her head, staring at the hands clasped in her lap. She did nod briefly, so Sophie knew she'd heard.

"Is the pain bad?" Beulah asked as Sophie lifted the hot pan from the ring.

Delora sighed, her small chest heaving. "Sometimes," she said, glancing briefly at Sophie. "Sometimes, it's bad."

Using a metal colander, Sophie strained the thick potion from the hot pan into a stoneware bowl. Steam inundated her, and she licked lips tasting of fruit and spice. She filled a teakettle with cool tap water and set it on the ring.

"Best you come in on the bed." She indicated a back room. "This has to set up a while before you get up."

Delora followed Sophie into the bedroom. The double bed lay

centered on the west wall, piled high with more comforters and pillows than an unsealed, un-air-conditioned house in the Alabama bayou would warrant. Books, their jacket colors forming muted rainbows, lay in crooked stacks on every available surface. Delora studied them curiously. Many were about medicine or herbs; others appeared to be fiction.

"What about Mrs. Cofe?" Delora asked, unfamiliar with the proper protocol.

"Grandam's been slowing down for a while, her leg's numb from a stroke last year."

"I'm sorry, I didn't realize."

Sophie smiled at Delora, and Delora's heart jumped up and ran away in her chest. "It's okay. She's been teaching me since I was a kid. She says I have it all now so I do most everything. Go on, lay there." Sophie nudged Delora toward the bed. "Stretch out, so I can put this mess on you."

Delora eyed the bed doubtfully. "Don't we need something under, so we won't ruin these covers?"

Sophie studied Delora and nodded toward a stack of folded towels on the bureau. Delora shook one out and spread it with careful precision atop the counterpane, then scooted her bottom into the center.

The glimpse Sophie had of the wound as Delora shifted made water well in her eyes. It could have been the steam from the pungent potion or it just might have been the twisted skin around the small pink gash of Delora's sex. The lack of hair there furthered the illusion that she was a child, though the frank blue eyes judging Sophie's reactions were old as the bayou's interior. Sophie allowed her gaze to meet those eyes and felt her stomach plummet into a separate dimension where time stood still.

"So this is it, Lord," she almost muttered aloud. "This is what it feels like. Why'd you wait so long?"

Breath caught in her throat, and she wondered if she had said it aloud. Delora's expression had not changed, however, and she seemed to be as enthralled as Sophie. Sophie felt a weird panic underlying her usual calm. She could sense the shift in energies as the two of them touched without touching. Delora was affected as well; her shallow breathing had deepened.

Sophie moved forward, finally pulling her gaze from Delora's. Hands shaking, she moved next to the bed. Delora had dropped her chin to her chest and seemed to have gone away again. As Sophie moved close,

Delora reclined farther until she rested, flat and defenseless, awaiting Sophie's ministration. Pulling up the T-shirt, Sophie studied the area, trying to determine how best to apply the ointment. Absently, her hand dipped into the heat of the healing salve, and her mind slammed back to dipping her hand into Kinsey Phelps, her first lover. They'd been so young then, mere babies, although they thought themselves so wise in the ways of mystery and life. Their stolen kisses behind the huge cypress below Wichita's Store had been the finest in Sophie's life.

Delora gasped when the heated material met her skin, then exhaled with deliberation.

"Just relax," Sophie soothed. Her hands were large and powerful, and she used all the magic she knew slathering on the ointment. She spread it thick and made sure she layered it past the edges of the burned skin. Her hand sought more from the bowl, then slipped fearlessly between Delora's thighs.

"This may sting a little, but it's for the healing," Sophie whispered. Slowly she pressed her laden fingers part of the way inside Delora's body. Delora's eyes, which had been screwed shut in denial, finally flew open and her mouth fell into a grim line.

"Am I hurting you?"

Delora looked away, toward the window that framed a view of Spanish moss twining into Spanish moss. "No, I—I don't think so. It feels hot."

"Good. That's what we want." Sophie withdrew her hand and spread the remainder of the concoction along Delora's groin and upper thighs.

Rearing back, she took a deep breath and transferred the empty bowl to her right hand. With her left, she pulled down the shirt partway and flipped the edge of the towel across Delora's nakedness.

"You just stay here now. Rest. I'll be right in the next room."

She avoided Grandam's eyes as she made her way to the kitchen. At the sink, washing her hands, Sophie found herself filled with song. She tried to burden it down but ended up humming praises of joy. She could feel change nibbling at the edges of her life and the nibbles felt just that good.

CHAPTER EIGHTEEN

She dialed the number from memory. Strange how quickly she memorized each new long distance phone card. He answered almost immediately.

"Delora, is that you?"

He sounded half asleep, and alarm jangled through Delora. She didn't want to abuse their friendship. Sleep was a precious commodity for both of them and stealing it was a dire infringement.

"My gosh, I'm so sorry. I woke you, didn't I?"

"S'okay," he replied, stifling a yawn. "Sleep is boring."

"Maybe. But you don't sleep too well, like me, and I hate to wake you."

"It's good to hear your voice, anytime. You sound wide-awake. What's going on?"

"I'm confused."

"How so?"

"There's this woman I met. Well, two women really. An older healer woman and her granddaughter."

"Where did you meet them?"

"At their house, on Bayou Lisse. I fell and tore one of the skin grafts at the greenhouse yesterday and I needed some help with it. All the people around here talk about how good they are as healers."

He laughed dryly. "Couldn't bear the thought of going back to the hospital, huh?"

Delora smiled and looked around. Her cell phone battery had gone down, so she was at the phone booth attached outside Manning's Grocery off Front Street. It was creepy there at night. One weak incandescent bulb was all that lit the front sidewalk. A soft glow emanated from the nightlights inside, but Delora still felt vulnerable to the wide expanse of darkness around her. "No, I don't want to do that. I'll get all that crap about applying for disability again."

They fell companionably silent. Delora pulled chewing gum from her mouth, stretching it like saltwater taffy a few times before tucking it back in.

"The one woman, her name is Sophie. There's something about her..."

"How do you mean? What kind of something?"

"It's like I have a hard time looking away from her face. She's really beautiful with long blond hair and it's not that thin hair either; it's like all these fuzzy curls. She braids it up so it kind of curls all around her face. Like...like a halo."

"So, are you thinking she's pretty and you'd like to look like her?" He was struggling to make sense of her words.

"Well, yeah, but I'm hypnotized by her, when our eyes meet and..."

"What color are her eyes?" he interrupted.

"Deep brown, but like an otter."

"An otter? What the hell's an otter?"

Del laughed. "Like a seal but littler than a beaver. They live here in the bayou. They have shiny brown fur and the color and shine is like Sophie's eyes."

"So what do you think it means?"

"I don't know. What do you think? I can't stop thinking about her. There's some weird magnet thing going on like she's pulling me into her. How strange is that?"

"Maybe you're attracted to her."

"What do you mean?"

"How do you feel when you're with her?"

"I told you. Excited, real excited. I don't want to go, to leave her, even though I know it's time to. I let her touch me there, too, where I'm burned."

"It's like a crush," he surmised.

Delora could hear him nodding, having solved her dilemma in his own mind.

"What?" She suddenly had a hard time understanding what he meant.

"Like you're in love with her. Infatuated."

Infatuated. The word hung between them.

"Do you think that's possible?"

"Babe, in the world you and I live in, everything's possible. Have you ever been attracted to a woman before?"

Delora had to pause and think a few moments, Bucky Clyde's breath regular in her ear. "I used to like this little girl, Tabitha, in fourth grade. I used to pack extra stuff in my lunch for her and stayed with her as much as I could. Then Mom and Dad died and everything changed."

"Maybe you're a latent lesbian. Have you ever wondered?"

"It's such an ugly word," she sighed. "'Lesbian.'"

"Why?"

"I hate labels, that's all." She paused. "Look, go back to sleep. I gotta go."

"Wait. So what are you going to do?"

"Nothing. I'm gonna go home and go to bed myself, and tomorrow I'll go to work just like I always do."

Bucky Clyde sighed deeply. "All right. I understand. Love you, though. Please be careful. There's so much changing for you right now. You gotta find yourself somewhere in the middle of it all, okay?"

"Okay, I will. Sleep. Have a good day tomorrow, okay?"

"Okay."

She hung up and studied the night. Lightning bugs waltzed off in the trees and moths fluttered around the light bulb overhead. She could hear the distant sound of traffic farther into Redstar. Her mind rebelled and envisioned her body entwined with Sophie's. Then she thought of beautiful Sophie leaning to kiss the scarred skin of her abdomen, and blistering tears stung both eyes. Sadness filled her and the pain of it made her suicidal.

After a moment of deep thought, she laid her left hand against the brick wall of the store, spreading the fingers wide. Without further thought, she held the phone handset like a hammer and slammed it into her little finger. Harsh, throbbing pain raced all the way to her shoulder and, gritting her teeth, she calmly replaced the handset and held the wounded hand delicately in her other palm. She walked to her car, ready, finally, to go home.

CHAPTER NINETEEN

"So. What do you think of her?"

Sophie had directed the question to Grandam, but Clary looked up from the magazine she was studying. "Who?"

"Little gal from town," answered Beulah. "Had a burn that needed work."

"Hmmm," Clary said. "What was she like, Sophie?"

Sophie shrugged, a little embarrassed. "Little, like Ellie St. John's people. And a blonde, like me."

"Cute?"

Sophie smiled and felt a strange rush of emotion rise up.

"Well, isn't this news," Clary said.

"Mmm," began Beulah with a chuckle. "You should have seen them, Clary. Made my heart warm."

"So she came to the house here?" Clary repeatedly looked from Beulah to Sophie, trying to become part of this new facet of the Cofe's life.

Sophie rose and placed her empty coffee mug into the sink, ready at last to share Delora. By doing so, she knew the doors of the Universe would open and the little blond woman would be fully imprinted and made a part of their reality.

"She came by late last night. She'd been in a fire some time ago, all across her lower body…"

"From just about her waist all the way to her thighs. It was strange how it was only there. I didn't see any scars anywhere else, except where the surgeons had taken some skin," added Beulah. "I like her, by the way," she directed toward Sophie.

Sophie nodded and continued. "What brought her to us was a fall that tore open one of the grafts." She paused. "The strange thing was that the fire went up inside. I've never seen anything like it. I think someone did it to her on purpose."

Beulah lifted her head and studied Sophie with keen eyes. How had she not sensed that? She used her fork and absently pushed scrambled eggs around on her plate as she pondered this new idea.

"Who would do something like that?" asked Clary, lifting her mug and taking a sip of coffee, eyes thoughtful. "That just don't seem right."

"You know anything about her people, Clary? They're the Clarks from on Cox's Creek. She's a…what's her name?" Beulah snapped her fingers, trying to awaken her memory.

"November. She's Delora November," Sophie supplied wistfully, her gaze studying the early morning haze above Bayou Lisse.

Clary sat straight and her mouth fell open. "I know about this," she said excitedly. "It was about two years ago. Her husband Larry, no, wait, Louie. Louie November. Drunk on his ass one day he set their house on fire. He was burned too but still lives here in the area. I thought the wife left him, moved away, though, to Georgia or something."

"She's back, I guess," said Beulah, gnawing halfheartedly at a piece of toast. "Maybe they got back together. I wouldn't give the son-of-a-bitch *beng* the time of day, though, 'twas me." She threw the toast onto her plate and pushed the plate away.

Sophie smiled, knowing that Grandam always fell into the old language if her emotion ran high. Delora's plight must have affected her deeply.

"*Jin, puridaia, Devel dan bengs, doldi,*" Sophie said softly.

Clary snorted. "Hmph, if God punishes devils, why are there so many fat, rich ones walking around?" She rose, carried Beulah's dishes to the sink and began washing them busily.

The creak of an oarlock outside drew Sophie's attention, and she moved to the front door. "Kith is meeting," she told the others.

Clary and Beulah moved to peer through the screen with Sophie.

"I wonder what the topic is," murmured Clary.

"I haven't heard anything," answered Beulah. "Usually Irma Geneva tells me."

Sophie had to admit the boat passing by would easily strike an ominous alarm in the hearts of all who viewed its passage. At meeting time, the boat, owned by Kith member, Tomlin Sirois, would stop at every one of the nine homes along the bayou collecting the members. Usually they met to discuss the maintenance of the laws and people, but extra meetings could be called when decisions, usually related to crime, had to be rendered.

The boat was long, twenty-five feet, and carried a somber collection of Manu Lisse. Most were older men, well-respected in the Roma community of Bayou Lisse, each representing a specific tribe. They were dressed in traditional garb, wearing long dark robes over their daily wear and high leather boots, each decorated according to their tribe. Black, low-brimmed fedoras covered their ebony-haired heads, each with a short feather set off at a jaunty angle. They were talking softly among themselves. Jaul Fauster, representative for the Chovihanni tribe that the Cofe families belonged to, waved at them from his perch standing along an upright. He extended one leg and hung off the side of the boat as he waved. The other Kith turned and eyed them, most lifting a hand in salute. Beulah or Sophie had treated every one of the nine at some point, so their home was well-favored by the governing board.

Within moments, they were out of sight and the women returned to the kitchen table. Sophie studied Grandam's olive skin and wondered again at her own coloring. She'd wondered many times before, at each family gathering, why that, although she had the dusky skin of her people, her hair was as fair as a morning sunrise. Where was the dark hair and brows of the others? She and her mother Faye were the only two in the tribe who bore heavy blond curls and hair that grew absurdly fast, like a field afire. Grandam attributed it to her great-great-grandmother, Maddy Cofe, who was the first to be born with silver hair. According to family lore her gift had been the most extreme, for she communicated entirely without words and could heal from a distance if brought a comb bearing the ill one's hair.

Although the blond coloring set Sophie off from her people, there was also the additional respect accorded her due to her own healing prowess. Thus, she'd never regarded the difference as a painful one and moved easily among those she helped.

Sophie's thoughts turned to Delora, who was also blond but with pale, freckled skin and huge, blue eyes. She listened with half an ear to Clary and Grandam's conversation, but her being focused on Delora and certain unmentionable fantasies.

CHAPTER TWENTY

The ache of her broken finger lingered, throbbing like a toothache. By six Delora had had enough. Bidding Esther a pained goodbye, she gave the bar a last swipe, with keen eyes scanned the club making sure everything was in order, then slipped out the back door. At home, she eased into the front hall, quiet as was her habit. The TV droned quietly in the darkened living room, the flickering light strobing against the walls.

The sound hit her first—sly chuckles and strange, short moans. Slowing her tentative stride even further, Delora peeked around the corner and recoiled. Louie was resting in his usual chair in the darkened living room, head thrown back and mouth open. Light from the television flickered across his scarred face, making his visage horror movie quality. The sight frightened Delora, but she wasn't quite sure how she felt about Rosalie's head bobbing up and down in his groin area. Delora's eyes grew wide as she watched Rosalie move high and shift her bulk above Louie, lowering herself onto him. She rocked herself up and down as her loose housedress billowed around them.

Revulsion stirred in Delora and she backed against the wall of the dim hallway, heart pounding and mind racing. How long had this been going on? She peered around the doorframe again and watched long enough to see Rosalie lean forward and press her sloppy mouth onto Louie's scarred, minimal lips.

Hell, she thought with surprisingly little anger, they could have been carrying on since she and Louie moved here. Perhaps this was the real reason Louie had not approached her for sex since the accident—a great fear she had lived with for the past two years. She should have realized he wasn't leaving her alone out of some charitable inclination. Damn his ass.

Edging toward the door to outside, she passed through carefully. She didn't want them to know she'd seen. Odd. She should have been filled with anger and hurt but felt only resignation. So be it. There was no need to rock the boat.

Standing in the front yard, hand pounding, Delora realized that for the first time in her life she felt homeless. Even when her parents had died in that horrible hurricane that had passed through like the wrathful hand of God she had not felt that way. There had been a childlike knowledge—no, a certainty—that the state welfare people would find her a home. And it wasn't until later when she had a foster home that she realized how much her parents' death had changed her life. Yet she had had a home.

Now all was different. She felt abandoned. There was no place to go.

As if denying the realization, her feet started scissoring, taking her to the car and the road south. She entered Redstar and sat outside the darkened diner chewing aspirin she'd picked up at Albie's Drugstore. She watched the black boys talk up passersby for a few coins and knew she did not want to stay there. Frustrated, she gunned the engine. Feeling a twinge of pain in her abdomen, she suddenly knew where to go.

CHAPTER TWENTY-ONE

Delora stood before the small wooden house. The last gasp of spring flowers stood guard on either side of the door, their feet hidden in window boxes. Delora felt a stirring within her, a funny anticipation. Or fear. Soft light spilling from the large front window made her believe Sophie was home, even though the stillness of the night made this faith waver. A low drone of grasshopper song reached a crescendo as she moved toward the porch. The sound of her footstep onto the bottom step ratcheted off into the night like a harsh moan, and she paused, a deer in car headlights. There were no sounds from inside, so she stepped carefully onto the weathered floorboards of the porch.

The door opened just as her weight shifted from step to porch and gentle candlelight leapt upon her. Sophie waited for her, framed in the doorway, a calm silhouette. Their eyes met and Delora passed from the disturbing night into the quiet sanctuary of Sophie's home. Inside, Sophie motioned Delora into one of the easy chairs and disappeared into the back. Delora looked at the chair and realized it was the most inviting thing in the world. Gratefully, with just a hint of wonder about why she was here, she settled herself into the chair, angling her head back. A vision of Louie's scarred face in that same position disturbed her so she jerked upright.

She reluctantly replayed the scene in her mind. They'd been at it a long time; they were too comfortable with one another. Delora knew she should be angry, knew she should be seething about the burning as well, but there seemed to be nothing left in her to care. She was an empty husk, the sweetness inside having all been burnt away as easily as the outer flesh.

As if she'd had it ready and waiting for her, Sophie appeared with a cup of hot, brewed tea.

"It's black tea with a little chamomile for calmness," she said as she handed it to Delora.

"Mrs. Cofe?"

"She's in bed. Usually goes early these days."

They sat in silence for a long time and, strangely, Delora felt comfortable. Sophie wore like a comfortable pair of jeans, yet Delora felt exhilarated to be with her. There was an odd electric hum, and, if she thought about it too long, she realized there was some eroticism to it. Since the time their eyes had met and Delora had trusted Sophie's hand there in her most intimate, wounded place, there had been this unspoken energy between them.

They sat in silence for some time, sipping tea. Delora closed her eyes and pressed her cheek to the warm exterior of the porcelain mug.

"Do you want to talk about it?"

Delora opened her eyes. Sophie was watching her, eyes sympathetic and ridiculously warm in the lamplight. She shook her head, letting Sophie know it was not something she wanted to deal with tonight. Instead, she began talking about her childhood, about the death of her parents, the aftermath of that storm.

The description of Delora's loss was so vivid that Sophie could taste the copper of Delora's desolation, could smell the resignation Delora wore on her skin.

"Hold me," Delora said suddenly and so quietly that Sophie was afraid she hadn't heard correctly.

Sophie placed her cup carefully on the end table and sat back. "Come sit on my lap," she invited, her eyes unreadable.

Delora rose with slow uncertainty, and Sophie wondered why this movement should seem so natural, so inevitable. Delora fell into Sophie's arms, a feather wafting through the Guf, the hall of souls. Sophie's arms found a home in Delora's slim curves, and they remained silent, breaths catching as they tried to stifle an inner excitement the contact wrought. Grasshoppers sang mournful ballads outside the walls while the bayou water beat a bass note against the shore.

Delora drifted off, and Sophie studied her beautiful sleeping face for some time. Her fingers lay softly curled against Delora's cheek, and she tenderly pressed her lips to the warmth of the sleeping woman's forehead. It was then she noticed the subtle darkening of the left little finger. Carefully she worked it loose into the light. Delora muttered in pain but did not awaken. The finger was broken and needed tending. Loathe to awaken Delora, however, Sophie decided it could wait. A different comfort seemed more necessary at the moment. Resting her head against Delora's crown, she closed her eyes, basking in the essence of the woman she knew she would love.

CHAPTER TWENTY-TWO

Her hands reached to caress an imaginary form. She could see Delora's head indenting the pillow next to her. Sophie rolled onto her left side, right hand stretching toward where she knew Delora belonged.

"Are you there?" she asked, not entirely sure she meant Delora or the creatures from the other side. Perhaps the Others would see the extent of Sophie's desire. No, her need. How could this gnawing be mere desire? Though powerful, desire could not match this aching for Delora in her life.

This was a new experience, this need. Bayou born, she'd learned early that whatever she did set universal forces in motion and these forces were usually unpredictable. Only ritual and daily direction could sway these forces and sometimes even these were useless.

"It must be time," she entreated to the powerful minions of the Universe. "Since you brought her to me and gave me this craving."

She wasn't sure whether to thank them or curse them.

Her fingers brushed across the soft cotton fabric caught taut across the mattress. So smooth, like the inside of Delora. She had relived that brief moment of possession time and again. The sensation of slipping her hand inside would wash across her unexpectedly, snatching her breath and causing her to drop everything just to remember it in detail.

If she tried hard, she could capture a little of Delora's scent. Her smell was an intriguing blend of lemon, fried food and cigarettes. Delora had stayed until about four in the morning. About midnight Sophie had led the sleeping woman to the bedroom, all the while muttering calming words. Then Sophie had cuddled her close as they lay together and all protestation vanished. Sleep had returned to the smaller woman, but Sophie had lain awake a long time, part of her thrilling to the physical closeness, allowed at last to hold Delora. Another part of her chewed worry until it was bitter gall.

Then, just before daybreak, Sophie had awakened to Delora's panic. With whispered apologies for the intrusion, Delora tried to hurry away so she wouldn't be missed at home. Sophie had practically barred the bedroom door.

"You can't go yet," Sophie whispered firmly.

Cradling her wounded hand, which must have hurt like a son-of-a-bitch, Delora stared wordlessly at Sophie with wide eyes.

"I know why you need to go and you can go," she whispered. "Just let me take care of that, okay? I don't want you hurting, Delora. Fifteen minutes, I promise."

Delora lowered her head and nodded assent. They walked together through the dim house, and Sophie gave new fire to one lone candle. She gathered supplies while Delora waited next to the wooden worktable.

"How'd you do this?" Sophie asked quietly.

Delora remained silent but watched Sophie with avid eyes, only hissing once when Sophie straightened the break and bound it to the splint. Sophie's eyes found Delora's, and their gazes locked. Sophie saw so much there and she ached to kiss the other woman. Delora's expression silently welcomed her. Yet after a long moment, Delora looked away, nervously, toward the door.

Sighing, Sophie finished and pressed a bottle of pain pills into Delora's other hand. "One every four hours and lots of water, okay?"

Delora nodded but returned the bottle to the worktable and turned away. She opened the door with care and stepped through.

"Delora?"

She turned back and studied Sophie's face.

"Watch out for deer. They're everywhere this time of the morning. Be careful."

Delora smiled and Sophie's heart took wing.

Now, arising for the second time, sweeping her legs over the side of the bed, Sophie stood and moved to the bathroom, wondering how her newest patient was doing. Her workload was light, but she did need to go into town and check on Alvin. Maybe, just maybe, she'd have a little time to stop in and see Delora too.

CHAPTER TWENTY-THREE

A group of mourning doves had taken up residence in the shrubbery in front of Spinner's Fen. Their cooing conversation usually welcomed Delora—at least until her crunching footsteps announced her closeness and silenced them. Today they were strangely quiet, the only evidence of their presence the sporadic flutter of wings.

Long a believer in omens, Delora paused on the gravel walkway. What did this silence mean? Such quiet, after more than a year of noisy greetings, had to be significant. She was not a seer, however, and had no easy answers. She slowed her pace and studied what she could see of their gray and white bodies through the heavy leaves.

There was no indication by the sound of what the message entailed. Sighing, Delora moved past. There was work to do. Annie had called earlier to say she'd be late. This didn't worry Delora. She had opened the greenhouse many times on her own.

Moving to the heavy front doors, she laboriously propped them open, then took her time arranging the sale items to their best advantage on the shelves flanking either side of the doorway. There was no rush, really. She wouldn't water the bigger plants in the back until Annie arrived.

When all were arranged to her satisfaction, she walked around the fragrant greenhouse, randomly choosing good-looking midsize potted plants to place out in front of the building.

Delora liked being alone at Spinner's Fen. It was as if her hearing grew more acute. Without Annie there, even quiet, slow-moving Annie, the air was more rarefied, not cluttered by bodies displacing the sound.

Listening to the whisper of dry grass rubbing against the greenhouse wall, Delora continued on, her movements silent and precise. Watching out for her bandaged finger, she set out flats of adolescent tomatoes, their spicy leaf-kisses welcome on her skin. Neatening the rows of gardening books, she found a misplaced praying mantis. Crooning to her, Delora studied the beautiful young creature, marveling at the fine work of nature. She felt blessed to have been able to see—and have time to study—such a well-structured insect.

"Go on with you," she said finally as she walked outside and placed the mantis in a blooming Rose of Sharon bush. She was fiddling with the watering apparatus, preparatory to watering the inside plants, when she heard a car engine approach.

Expecting Annie's truck, she was surprised to see a small silver car meandering up the drive toward Spinner's Fen. Delora dropped the hose, realizing she needed to give the customer her full attention. To her surprise, Sophie Cofe unfolded herself from the small car.

The two women stood and regarded one another for a long time. The healer woman's presence once again affected Delora powerfully. Her heart hammered rapidly in her chest as she drank in Sophie's appearance. The long mane of blond hair was bound into its usual untidy braid, but her cheeks were unusually pink from time spent in the sun. Her eyes were still warm as they studied Delora, waiting for her to speak.

Delora took in Sophie's long lean body clad in faded jeans and a simple, pale blue T-shirt and felt as though she couldn't speak.

Sophie shifted restlessly, although her welcoming smile never faltered.

"I wanted to check on you." Sophie's voice was soft, bearing a strange intimacy that moved Delora in the center of her being. The voice compelled her to new heights of feeling and her breath fractured as it left her lungs. She still could not quite get words out.

Sophie waited, but when it became evident Delora wasn't going to answer, she shifted her stance and her smile was empathetic, understanding. "So, you're okay." It was a statement, not a question, and she let her eyes leave Delora and roam across the greenhouse. The gaze returned to Delora moments later and Delora felt as though a warm blanket had engulfed her.

"You know where I work," Delora breathed finally.

Sophie nodded. "Yes. All of them."

Delora was pleased that Sophie would go to the trouble to find this out.

Sophie moved closer to a hibiscus and gently teased the edge of a blossom. "I need rue. Do you have rue? I need to fill a bare patch."

Delora could have kicked herself. Of course Sophie was here for plants. She felt chagrin for making Sophie wait. She wanted to do a good job for this magnificent woman. She found her voice and discovered it to be low, filled with vibrancy. It matched Sophie's tone, low and sexy.

"Over here," she said, moving to her left. Sophie followed silently, but Delora felt as if the air between them swelled with other words, a language new to her but compelling.

She led Sophie to a collection of good-sized rue in pots. Rue was hard to start and hard to grow for long in containers so these had been on their way to the perennial garden out back.

"How many do you need?" she asked.

Sophie knelt and examined the plants from underneath, careful not to touch the leaves, obviously knowing about their blistering effect. "I'll take three."

She indicated the bandage on Delora's hand. "How's your finger feeling?"

Delora smiled down at the other woman, wanting to touch her but so very afraid. Suppose all this chemistry between them was in her imagination only? Suppose Sophie was put off by Delora's admiration, her scars?

"Oh, okay," she stammered, remembering acutely how tenderly Sophie had bandaged the hand after Delora woke in her arms in the early morning hours. "It's much better. Thank you."

She paused, searching for a new subject. "I'm glad these babies found a good home. They're scheduled to be put in the ground tomorrow. Be sure and get them out of the pots as quickly as you can and give them lots of leg room."

Sophie rose and was standing very close to Delora. "Will do," she whispered. She moved even closer and their eyes met just as Annie's truck rattled into the parking area.

Both women sighed, realizing another precious encounter had been thwarted.

Delora bent and lifted one of the pots and Sophie hoisted the other two.

"Sophie, how are you?" Annie exclaimed as she left the truck. "You and Beulah need rue, I see. How's she coming along?"

"Good," Sophie replied. "Some days it's like she's never been down."

"Well, I'm glad to hear that. They say the brain is incredible, able to recover a good bit after a stroke." She helped Sophie load the rue in the backseat of her car, then fetched the other from Delora and loaded it as well.

"I read that too. It's like it creates new pathways and communicates with the body through different channels than before," Sophie agreed.

"Well, if one's willing to try. I think a willing spirit is a big part of it."

"Well, that describes old Beulah to a T now, doesn't it?"

Annie laughed and agreed as she moved to the side of the greenhouse.

"Her money's no good here, Delora," she called as she disappeared.

Sophie already had money in her hand; she shook her head and motioned for Delora to take the money and be quiet about it. Delora shook her head no, so Sophie grabbed her hand and pressed the money into it.

"So, you're okay? Sure?" Sophie asked in a low whisper.

"Much better," Delora replied, her hands automatically placing the money in the money box and making change of the same amount. She continued to study Sophie's dear face. When she extended the bills, Sophie took it by placing her large callused left hand below Delora's so her palm cupped the back of Delora's hand. Sophie's right hand moved to collect the change and for a brief moment, Delora felt encased by Sophie's power, her presence. It was breathtaking. Moments later, she was gone with a promissory smile.

"I really like Miss Sophie," Annie said sometime later. They were eating peanut butter and honey sandwiches that had been warmed by the sun. Delora hadn't fully recovered from Sophie's visit. Her head felt stuffed with wool.

"You know, she got my dad well from pneumonia while he was at University Hospital getting pins removed from a broken ankle. The docs there weren't making much progress so Mama called the healers. Here comes Miss Sophie with her packets of herbs and thermos of hot water. She spread mustard and onions on his chest, tied onions to his feet and had him drink this awful tea made from thyme and God knows what else. And don't you know he got well in just a few days. The nurses said his room smelled like he'd been eating hot dogs."

She laughed and balled up waxed paper into a tight wad. "It's amazing what those healers can do."

"It is," Delora agreed. She knew Sophie's hands intimately; the thought of them—and Sophie's eyes—stayed with her the rest of the day.

CHAPTER TWENTY-FOUR

"They're having an affair."

"Who?" Bucky's puzzlement showed even through his mangled voice.

"Louie and Rosalie."

"No shit! What are you talking about?"

Delora sighed and glanced at her booths, assuring herself they were okay. Marina was on a bank run, so Delora was minding the entire diner. Everything was going smoothly so she had taken the opportunity to give Bucky a quick call.

"I saw them the other night, going at it," she explained.

"No! What did they say?" His disbelief echoed in her ear.

"I didn't let them know. I snuck out after I saw them."

"Oh no, you should have said something. This is a perfect out for you. If he's fucking around it's grounds for divorce, Delora."

"I know, Bucky." She lit a cigarette with her right hand, holding the phone carefully in her left. Sophie had splinted her finger and taped it to her ring finger so holding the phone in her left hand was awkward. "I'm just not ready to go there yet."

"What's that supposed to mean? Is he or is he not sleeping around on you?"

"Yes. But he has every right. I can't be there for him anymore. I don't care if he is making it with Rosalie. I certainly don't want him."

There was a long silence. Bucky sighed finally and spoke bitterly. "So, what did you do? Nothing?"

"I went to Sophie's." She drew on her cigarette and studied the customers again. They seemed okay, but she knew she'd better not stay on the phone too much longer.

"Where?"

"Remember the healing woman? From the bayou? I went there and we...talked. She splinted my broken finger too." She placed the cigarette in the ashtray under the counter.

"You have a broken finger? When did that happen?"

She sighed and noticed that one of the couples had finished and were coming to the register to pay. "It's a long story. I've gotta run. You know..."

Bucky waited a moment. "What?"

"I think maybe I am what you said. I mean, there's definitely something there. I just wanted you to know."

"Call me later, okay?"

"Okay, will do. Love you."

She closed the phone and dropped it into her pocket. She thoughtfully touched her bandaged fingers, then turned a brilliant smile on the customers.

CHAPTER TWENTY-FIVE

Louie was waiting for her at the edge of Manahassanaugh Park in his usual spot. He liked a specific bench over on the eastern edge of the park. Though he never explained why he chose this spot, Delora felt it was because he could sense that it was more secluded on this side than on the busier western side. The younger folk tended to congregate on the western half because they had closer access to the playground equipment and food kiosks.

Also, there was a smallish swimming pool that had been voted in during the late 80s and in summer it was well-used. The crowd of young people there might mock Louie with his sightless eyes and molten lava face. She was sure the threat of this was what kept him on the quieter side of the park.

She was actually surprised he went out at all, although she couldn't fault him for wanting fresh air and sunshine. He had a few old buddies there too, mostly winos who didn't care much what old Louie November looked like. There were few friends left. He'd never been popular in school and his contrary behavior had alienated the few adult friends he'd been able to make.

Parking the car in the graveled area bordering the lush greenery of Manahassanaugh, Delora left it running and ran around to open the passenger door. She strode across the grass, enjoying the heady summer smell of a well-tended plot of land.

He sat there, his wide wooden-plank body reared back, one arm holding his walking stick, the other riding along the back of the bench. Surrounded by unemployed cronies, he was pontificating about something. She could hear the low rumble of his monotone as she approached. The men with him eyed her warily, as if wondering at her nerve, intruding upon their exclusive male domain.

Uncannily feeling their sudden silent detachment, Louie turned his head her way and queried, "Who's that?" he asked imperiously. "Rosalie? Delora?"

"It's me," Delora said.

"What the hell's took you so long? I'm about to starve out here."

"I'm sorry, Louie," Delora said, approaching and touching his forearm. "Let's get you home. I'm sure Mama has supper ready."

One old guy, with hard eyes and reeking of alcohol, watched her with keen interest.

"Who is this little bit, Louie? You ain't expectin' us to believe this is your wife, are you?" he asked.

Louie laughed and brushed Delora's hand away.

"This is her. Pitiful, ain't it? And she ain't never been in time for anything. I swear you just can't get good help these days."

"But she's a pretty thing," Hard Eyes said loudly. "What the hell's she doing with an ugly old bear like you?"

Apologetic laughter floated on the sun-streaked air. Two of the men hunched forward as if ashamed of their involvement.

"I guess she looks all right," Louie agreed, "but can't say that much matters to me anymore." He laughed, but the others muttered lamely, clearly embarrassed by his reference to his disability.

Hard Eyes still watched Delora with a gaze that had her squirming uncomfortably. What was he looking for? Anger flared in her.

"Come on, Louie, let's get you home now," Delora said, grasping his arm and endeavoring to pull him to his feet. "I've got your cane."

Louie rose reluctantly and hitched his belted jeans.

"Well, fellas, guess I'll be on. The little lady wants her way with me and who am I to say no?"

Delora blushed and pressed her lips together in a firm line so she wouldn't say anything. The men laughed, including Hard Eyes, who never stopped watching her. His gaze made Delora feel dirty.

Louie held her bicep as she led him to the car. After he was in, she almost slammed the door harder than was necessary—but memory held her hand. One of her worst black eyes had come from slamming a car door once. Instead she shut the door with a firm push.

"Took you long enough," he repeated as soon as Delora had settled herself and shut her door.

"I'm sorry," she said again.

After Louie asked her to light a cigarette for him, the two sat in silence the entire way to Royale Court. Rosalie's van wasn't outside the small ranch-style house and a feeling of dismay washed through Delora. If Rosalie was there, Louie would be distracted and busy talking to her. As it was, with only Delora there, he would be as annoying as hell.

Sighing, she parked and moved around to lead him from the car into the house.

The two remained silent as they entered the large kitchen area. Delora wriggled free of Louie's grasp and muttered something about getting dinner. He wandered toward the living room, and she breathed a sigh of relief. Busying herself, she took pork chops from the refrigerator and laid them on the counter. Rosalie had left cans of vegetables on the counter as well as a bowlful of potatoes so Delora had a good idea of the evening's menu.

As she peeled potatoes, she thought of Louie in the other room. She could hear the TV and thought how nice it must be to have nothing else to do.

He's blind, fool, an inner voice whispered.

An uncharitable part of her mind persisted, however. *His fault,* it screamed. The paring knife slipped and came dangerously close to her thumb. Just what she needed—another bandage. She placed the knife in the sink and took a deep breath. She didn't need this crap today. Her thoughts flew to more pleasant things—Sophie and Salamander House. She daydreamed she was there, the lazy slap of Bayou Lisse sounding in her ears. She saw Sophie's warm brown eyes lit with the inner fire of her wholesome spirit.

Delora smiled and picked up the knife. She peeled a potato completely before she thought another thought. The first thought was still Sophie and insanely it was a memory of Sophie's hand pushing insistently between her thighs. The memory evoked a strong plummeting feeling in her body and a shudder of desire raced through her. It took a minute for her to recognize it and when she did, it frightened her. She knew what Bucky said was true. Delora didn't much care. Deep down she believed most people were capable of bisexuality if they allowed themselves to be, but what rankled was, why now? Coming at this point in her life, this desire for Sophie was a moot point. Sophie had seen the worst of Delora; she wouldn't want her.

She thought of her gaze at the greenhouse. Hadn't she still liked her? They meshed together so well. Delora frowned at a difficult potato. She probably just wanted Delora's friendship. This desire for Sophie's touch was Delora's burden to bear alone. Secretly.

She awkwardly cut each peeled potato into cubes and started them toward boiling in a pan of water on the stove.

She got the frying pan ready for the chops after debating a minute or two about how Rosalie wanted them. Often she cooked them in the oven with breading sprinkled on top.

The decision was taken from her hands by Rosalie's entrance. She came in the kitchen door, a plastic grocery bag in one hand. She lumbered up the short stoop and through the screen door, breath bellowing in and out in harsh gasps.

Delora hurried to take the bag from her.

"I started dinner. Got the potatoes on but wasn't sure how you wanted the chops cooked."

Rosalie laid her pocketbook on the table and moved to the stove. She peered into the pan of slowly rolling potatoes and made a tsking sound. "I was gonna slice and fry them," she said sadly.

Delora paused at the refrigerator a head of lettuce in one hand, a block of cheese in the other. Anger filled her, but she beat it down. "I'm sorry, Mama. I didn't know."

Rosalie sighed and rinsed her hands at the sink. "That's all right. We'll have mashed."

She hid the pork chops with her bulk, effectively dismissing Delora.

Delora, feeling chastised, lifted plates from the cupboard and placed them on the table. She laid out paper napkins and silverware with great care, then stood wringing her hands wondering what to do next.

"How's Louie this afternoon?" Rosalie asked finally. She turned to look at her foster daughter.

"He's fine. Quiet."

Rosalie snorted. "I'm hoping that's a good thing."

Delora smiled timidly. "Hope so."

"Listen, there's laundry that needs to be done. You work on that while I do this."

"Okay," Delora said, glad to be freed from Rosalie's territory.

Surrounded by the pleasant fabric-softener-and-detergent smell of the laundry room, Delora felt more at ease. Hearing Rosalie's heavy step in the kitchen, she moved around the partition that separated the laundry area from the storage half of the room. There, in the dividing wall, rested Rosalie's treasure. Sliding a large carton to one side and partially pulling aside a wooden panel, Delora could see it.

Each of the oversized pickle jars was packed full of tightly wadded bills. There had to be a million dollars stored there. She bet Rosalie didn't even know how much she had saved over the years. The jars were about two feet tall each, the folded bills pressed tightly into each one. Three of them contained change; the money winked at Delora in a stray beam of light.

"I see you," she crooned softly.

The money had been there a long time. Delora hadn't known anything about it until she noticed a pattern to Rosalie's behavior. Every time Delora paid her in cash, Rosalie would find some excuse to come to the laundry room alone. Delora was no dummy and soon noticed, by several weeks of detective work, slight movement in the position of the cardboard crate. Then it was just a matter of time until her keen mind had fastened on the truth hidden in the partition.

At first, she had been amazed, and then she went through a period of seething anger. Rosalie cried poverty all the time, extorting more and more money from Delora's earnings. She also took Louie's disability checks, cashed them and ferreted the money here. Delora found some satisfaction in knowing that in reality, most of the money stored there was her money. Rosalie's only income was a veteran's check from her dead husband, amounting to just about five hundred a month. The rest of it had come from Delora and Louie and her foster sisters when they moved back home.

Later, sitting across from Rosalie and Louie at the dinner table, knowing about the affair and the cash so close by gave her a sense of power. She knew Louie had no inkling the money was there, otherwise he'd be spending it as fast as he could. She also knew that Rosalie didn't know this one fact about her, that she knew about everything now. This one nugget of knowledge allowed a type of one-upmanship that she cherished.

CHAPTER TWENTY-SIX

"She's in love, is all," was Clary's response to Stephen's inquiry about Sophie's distracted presence.

Sophie sat forward. "It's not like that...just, we don't know that yet, okay?"

Stephen's smile crept across his face like a slow crack in a plaster wall. "Oh, my gawd. You don't mean to tell me...who is it?"

Sophie blushed and sat back, motioning for Clary to carry on with the gossip she'd started.

Clary obliged. "Well. Her name is Delora November and she lives over on Royale in Redstar."

Righteous, still recovering from work the night before, yawned widely before speaking. "Tell us more. Where'd you meet her?"

Sophie leaned forward, eyes twinkling. "She came to me."

"She did," Clary added playfully. "She had some burns that needed tending."

"Damn. Is she okay?"

"They're old," Sophie explained. "She just needed some patching."

"Well, we need to meet her. Invite her to dinner." Stephen was eaten up with curiosity.

"What else do you know about her?" Righteous directed his question to Clary, clearly believing her to be the more responsible of the women present.

"I didn't meet her that night—I wasn't here—but I think I've seen her around. She's that little blonde that works in Blossom's, over on the highway."

"She works at the French Club too," Sophie added. "And out at Spinner's Fen on Carelton."

Stephen frowned. "Now wait a minute. How many jobs does this girl have?"

"Too many for my way of thinking. I think her husband is pretty much useless so she has to." She paused as she felt incredulous eyes on her.

"She has a *husband*?" Righteous breathed. "What are you thinking? Do you know how crazy that is?"

Stephen eyed his partner with exasperation even as he agreed. "Yeah, Sophie. Can't you find a single woman?"

Sophie shook her head ruefully. "Wouldn't matter either way. She is who she is."

A prolonged silence fell.

"Well, what the hell does that mean?" Righteous asked.

Sophie watched Righteous as her eyes twinkled. "It means I have faith that everything will turn out okay."

"By this you mean she'll leave him and come to you?"

"That sounds reasonable," she agreed with a shrug.

"Ha!" Righteous insisted loudly. "You really think it'll be that easy?"

"Why not?"

"Things just don't work out that way. You can't snap your fingers and have everything the way you want it."

"Why not?" Sophie's gaze was calm and patient.

Beulah chuckled. "Give it up, boy. You know you can't get past her when she's this way."

Righteous hung his head. "Okay, fine. We'll see how it all plays out. I ain't holdin' my breath for no happy ending though."

"Well, I am," Stephen said in a campy, queen voice. "I believe Sophie'll get her little diner girl. What I want to know is just how far has this relationship gone. I mean, do you even know for sure she's, you know, like us?"

"Not for sure," Sophie replied thoughtfully, her mind working possibilities. "Sure seems like it though."

"But she's married!" Righteous persisted.

"Doesn't mean a lot. I don't think it's a match made in heaven."

"He's mean, isn't he?" Clary watched Sophie closely.

"I think so." Sophie sighed. "That and the accident have beaten her down some."

"What happened? Was it a house fire like my grandma?" Righteous asked.

"Yeah, but it was set by her husband," Clary interjected. "Word is he was drunk and tried to burn the two of them up."

Righteous's mouth fell open.

"You don't mean it," Stephen said, his voice horrified.

Sophie sat back in her chair, the fingers of her right hand tightening around the base of her glass. The cool moisture of the condensation erupted and slid along the back of her hand.

"Aye, the past is past," Grandam said. "Y'all leave Sophie be and come get some of this peach ice cream Tass churned for us this afternoon. Clary, you got some of that whip for the top?"

Clary laughed as she rose and headed toward the refrigerator. "You got such a sweet jones, Miss Beulah. It's a wonder you ain't got sugar in the blood."

Grandam laughed and lifted the dessert plates from the counter behind her. "Probably do at my age. Can't live forever, though, and I can't think of a better way to go than eatin' that whip spray."

Stephen leaned over to pat the hand that lay supine in Sophie's lap. "I'm real happy for you, Sophie. No one deserves love like you do. I think it'll all work out. Are you gonna let us meet her soon?"

Sophie studied Stephen's all-American features. "I'd be honored for y'all to meet, sweetie. I'll set it up as quick as I can."

Stephen had cocked his head to one side and was studying the healer. "She's special, isn't she?"

Sophie nodded. "Yeah. I believe she is."

CHAPTER TWENTY-SEVEN

"So, why won't you marry me?" Hinchey's voice was calm, bordering on nonchalant. He leaned against the bar, twirling an empty beer bottle on the polished bar. The repetitive sound of its passage was making Delora a little crazy.

Some teenager had come into the French Club and drawn crayon-marker farmscapes across the glass front of the jukebox. Grimacing, Delora worked at it with a green plastic scrubbee.

"Because I'm already married," she answered. "You know that."

"Louie November's not a husband. He's a waste of breath and flesh."

Delora paused to lift one eyebrow in his direction. "So sayeth Hinchey Barlow."

"Just get me another, will you?"

She gave the jukebox one last strike with the cleaning cloth and moved to fetch him a fresh Michelob from behind the bar.

"Louie's all right. He has his own issues just like all of us." She leaned on the bar and studied Hinchey's pouting face.

Hinchey was never the handsome one at school. But he was fun. Had a ready wit and a smile for everyone. She and Nita May had talked about him some, as they did all the boys at Tyson County High

School, imagining how it would be to kiss him and have him "lay on top," their freshman euphemism for sexual congress. How would it be to lie in Hinchey's arms? she wondered idly. She could almost feel his hands on her and when he raised his eyes to hers, she dropped her gaze, afraid he might read her thoughts and be encouraged. Her hand strayed low, protectively covering that tender area of her body that no one must see.

"There's lots of girls who would want to marry you, Hinchey. How come you're not hanging out with them? I'm a lost cause and you know it."

Hinchey took his turn studying her. "No. I don't know that. All I do know is there's no one out there like you. I've wanted to be with you since we were in school together and that's not changed."

Delora's fingers tugged on loose threads in the white cleaning cloth. "So much has happened, Hinchey, so much changed. You have no idea."

He pulled her hand into his. His fingers were soft, hot, possessive. "My feelings haven't changed. Not one bit. Louie don't deserve a fine woman like you. I remember how he treats you and it's no better since the fire. I bet that's exactly why God took his eyes. Things like what he does have a way of circling back."

Delora had a crazy urge to touch the back of his neck, the place where the skin folded over his collar like a pudgy pink envelope. She knew how it would feel without touching it—soft, yet puffy firm.

"I know," she sighed. "He can be mean as a copperhead, still is. That doesn't mean I can step out and ignore my responsibilities."

"What?" His grip on her hand was painful. "Driving him around town? Working two, no three, jobs to support y'all?"

"You know what I mean." She gently loosened his fingers and stepped back to light a cigarette.

"Tell me the truth, Delora. Do you love him?"

Delora let smoke trail from her mouth as she mulled over his question. She had asked herself that exact question hundreds of times and still had no answer. "Hinchey, I don't know what love is," she said finally.

"I do," he said, leaning across the bar, his eyes roaming, as if mapping every inch of her face. "It's being willing to give up the world for someone. It's wanting that person to be happier than you are yourself. It's the way I feel when I see you after working my ass off all day selling those damned cars. That's all."

Embarrassed by his passion, Delora laughed lightly. "How you do go on, Hinchey."

"I bet you've never felt any of that for Louie. Admit it."

She thought a minute, eyes playing across his lips. "Would it matter? Here I am. Here we are. Nothing is going to change any of that."

"Listen to me. I want you, Delora. I want to hold you in the evenings, fall asleep beside you. I want to kiss you anytime I please." His pale face flushed quickly; he looked as if he'd been in the sun all day. His pastel blue eyes pleaded for her to hear him.

"Hinchey…"

"You're so beautiful, Delora. Can't you see what you mean to me?"

She watched him evenly, trying not to buy into his emotion. "Me, beautiful."

"Yes, you. I always thought so." He was whispering urgently, working hard to make sure she heard him.

She heard him but felt bound by helplessness.

"Hinchey, look. There's things you don't know about. Problems with me. When we had the fire, well…it was bad, Hinchey."

"I know, Delora. God, it almost killed me. I just knew you were gonna die over there in Mobile. And I'd never see you again. I think that's when I realized how much I do love you. The thought of losing you almost did me in."

His voice, low and weighed down by southern drawl, usually comforted her but not today. Friends with him since high school, Delora often puzzled over their relationship. It was superficial, manifested because there was so much she would never tell him and because she knew he believed—no, expected—the two of them to be together as a couple someday.

Delora felt derailed and a small whirlwind of anger stirred within. It was always about everyone else, wasn't it? None of them really gave a damn about what she wanted to say.

Now, as she saw the way he looked at her, sorrow and guilt beset her. She had tried so many times, gently, to tell him there could be nothing more between them. He didn't know about her scars and exactly how she got them, and she liked it that way. Pity was too easy and she'd have none of that. He knew she'd been at the hospital for some time but not the extent of her injuries. Better not to speak of what Louie had done. Best not to give it new life by voicing it. Hinchey didn't think much of Louie anyway and this knowledge would only confirm his feelings. Delora didn't want anyone knowing how a marriage could descend into such a hellish place.

Yet there was no help for it.

"Hinchey, I can't fuck you. Ever. The burns from the fire go up inside and I can't have sex anymore. The rest of my life."

Hinchey grew silent, and Delora could feel the sadness building between them. And regret. She set her mouth in a firm line. She would not cry about this mess anymore. There'd been too much of that already.

"But Louie...Don't y'all...?"

He actually seemed surprised. And she was surprised he hadn't guessed. It seemed to her that people, knowing she'd been burned bad by a house fire, would've figured out that if her face wasn't burned, her body had to be.

"No." She shook her head. "Not since the fire. Never will again."

He settled back, away from her, his mind masticating each morsel of information until it became fuel for a new reality. This new reality spilled from him in a glorious defecation.

"You know what? I don't care." He took her hands in his. "There's ways around that Delora, for two people who love one another. There's other ways to please a man."

"To please a man." Delora's feeling of grimness grew. "And me?" she asked. "How will you please me?"

He stared blankly. The idea hadn't even occurred to him.

"Any way you want, honey. You call the shots. All I'm trying to say is, I need to be with you. I'll work with you, I swear. Just tell me what to do. We'll work it out. Leave Louie and come with me."

"Where?" she asked calmly.

"What do you mean, where? Anywhere you want to go. I don't care. I can sell cars anyplace. Where do you want to go?"

Delora thought about it, her hands twisting out of his. She thought of the maps, waiting for her in her bedroom.

Esther Fifth entered from the kitchen and approached the bar. She draped one heavy arm across the top, then leaned on it, her upper body almost horizontal. "I swear that man is just asking for trouble, spouting all that Jesus crap."

"Aww, Esther, you're gonna go to hell for sure," Delora told her.

"What are y'all talking about?" Hinchey asked. He seemed composed, but his eyes were pained.

"It's the new dishwasher, Munsy Braun," Delora explained, her gaze apologetic. "He's got religion and wants us to have it too."

"I told him I go to Freedom Baptist, but he just ain't listening," Esther complained.

"What church does he go to?" Hinchey asked. He looked away from Delora.

"One of the holy rollers, I'm thinking," said Esther. She rose from the counter and surveyed the mostly empty lounge. "Where the hell is everybody? Is the Dollar Store having a sale or something?"

"Probably over looking in the Jobes's windows." Hinchey took a deep swallow of his new beer.

"What happened to the Jobes?" Esther watched Hinchey, eyes roaming curiously across his face.

Hinchey looked pointedly at Delora. Delora ground out her cigarette.

"What now?" Esther persisted.

"The damnedest thing. Mary Jobes is married to Peachy, right? And you remember they were best friends with the Moyers who lived next door?"

Esther nodded and Hinchey continued in a sarcastic tone. "Well, turns out that Mary and Danny Moyer have been having a little thing on the side and they've fallen mad in love, of course, so Mary decides she's telling Peachy that she's leaving him for Danny."

"Platter up," said Michael as he slid Hinchey's roast beef sandwich onto the warmer that separated the bar from the kitchen. Delora moved to place it in front of Hinchey.

"So what happened?" Esther asked.

"Well, she moves out and Danny moves out, of course leaving Nora all alone. So, wouldn't you know it, now Peachy and Nora are keeping company." He methodically spread prepackaged horseradish sauce across the top bun of his sandwich.

"What happened with Danny and Mary?" Delora asked, filching one of his steak fries and dipping it in the horseradish sauce.

"I told you, they ran off together."

"Yeah, but where?" Her eyes roamed Hinchey's features as she chewed.

"Sammy at the car lot says Goshen. He sold Danny a truck on his trade-in."

"Isn't that something? And her working for the county administrator, I guess she had to give up her job?"

Hinchey chewed and swigged his beer, wiping his mouth with his paper napkin as he looked away from Delora. "Uh-huh. Jean Painter got it."

"Blink your eyes in this town and things change," Delora said thoughtfully.

"Peachy's much cuter than Danny," Esther added. "What was Mary thinking? I went to school with her, you know. Always was a wild thing."

"Poor Nora, though. I hope she and Peachy do okay."

"Just rebound," Hinchey said. "I bet it don't last six months."

"Eat your sandwich, Mr. Negativity," Delora said. "Esther, I'm gonna go do the bathroom while it's slow, okay?"

"Sure, honey. I don't think it's too bad, though."

Delora thought about seeing another man, having an affair. She knew it was physically impossible, but still she tried the idea on for size as she absently changed the empty soap cartridge in the ladies' bathroom. There was no way she could relate. Though she'd desired men before, or perhaps desired their need for her, she couldn't imagine instigating such a major life change just for that feeling. Did other people feel more strongly than she did? Why wasn't she plagued by the hard needs that could destroy lives?

Maybe it was her inexperience. There'd been only two men before Louie, each lasting about eighteen months. She had really liked Mitch Payne. He was a tiny fellow, not much bigger than she, and had always treated her well. Their fumbled lovemaking had been filled with goodwill and laughter. She'd never be good enough for him, however, according to his mother. Being the wife of renowned lawyer Patrick Payne had really done a number on little Maryanne Garrett: she became someone who hated her past and certainly wanted her son to have better than an orphan based in Redstar, Alabama. So off the Paynes had gone, to rural New York where things were more to her liking. Mitch had promised to write, but the letters never came.

Delora thought he might understand what she was going through, might be able to deal with it. Yeah, she'd see him on the side. For companionship. Good thing she didn't know how to get in touch with him. She wanted some change in her life but nothing that drastic. Thank goodness for the phone calls with Bucky Clyde.

Sighing and pushing the ridiculous ideas away, she swabbed out the toilets, filled them with deodorizing liquid and used paper towels to mop the floor haphazardly. The ladies' room really wasn't bad. A good thing, as her belly ached if she bent too much.

Hinchey wanted her and that didn't seem to have changed. She could see it seething from his pores every time they were together. All she had to do was say the word and Louie would be history and Hinchey would be in. She thought of how her life would be different—no blind, hot-tempered Louie to deal with, just placid, easygoing Hinchey. It would be a better deal certainly, a great trade, but she just wasn't up to it. That hard need just wasn't there. And no matter what she did, someone, somewhere would want sex with her. It was unavoidable.

Louie knew better than to touch her since the fire and that was just fine with her. Trying to explain to someone new why she could never be sexual or repeatedly rebuffing Hinchey's advances would just be too much to bear. She was better off leaving well enough alone.

Stepping back into the restaurant, she saw Hinchey and Esther still locked in conversation. She peeked around at the clock above the bar, hoping Hinchey and Esther weren't talking about her. Only two more hours to go and she could go home. She thought of the new bottle of vodka chilling in the closet, in the ice chest, and closed her eyes, leaning her head back against the rough paneled wall outside the ladies' room. She stayed there a long time.

CHAPTER TWENTY-EIGHT

Thoughts of Delora had filled Hinchey's mind as he drove home that evening. He'd had a few beers—well, four beers—so he was driving cautiously. Pulling into the drive, he breathed a sigh of relief and switched off the engine. Delora. She reminded him of Tinkerbell from the Peter Pan stories. A Tinkerbell with smudges under her eyes and chewed fingernails. He had often wondered about the demons that haunted her. Now he knew.

He'd loved her long before Louie had come into the picture and taken her over, though he'd never told her then. Delora was a different girl today than she'd been in high school. Tinkerbell would have been an apt description then—full of life and laughter. Even with her parents gone, she had managed to find some enjoyment in life. Since marrying Louie, however, she'd become strangely withdrawn. Hinchey still couldn't believe what she'd told him. Pain stabbed at him as he thought of what she must have endured. God, he hated Louie.

Hinchey sighed again and slid from his truck. His mother was probably watching television so he eased the truck door closed and entered the house as quietly as possible. Passing through the kitchen, he saw, by the light of the range hood, that his mama had left dinner for him, a full meal—pork chops, mashed potatoes, gravy, corn and applesauce. He pressed his hands against his abdomen. Was he hungry again? He couldn't tell. Knowing how hurt his mother would be if he didn't eat her food, he sat at the table and ate the lukewarm food, almost every bite.

At seven thirty, Hinchey switched off his bedroom television and took a seat at his desk. He laid the notepad bearing Keychain's number reverently on the desk blotter. He was looking forward to hearing her voice.

"Hinchey, come help me move this."

Hinchey sighed, laid down his cell phone and rose. His mother had been vacuuming for the past fifteen minutes and was driving him crazy.

She stood next to her bed, the vacuum roaring. "Lift that end table. It's been forever since I cleaned behind it."

Hinchey knew better. He'd lifted the damn thing for her just a week ago. "Mama, what are you doing cleaning house so late at night?"

"I had to work extra this week, you know that. Saturday's my cleaning day."

"What about your shows?" he shouted as he lifted the table, allowing her to poke the hose under. With her free hand, she indicated the television on its stand in the room. A fifties-style couple was arguing on the screen. Hinchey shook his head and manipulated the table so it rested in the exact same carpet dents as before. He eyed the clock on the bedside table. He needed to call Keychain in fifteen minutes. He didn't want to call late, in case she thought he wasn't interested, and he'd really hoped to get a few minutes to clear his mind and get ready to talk with her.

The vacuum switched off and the sudden silence was deafening. Hinchey looked at the television only to find that it had been muted. His mother reached behind him to lift the remote and switch off the television.

"I'm going downstairs now. You put the vacuum away, okay?"

"Sure," Hinchey said eagerly, glad his mother was going to be out of his hair for a while.

Back at his desk, Hinchey drew in a deep breath and lifted his cell phone. He thought about Keychain and what he knew about her. Excitement stirred in him. Keychain was foreign to everything he knew. She was in New Mexico. She was young, his age, and enthusiastic. She seemed smart, much more so than Hinchey. He had a sudden thought. He could go there. He had some money saved. Then he thought of his mother and grunted. What would he tell her when he left her? What would he tell Delora?

Pushing all doubt away, he dialed the number, his body hunched forward with anticipation. The phone rang twice and then silence.

"Hello? Country?"

Hinchey cleared his throat and blushed, even though he was alone in his room. "Yes, yes, it's me," he replied.

Keychain sighed and Hinchey thought of her chest swelling with breath. The thought surprised him. "So, tell me more about yourself," she said.

He liked the sound of her voice. It was even and not too high. He liked that.

"What do you want to know?" he asked, voice lowering, growing intimate.

She laughed and Hinchey fell a little in love. "Everything, silly. Tell me anything you want."

"Well, I never told you this, but I still live at home. My mom needed me after Dad died and I just stayed on…"

"Oh, my gosh," Keychain broke in, her voice excited. "I just moved out six months ago myself. Sometimes it's easier to just stay on and I was saving money."

"Totally," Hinchey agreed. "Don't they drive you a little crazy, though?"

"Absolutely. That's why I finally had to go. I have a small place, but at least it's mine and I can live by my own rules. You should come see it, I've decorated it with Southwest colors and I just love being here."

"I'd love to do that," Hinchey said, excited by the prospect and the invitation. "I'd like to get away from here. Have I ever told you about where I live? It's a small southern town."

"A little, but tell me more," she replied.

Hinchey carried the phone to his bed and reclined. "Let me tell you about the people here. You just won't even believe it."

CHAPTER TWENTY-NINE

Delora lay in darkness, exhausted from a long night at the French Club. A few late season fireflies winked at her playfully from the other side of her open window. Of course their brightness reminded her of Sophie's eyes, sparkling when she laughed.

Rolling onto her back, Delora sighed. Everything reminded her of Sophie these days. She felt positively infatuated with the woman. She admired her talent, her quiet thoughtful nature, her ability with the uneducated people she mentored and her untamed beauty. Her beauty.

It was time for Delora to examine her own sexuality and face the truth about it. Not that it was so very important. Knowing she was one way or another would not make her magically able to have sexual congress again. Still, the thought was intriguing. Looking back on her life, she could remember episodes of female attraction. There was a time, before she met Louie, in which she had questioned her sexuality. It happened after she had almost kissed Nita May. They had been swimming at Kiley Hole all morning and had tired themselves out swinging on a rope and dropping into the warm water. Later, stretched out on a blanket surrounded by the fragrant coarse grass on the bank of the river, they snoozed for a long time in the warming sunlight.

They talked drowsily and, waking more fully, Delora, lying prone, had lifted herself on her forearms and looked down at Nita May. In that moment, looking at Nita May's sweat-dappled skin, she had wanted to kiss her. First she had wanted to press her lips to the closed eyes, fringed with thick dark eyelashes. Then the cheeks had beckoned, their softness intriguing below the covering of fine translucent hair. Then the lips, full, dark pink, slightly chapped from a day in the sun. They were parted just a little. Delora's tongue had pressed hard against the back of her teeth, and she craved to moisten the rough dryness of Nita May's mouth with her own.

Shocked, heart racing and breath catching in her throat, at that time Delora had dropped her head onto her folded arms and closed her eyes until calm returned.

Did this mean she loved women more than men? Delora didn't know. She knew she had never wanted a man in exactly the same way. She'd been interested in their skin, the hardness of their muscles, the funny way their faces screwed up when they worked on cars. Still, it always felt like something was missing, and she hated to admit it, but it was that something that she had found with Sophie these past few weeks.

She sighed and, with her head turned to one side, studied the pattern on her comforter, one finger tracing the outline. Damn. What was she going to do if her feelings continued to grow?

Her thoughts flew back to Sophie. Her body was so sturdy, well-muscled under tanned skin, wrought from years of wandering the Bayou Lisse. There was a beguiling wildness about her, imparted by the slow water and lush greenery of Lisse. She was magic, pure and simple, manifesting into the lives of those she helped. An image of her pushing wild curls back from her forehead came to Delora, and she imagined herself pressing her lips to the forearm as it descended. She could imagine Sophie's surprise as Delora's lips touched her skin. Delora knew she would smile and welcome her into her arms. Would Sophie kiss her lips? Yes, Delora knew she would. The kiss would be slow and hot, Sophie's lips pressing hers open, hot breath passing. Maybe Sophie would pass Delora just a little bit of that magic she carried within her so Delora could be magic too. Yes, she could almost feel Sophie above her, could imagine the sun-smell and the heft of her body against her own.

Delora's breathing rate had increased and her hands crept to her breasts to skim gently across erect tips. She gasped when she realized what she was doing and felt awe at the sensation stirring low in her body. It had been so long since she had felt anything there except pain and stiffness, the stinging of the burns. Now there was a gentle nudging of wanting, a nibble of need there. She pinched her nipples gently and felt an ocean wave surge low between her legs. Could it be? Could there be something there—a child composed of desire waiting to be born?

Delora, without hesitation, gentled her breasts some more, cupping their fullness in her palms and teasing the erect nipples with her fingertips. More sensation stirred and images flashed across her mind. She saw a small furred animal stirring in its den, then Sophie smiling at Delora, her eyes warm and filled with a welcoming joy and acceptance. She saw the curve of Sophie's waist, between her jeans and her shirt, shown when she stretched her arms overhead. What would Sophie look like without jeans? Without a shirt? Delora could imagine her breasts. They seemed small, as her long body was lean. Would they grow hard as Delora's were now if Delora caressed them? Delora saw herself capturing the nipple with her mouth, could actually taste Sophie's flesh in her mouth, and alone in her bedroom, her mouth curved outward as if pressed to take in Sophie's breast.

Eagerly, guided by a cellular memory more than by Delora's consciousness, her hands moved lower, across skin rippled into a volcanic landscape until her finger pressed like a shield over the gash of her womanhood. The fingers moved in unison back and forth, side to side, the pressure increasing. The feeling within her grew, the waves of desire rocking against the shore of her sensible being ever more insistent. She fought the feeling with her mind, but this event was beyond conscious control. Her body had become a creature alien to her. The hand moved and moved, while Delora could only follow limply along, gasping and moaning in disbelief. Then electricity moved through her and she stopped breathing, yet screamed without breath, her mouth wide and eyes pressed shut. Her body arched high off the bed and bucked until her hand fell away. A low cry escaped her after the onslaught of breath returned to her lungs. Still moaning, she opened her eyes and stared groggily at the ceiling.

Was she okay? The throbbing spread from her toes to her scalp. Her hair was standing on end. Her arms were lying limply at her sides, and she moved her hands gingerly to see if she could feel them. She could. Her toes still wiggled and feeling was returning to her legs and heart. She was afraid if she touched any site in the center of her body from breast to groin, she would find a black hole where her desire had crisped the flesh away. She lifted her head and looked down, her bottom lip caught between her teeth. It was all still there, still throbbing every time she moved. There was no pain, just a feeling of fullness. She dared not touch it. Suppose her skin caved in under the rippled scar tissue? She closed her eyes, the thought too horrible to contemplate.

Sophie appeared in her mind, her smile sweet, her face encouraging.

Delora drew in a deep shaky breath and blew it out. It was going to be okay. Everything. She turned her body carefully onto her side and curled into a ball of cooling star energy. Feeling a new peace steal across her, Delora fell asleep, smiling.

CHAPTER THIRTY

They were wonderful, these people who populated Sophie's life. The names flew by Delora like so much fairy dust. They were unfamiliar, bordering on foreign. There was a beautiful black woman named Pyree, another named Clary. A beautiful, effeminate gay man named Stephen. His partner, Righteous, a tall, thin man of color with wide cheekbones and slanted eyes. Someone named Salty was there, wearing a comically attractive black bowler hat made of felt. Children were everywhere, some with olive skin and sleek, jet-black hair, others with copper skin and tightly curled hair that clung to their scalps like damp wool. A few pale, blond-haired children rounded out the color wheel.

Sophie was in her element. Obviously, her family was well respected and treated with a measure of deference. No doubt she had healed most of them at some point. Delora's eyes caressed Sophie from a distance, admiring her easy way with these people. She did something not many others do. Truly listen. Even to the children. Most adults brush children off when they talk to them. Not Sophie. She would stop whatever she was doing and bend down to listen. Not talk. Listen. Delora found that fascinating.

Even though Sophie was mingling among the huge crowd, she would often catch Delora's admiring glance. Her smoldering gaze made Delora feel a heavy emotion she'd never felt before.

Delora decided she liked Salamander House very much. It was worn and cozy and filled with odd magical scents that Delora couldn't identify. Separated from the bayou by several thick pilings, the wood-sided, six-room house fronted on the water and was like part of the landscape. A spit of grassy land stretched to either side and to the back, carved from the surrounding bayou by a curving drive. If the water got too high, the only access to the house would be by boat. A wide, heavy plank deck supported by pilings surrounded the entire home—rather daunting without swamp water immediately below it.

Picnic guests littered the grassy slope on the western side. They wore a wide array of colorful clothing. Delora, in jeans and a red button-down blouse, felt positively drab.

There was something especially unusual about the women and men of Beulah's family. They had hair dark as a moonless night and thick brows that framed piercing black eyes. Their smiles flashed often and the white teeth were big and bold. They wore beautiful clothing—shirts that appeared to have been hand-stitched or at least hand-designed on a sewing machine. The designs were loose and flowing, bearing butterfly colors and the occasional web of silver or gold embedded in the fabric. They looked Italian or Spanish. Maybe Middle Eastern. She made a mental note to ask Sophie about it the next time they were alone.

Three long tables, dressed in white cloths, supported a huge amount of food. One table bore hot offerings, another cold and a third was stacked with potato chips and other salty treats amid bottle after bottle of soda and tea. The beer and other spirits lay displayed on a smaller table set up on the deck. Most of the adults had found their way there already, and moods were light.

Delora felt happy and light herself, certainly more than she had in a long time. She found herself surrounded with new faces, faces that didn't even know Louie existed and certainly had no inkling that she bore scars from his whim. This anonymity was refreshing.

Her eyes flew once more to Sophie. Although she was young, certainly no more than thirty, she obviously possessed an old spirit. She was wise in the ways of man and nature. Delora wondered if she ever lost her cool. She had yet to see Sophie angry or upset.

Sophie must have felt her gaze for she excused herself from the gaunt man with long black hair she was speaking with and strode toward Delora. Delora blushed and dropped her eyes only to raise them helplessly to watch Sophie's lean form approach. There was something about her, something about that calm, confident smile.

"How are you holding up? It's a little overwhelming, I know."

Delora studied Sophie's face but pulled her gaze away when Sophie's interest deepened. "Your call was a surprise. How'd you get my cell number?"

"Ahhh, the ways of the bayou are mysterious," Sophie said, laughing when Delora pulled a face of mock annoyance. "Sorry for the short notice. So what do you think of the family?"

"They're amazing. Beautiful. Surely they're not all family?"

Sophie's sweeping glance took in the crowd as she viewed it from Delora's vantage point. It was a motley crew, no doubt about it. Grandam's sister, Yarrow, was there with her husband, Lemley Banks. They lived inwater on another piece of Wassel Cofe's land. They lived even further into the old ways than did Grandam and Sophie. Visits to their house had always been like stepping into an ancient dimension when people were ruled by superstition and sorcery in equal measures.

A good number of the revelers were patients, however: men, women and children that they had led toward healing during the years. If taken to task, Sophie could have named every injury or illness. She couldn't remember to tie her own shoes sometimes, but she could remember every patient she'd treated. She turned back to Delora. She didn't want to think about other patients today.

"Some are other families from the Bayou Lisse. They live all up and down the waterways. Some, like Alvin and Doris Borrows, live over in town, Redstar, but most are from the water."

"Your grandmother..." Delora began, but broke off, unsure how to broach the subject of Sophie's ethnicity.

"What about her?" Sophie pulled Delora toward the food table.

Delora eyed the food-laden table. There was everything from a planked fish to a full roasted turkey, all the way to ice cream in a big bowl resting in an ice-filled barrel. It was a lot of food.

"Glory, who cooked all this?" she exclaimed.

Sophie laughed and sliced off a huge chunk of chocolate cake packed with pecan halves. "Everyone. Clary did some of it, but everyone brings something to these things. Didn't your family ever do this?" She paused. "When they were still with us, I mean." She watched Delora even as her hand lifted two plastic forks.

"No, not really. School functions. And church things with Rosalie. But never this much food."

Sophie laughed at the other's wide eyes. "Come on, Miss Innocent. You've got to try this cake. Myria Pulet makes it and I swear I could eat the whole thing by myself."

"Come on here, Miss Sophie. Y'all can sit here," Tassidy Myer said as he rose and offered his chair and the empty one next to him.

"Thank you, Tass. Your mama is smiling on you from heaven," Sophie told him.

He grinned and ducked his head as he moved away.

Delora studied the man with his straight ebony hair worn long beneath a limp-brimmed Stetson and colorful shirt over metal-studded jeans. "Is he a relative?" she asked.

"Oh, I'm sorry. I should have introduced you. Tassidy is Grandam's baby brother. Let's see that makes him my, what? Great-uncle? We always called him Uncle Tass."

Delora glanced after him as they sat. "He looks nice."

Sophie nodded her agreement as she dug into the cake. "Salt of the earth."

Delora lifted the fork Sophie had passed to her and used it to pick at the cake. "About Miss Beulah. Are y'all Italian?"

Sophie turned wide, astonished eyes on Delora. "Italian?" She laughed and used her fork to push a small bite of the cake into Delora's mouth. "We're Egyptian, but don't tell anyone. We don't talk about it. Isn't that good?"

Delora lifted her eyes to Sophie. The rich sweetness of the chocolate in her mouth and the sheer sugar of Sophie's gaze made Delora tremble deep inside. The moment was too perfect and it terrified her. Sophie seemed to sense her fear and her face went tense.

"Delora, it's all right, honey. I'm right here. Tell me what's wrong."

Delora was too embarrassed to admit her feelings or her fear. She realized she loved Sophie. What was she to do with these feelings? Surely Sophie wasn't interested. But wait, another part of her whispered. *What about the way she looks at me?*

Delora shook the optimism away like shrugging out of a winter overcoat.

"It's good cake. I think it's the nuts. Lots of nuts add richness."

"So, you cook?" Sophie tilted her head to one side as she regarded the other woman.

Delora laughed, determined to ease up and not allow Sophie's nearness to twist her stomach into knots. "I'm not sure I know the meaning of the word. I do what I have to do to get by."

Sophie laughed, broke off another small piece of cake, then handed the plate to Delora "Okay, chocolate limit reached. The rest is for you."

Delora grunted and studied the plate with suspicion.

They fell silent and watched the milling, laughing crowd.

"You still live with him, don't you?" Sophie asked quietly.

Delora snapped her gaze back to Sophie. How much did this woman know about her life?

"Does he still hurt you?"

Delora knew she should be incensed at this invasion of her privacy. She knew she should consider the question the height of rudeness and disregard it. Sophie was different and Delora could feel no indignation. She realized with the bright light of epiphany that Sophie would always be one step ahead of her. And that Sophie could see where others could not. She considered her answer carefully.

"No, he ignores me mostly and that's good."

"So, he won't do it again?"

Delora thought about telling her about the lighter fluid she'd found under his bed. It was too exhausting to open that door. "No. I don't think it matters to him anymore. He's blind now."

Sophie leaned forward and dangled her hands between her knees. Her voice was soft and carried to Delora on angel wings. No one nearby could have heard. Only Delora.

"Do you know how I am?"

Delora's puzzlement lasted only a minute. Sophie was trying to make sure Delora knew why the feelings were growing between them. She had to be sure though.

"Do you mean about the healing stuff?"

Sophie tucked her head and smiled, her eyes on the crowd. "No. The other."

"Yes. Yes, I know."

"Is that okay?"

Sighing, Delora mulled this question over. Was it okay? Did she want to give Sophie permission? A host of thoughts tumbled through her mind. She envisioned some possibilities, negated others. A part of her knew she had nothing to lose if others knew she was involved with Sophie, but the scars...how could she be what Sophie wanted and needed? She had to discourage Sophie. As soon as her mind was made up, however, Sophie lifted her eyes and snared Delora with a look of love and desire so pure that Delora quit breathing for a full minute.

"Yes," she said. "Yes, it's okay, Sophie."

Sophie continued to fall deeply into Delora's eyes, the contact broken only when one of the children, pushed by another, fell into the water with a loud howl. Infectious laughter swept through the crowd, catching Sophie and Delora up in it.

"I'd better get him a towel and something dry to wear," Sophie said as she rose. Her loving gaze lingered, however.

"Sure," agreed Delora. "I'll be here." She felt as though she could use a few minutes alone with her thoughts. And time to deal with the unfamiliar warmth spreading through her body.

"I'll be back soon and maybe we can take a walk, okay?"

Helpless, Delora nodded.

CHAPTER THIRTY-ONE

Bayou Lisse at night was even more incredible than in the daylight. Most notable were the insects. Here there was no subterfuge. Insects ruled openly. Next were the frogs. It seemed every step taken by the two women dislodged another resting amphibian.

"Frogs everywhere," Delora muttered, finally breaking the silence that had enveloped them for some time.

Sophie reached and took Delora's hand in her hot grasp. "Usually are, this time of year."

Delora rubbed her thumb along Sophie's knuckle. It felt good to connect with her.

Sophie paused next to a wide area of open water. Delora stood next to her and they watched the slow undulation of water.

"Can you see the lights?" Sophie asked quietly. "Watch the water. Deep."

Delora looked at Sophie's rapt face, then followed her gaze toward the water. And there it was—a chain of lights moving through the depths.

"What is it?" Delora whispered.

Sophie shrugged and pulled Delora's hand closer, tucking it under her arm. The fullness of Sophie's breast pressed against the back of Delora's hand. "I'm not sure. I call them fairy lights."

Delora nodded. Fairy lights. Yes.

"Life sure is an adventure, isn't it?" Delora mused quietly. Mosquitoes danced about them angrily, yet stayed away. Bayou water tapped gently just down at the end of the grassy patch where the two women stood. "Just when you think things are duller than dirt something happens to shake your world."

"Seems that way," Sophie agreed.

Delora watched her in silence.

Sophie tensed suddenly, looking at Delora. A message passed.

"So what has happened to shake up your world?" she asked.

Delora smiled. Gone was the resigned bitter woman she'd been. Sophie wasn't sure she knew who this new woman was, but she was sure glad she was having the opportunity to get to know her.

"Lots of things," Delora replied. "Seeing you with all your people, for one. I never knew how special it is—this healing you do."

Sophie smiled, her mouth gathering dusk and holding it. "It's addictive—like that sweet German wine they sell over in Goshen. Once you've tasted it, you've got to have it again and again. Even though the cost is outrageous."

Silence again for a short time. "And what else has shaken up your world?"

Delora grinned again, and Sophie saw the coy, flirtatious girl Delora had once been. Her heart flipped in her chest.

"Lord, Lora. I've got to tell you, I…"

Sophie couldn't finish. Delora's laughing gaze was pulling her in like water over a deadfall. She tilted her head and allowed herself to be pulled in. There was a small moment of doubt in Delora's eyes as Sophie leaned and pressed her lips to hers. The kiss was charming and chaste. Even as their lips moved apart Sophie stayed close, inhaling the essence of Delora. She'd read once that touching faces was the greatest intimacy two people could share. She wanted this with Delora. Surprising her, Delora allowed it, even seemed to encourage the closeness.

"You're healing me, you know," Delora whispered finally. Her sweet breath, still bearing the essence of chocolate, tickled against Sophie's cheeks.

"And you, me," Sophie answered. "I didn't even know I was broken until you came into my life. Now, without you with me, I am."

CHAPTER THIRTY-TWO

"What's your schedule today?"

The words next to her ear and the friendly smell of coffee wafted across Delora, waking her. Where was she?

Eyes opening slowly, they fetched up on Sophie's smiling face. Alarm fired along Delora's nerves. She sat up abruptly as the previous night replayed in her memory.

"Oh, my gosh, Sophie. I'm so sorry. What was I thinking, imposing like this?"

She tried to kick off misbehaving blankets, and Sophie laughed at her dilemma.

"Hold on," she said, cautiously placing a mug of coffee on the bureau. "You're going to hurt yourself."

Delora relaxed against the pillows. "I slept here all night, didn't I? Here with you."

Calmly, slowly, Sophie folded back the blankets. "Yes. Yes, you did. That's why I asked about your schedule. Where do you have to be today?"

"What day is it?"

Sophie smiled and handed the coffee over. Delora took it and sipped gratefully.

"Monday."

"Blossom's, all day until six. Then French Club after."

"I swear, I don't know how you keep it all straight," Sophie muttered with a shake of her head. Delora watched her, enjoying the haphazard twisting of Sophie's tawny curls, unbound this early in the day. She reached across and captured an escaping curl with an index finger. The curl grasped her back as if it were a sentient being. Sophie's eyes grew soft and dreamy as they regarded Delora.

Sudden laughter penetrated from another room, and Delora started, dropping the curl and grasping the mug with both white-knuckled hands.

"Who's out there?" she whispered. "I'm so mortified."

"Just Grandam and Clary, that's all." Sophie glanced toward the door and sighed.

"Oh no, what must they think of me staying here this way? I'm so embarrassed."

Sophie took the cup from Delora and helped herself to a healthy swallow before setting it to one side. "Don't even waste energy on that. They don't care. I'll get a little ribbing from them about getting laid but that's only words."

Delora looked curiously into Sophie's chocolate eyes. She still felt the weight and warmth of Sophie's body all over her. "We…I mean…"

Sophie regarded Delora, eyes beginning to twinkle in a familiar way. "Nope. You'd remember that and I would too. We've got it powerful, don't we?"

Delora tried to act innocent. "What do you mean?"

Sophie leaned in and captured Delora's lips with her own. The scent and taste of coffee on Sophie transported Delora to a sweet place. It plain didn't matter that Beulah and Clary were only a wall away. It didn't matter that Delora was married or that she was damaged goods, scarred by her husband's brutal whim.

Delora's tongue escaped her mouth and sought Sophie's. Sophie's lips lay warm along hers, and Delora could feel the shift in her breathing as the kiss deepened, the two tongues frolicking slowly as they explored new terrain. A bright heat descended along Delora's body and her hands trembled as they tingled. She brought those shaking hands up to push Sophie away, but instead they moved along Sophie's neck and breast and pulled their bodies even closer.

Abruptly Sophie broke the connection. Both women were shaken, barely daring to breathe, and Delora felt that strange dropping sensation in her chest.

"*Duvvel beng atchava*," Sophie whispered.

"What is that?" Delora breathed out, the language piquing her interest.

"It's a good thing we're not alone. No, wait, it's a good thing I *remembered* we're not alone."

She lifted Delora's hand and pressed it to the heated skin of her neck. "*Krisi kommoben krisi chooma chor nongo ozi.*"

"That sounds so beautiful. What does it mean?"

Sophie gazed into Delora's eyes and Delora knew. She smiled shyly, yet was determined. "What is that you're speaking, Sophie?"

"Romany. The language of the Manu. I picked it up from Grandam and her sisters."

"It says more, doesn't it?"

"Much more." She leaned in and briefly recaptured their kiss. She handed the coffee back to Delora and pulled her to her feet. "Let's get you ready for work."

Delora allowed the other woman to guide her out of the bedroom and into a short hallway. The voices of Beulah and Clary could be heard more clearly there; they were arguing about the price of canned asparagus.

Once they were in the bathroom Sophie unbuttoned Delora's red shirt. Delora watched her as one entranced, as if watching an approaching tornado, knowing there is no place to hide. Four buttons down, Sophie paused and rubbed the back of her fingers against the rounded swell of Delora's small breasts. The electric current generated brought Delora back to awareness.

"Sophie," she muttered in a warning tone.

Sophie grinned endearingly. "But it feels so good," she whispered.

Delora allowed her head to fall back. "I know," she countered. "But we're not alone."

Sophie pressed her solid hips against Delora's and moved their bodies together in a slow sinuous coupling as she sighed next to Delora's ear, "Rain check?"

Delora blushed and nodded quickly. Delora refused to remember the scars.

Sophie backed away and pulled the door closed. "Hand out your clothes and we'll press an iron over them. If they can't be clean, at least they'll be presentable."

Delora finished unbuttoning the shirt with shaking fingers. She hung it on the outer doorknob and it was whisked from her fingers.

"Sophie?" she whispered.

"Yes?" Sophie answered just outside the door.

Delora pressed her palm to the door where she imagined Sophie's face would be. "I just wanted to make sure you're real."

Sophie laughed low in her throat. "Hurry up, slowpoke. It's seven already."

Delora gasped and slid from her jeans, passing them out to Sophie.

Standing in the small bathroom wearing nothing but panties, Delora felt lost but oddly secure. The feeling was as if she'd found home again, that prehurricane world that fit her so well.

Touching a sheaf of cattail gathered together with wild honeysuckle as a binding, she knew Sophie had crafted it. Curious, she took a few minutes to look over the simple toiletries scattered about the bathroom. She touched the shampoos and conditioners, mostly store-brand products. A few looked homemade, and she lifted one vial and recognized it as the scent she most associated with Sophie.

A short time later, she emerged from the shower and found her shirt and jeans, still warm from the iron, hanging on a hook inside the door. Also included was a new toothbrush and a pair of panties and a camisole still packaged in the manufacturer's shrink-wrap. To her amazement they were her size. After she dressed, she wasn't sure what to do with the panties she'd worn the day before and eventually stuffed them in her jeans pocket. The hallway was deserted. Wandering to the left, she emerged into the bright kitchen. The door to outside was open and the air sweetened by garden herbs. Clary stood at one of the windows staring out. She lifted a mug of coffee to her lips but paused when she spied Delora.

"Well, there you are, little miss. A shower makes you feel like a new person, doesn't it?"

Delora nodded. "Sure does. Thanks so much for the hospitality. I must have been pretty tuckered last night."

Clary poured Delora a cup of coffee and handed it to her. She accepted it gratefully. "You and Sophie did most of the cleanup and you with a broken finger. I'm not surprised." She let her eyes drift back out across the bayou.

"What are you looking at?" Delora asked as she doctored her coffee with sugar.

"Nothing. Everything." Clary shrugged. "Do you like English muffins? I thought I'd scramble the eggs. Is that okay?"

Startled, Delora answered quickly. "Yes and yes, but you don't have to do that, Clary. I can get something at the diner."

"Don't get her riled, Lora, honey. She can be testy if she doesn't get her way."

With relief, Delora saw Sophie enter through the screen door, hands full of fragrant greenery.

"Make enough for me, will you, Clary?" She handed Clary the herbs and moved to pull out a chair for Delora.

"Not a problem," said Clary. "What have you got here?"

"That's that new volunteer mint that came up. We'll use it for poultices first if you'll powder it up."

Clary shrugged and placed it in the sink. "Scrambled eggs coming up. No bacon, though; I haven't been to the store for a while."

"Okay by us," Sophie said as she took a seat across from Delora. She winked at her.

"Where'd your grandmother go?" Delora found she missed Beulah's presence.

Sophie frowned and cupped her chin in one hand. "I'm not sure. She may be reading the paper. She likes to sneak off and read in peace."

"The party yesterday was fun, wasn't it?"

Sophie nodded. "It was nice seeing everyone all together. I'm sorry about Stephen and Righteous, though. I wish they could work all this stuff out."

Delora tilted her head to one side. "Yeah, what's going on with them? They were really tense late last night."

"Righteous cheats. Stephen seems to think it's because he works at the Thirsty Rogue over in Goshen."

The coffee felt good in Delora's cupped hands and the heavy chicory smell soothed her. "That's a shame. How long has it been going on?"

Sophie passed Delora a fork and a napkin. "From day one, I think. They've had a rocky road."

"What'd I miss?" Clary asked, sliding steaming plates before them.

Delora's mouth watered when she spied the rich butter seeping into the toasted English muffin.

"Just Stephen and Righteous. They picked a fight before going home," Sophie answered, shaking pepper on her eggs. "We were sitting along the water last night and saw them at each other."

Clary put her hands on her hips. "Shame I'm not a betting woman. Those two will never make it."

Sophie swiped at her mouth with a napkin. "No negativity allowed."

"Hmmph," Clary snorted and moved to the sink.

The fresh food was well prepared, and Delora embarrassed herself by how quickly she ate. Sophie ate more slowly, her kind eyes watching Delora with some amusement.

"You ready for work now?" Sophie asked.

Delora laughed. "I think so." She patted her stomach, then rose and carried her dishes to the sink. "Thanks, Clary. That was delicious. Exactly what I needed."

Clary dried her hands and held out her arms. Surprised, Delora stepped into a warm, full-body hug. "You have a good day now, little gal," she said next to Delora's ear. "I'll see you soon."

Sophie and Delora walked to her car in silence.

"She likes you," Sophie told Delora when they paused next to the car.

"Yeah. I felt it. Felt nice."

"I like you too, you know."

Delora lifted her face to look into Sophie's eyes. "I know."

Sophie moved her face very close. "Aren't you going to tell me that you like me?"

Delora captured Sophie's lips with hers and held them a long, long time.

"I know," Sophie murmured with a tender smile when Delora moved away and slid into her car.

CHAPTER THIRTY-THREE

Sometimes, when conditions were just right, Delora could see the sunset from the side porch. It was a short phenomenon. Widows Ridge to the northwest usually veiled the later, more colorful parts.

Finished with the dishes, Delora stood at the kitchen door, studying the sun as it bid farewell to another successful summer day. With a weary sigh, she opened the screen door and stepped out into the still evening warmth. She slipped her hands beneath her hair, palming sweat from the nape of her neck.

The loud pop and exhalation of compressed air let her know that Louie had beaten her to the porch. She started to retreat back inside, but indignation rose up in her. She had as much right to be there as he did, maybe more so.

He sat in one of the nylon banded chairs, slumped back like a great rearing toad. As she watched, he lifted the beer clumsily to his lips and slurped it noisily. Foam spattered the back of his scarred hand.

He swallowed with a mutter of satisfaction. "You know it's just by the sheer goodness of my nature that I let you live, don't you?"

Delora no longer reacted to the hollow wet noises he made when drinking. Or his threats. She looked away when he dabbed his fingers on the front of his Rolling Stones T-shirt.

"You hear me, Lora? You know how lucky you are?"

Delora remembered the shirt well. It was one she'd bought him when they'd traveled to Troutville to the monster truck rally during those first few months of freedom after high school. Those had been good times, in a way. She'd been so young and hopeful.

She sighed. The shirt now stretched taut across his thickened frame.

"Yeah, Louie. I know."

She turned from him and tried to empty her mind so she could enjoy the evening. She'd become good at traveling to other places in her mind. She continued to catalog her environment, however, every leaf that had moved since the last inventory. One thing about nature. It was never static. There was always an undercurrent of motion, probably insectile. Weather dealt a hand as well.

Delora read once that there were ten quintillion insects on the planet, outnumbering humans by ninety-five percent. She had no idea what a quintillion was, but it was odd to think of those unseen populations. Nature's constant ebb tide was evidence enough of their existence.

"You ain't got nothin' else to say?" Louie asked.

Delora thought about Rosalie's anger. She had lied and told Rosalie that she had gone early to work, but Delora knew her keen eyes had taken in the fact that her foster daughter still wore the same clothing as the day before. Had she said something to Louie? Delora really didn't care.

Delora took a deep breath and slipped inside as quietly as she could.

CHAPTER THIRTY-FOUR

One evening, depressed and reluctant to drive the forty miles into Goshen to work, Righteous decided he was just plain tired and needed coffee. He pulled into the French Club. Inside, the wooden paneled walls gave this steak house just the right amount of shadowed ambience. A polished bar stretched across the back wall on the right. To his surprise, he saw Sophie's friend Delora working the bar.

"Hey there, gal, how's life treating you?" he said as he slid onto a barstool. "I had forgotten you work here."

Delora smiled and he felt warmed by her sweetness. Sophie sure knew how to pick them. "Hey yourself," she replied. "What brings you out this late at night?"

"On my way to work, over in Goshen. Just need some coffee is all. Need some energy 'cause I sure am not in the mood to work."

Delora laughed and nodded her blond head in understanding as she moved to the coffee machine. Within seconds, a steaming cup was in front of him. "We're not one of those fancy coffeehouses, but Esther swears by this blend."

Righteous blew on it, then tasted it straight up without cream or sweetener.

"Good," he said. "She's right on about that."

"So what do you do?" Delora asked. "Bartender? Is that what I heard?"

Righteous snickered. "I do whatever. I started out as a grunt at the Thirsty Rogue back when I was in high school. I carried beer kegs, washed glasses, wiped up the tables, you know. The hardest thing was cleaning up all them bloody bodies off the floor. They really make a mess." His eyes roamed across Delora's face, waiting deadpan for her to get it. His hunch paid off as she broke into soft laughter.

"You are some piece of work, Righteous," she exclaimed, leaning her forearms and upper body on the bar. "How long have you known Sophie?"

"Man, years." He sipped his coffee. "Since I was a kid. My family grew up near Lisse and seems like she was just always there. She went to school, like I did, though a lot of the bayou people teach their own at home. She never had no brothers or sisters and me neither so we sorta talked. We had gaydar even back then I guess."

"Can I ask you something personal? When did you know you were that way? I mean, were you young?"

He thought a long moment, then sighed and spoke carefully. "Actual, I never gave it much thought one way or t'other. I was, you know, by my uncle when I was little. It's the way it's always been for me. I was seein' this older guy all through school so wadn't much time for girls. Then I met Stephen and that was it. I like the boys and all..."

He blushed and paused to imbibe more coffee. The rich brew was working its magic and he felt like he might actually be able to work his shift.

"The boys? I thought you were with Stephen."

"I know." He had the grace to look sheepish. "I guess the devil gets in me. I'm gwine stop, swear it. I gotta stop." He tucked his head and rotated his stool from side to side. "What about you. When did you know you was gay?"

"Shhh! Big ears in this place." Delora glanced back toward the kitchen. "I didn't know for sure until Sophie."

"No shit! She is great, ain't she?"

Delora's smile was soft and mysterious. "Yeah, she is. So great she scares me."

"How do you mean?"

"Like I might disappoint her or something." It was Delora's turn to blush.

"Y'all ain't done nothin' yet, have you?" he stated with keen insight. He squinted one eye and studied her. "You ain't!"

Delora closed her eyes and reached for her cigarette pack. "I'm not sure that's any of your business, smarty-pants."

"Oh, honey, you got to get on that thing. What are you waitin' for?" He puffed out his round cheeks and made a comical face.

Delora looked away as she lit a cigarette. Righteous grew serious.

"It'll work out, Delora. Falling into another person is just about the easiest thing you can do. All you got to do is let it happen. Miss Sophie is puredee gold and just about the smartest someone I know. You ain't got one thing to worry about if it's her. Believe me on this, okay?"

Delora looked at Righteous and was impressed by his seriousness. "I think I do."

"Good." Righteous stood and laid two dollars on the counter. "I'm goin' to work now. You behave yourself or, if you can't, don't get caught."

Delora grunted as she lifted the money and headed to the register. "I got a long way to go to get in as much trouble as you do, Righteous. You have a great night!"

Righteous threw back his head and laughed as he left the restaurant.

CHAPTER THIRTY-FIVE

Sophie slowed in front of Blossom's Diner, Redstar's finest low-priced restaurant. Delora stood by the wide glass doors, her face turned toward the stream of traffic passing by on Highway 65. Sophie gave herself a few minutes to enjoy the fineness of Delora's profile before calling to her from the open car window. "Hey, over here. I came the back way."

Delora turned when she heard Sophie's voice, and Sophie wondered if she would always thrill to this woman's sweet smile.

"Hello there," Delora said as she slipped into Sophie's car. "I was able to get the whole afternoon off, a rare event, let me tell you. So what is this big job we have to do?"

Her lemon scent washed across Sophie and Sophie realized that for the first time in a long time she felt completely happy. She remained silent, just studying Delora, a smile on her face.

Delora watched Sophie as well and the silence that fell between them was powerful. Their eyes explored one another with the curiosity and bliss of a new relationship. Delora laughed softly. "If you don't drive, I may kiss you here in front of everyone."

"Hmm. Doesn't sound like a bad thing to me," Sophie replied, but she did, with a sigh, return her attention to driving. "Okay. We're going to heal people."

"Heal people? I can't do that."

Sophie nodded. "Well, you've been asking me about my work so I thought I'd give you a firsthand look."

Delora studied the road ahead. "There won't be, like, gross stuff, will there?" She grimaced to Sophie.

The healer laughed. "Wouldn't that be something—first time out and we get a situation like that?"

They talked about their lives as Sophie guided the car into the depths of Bayou Lisse. Sophie learned about how Delora met Louie, about her parents' personalities and their cute quirks. Delora learned about Sophie's mother Faye, about how she loved men and money and used them to escape the bayou. And they talked circumspectly about the powerful attraction they felt for one another and how it could be poorly accepted by a heterosexual world.

"Hey," Delora said suddenly, peering out the passenger window. "Isn't that your friend?"

Sophie followed Delora's gaze and answered, "Sure enough. What the hell is he doing out here? Roll down your window."

She slowed the car, and they pulled up next to Righteous who was jogging slowly along the side of the road.

"Well, Lord have mercy," Sophie called through Delora's window. "What are you doing out in this heat? Get in."

Righteous, panting heavily and awash with a heavy sheen of sweat, opened the back door and fell clumsily into the car. "You gals sure are a welcome sight."

Delora turned and grinned at the tall, thin black man. "I know you're not out there trying to work off a few extra pounds."

Righteous laughed and swabbed at his face with a soaked T-shirt. "Just tryin' to stay healthy."

"Why out here, though? You're a long way from home," Sophie pointed out as she pulled the car back onto the road.

He nodded agreement. "Yeah, just like the bayou is all. It's awful pretty here. Better than the hot asphalt out my way."

"Does Stephen know you're out here? People have disappeared in this water, whether gators or Race's hoodlums." Sophie peered sternly at him using the rearview mirror.

"Race's hoodlums?" Delora asked.

"Cheetah Race," Righteous explained, apparently unwilling to talk about Stephen. "He's our local mafia."

"And one bad character if you get on his wrong side," Sophie added.

"But I'm not on his bad side. We all went to school together, so no problem."

"Still it's too hot for you to be out here," Sophie scolded.

"Easy on me, Miss Healer. Stop bein' my doctor and be my friend. What are y'all doin' out and about? Gettin' a little lovin' done, hmm?" he teased.

Delora laughed as she blushed and slapped his bare knee playfully. "Righteous!"

Sophie just shook her head. "I'm working, for your information."

"Yeah? Who's sick?" He leaned forward eagerly.

"Who isn't sick?"

"Now, Sophie," Delora chided.

"I'm kidding, I'm kidding," Sophie said, defending herself. "Firis Skope thinks she's pregnant, and then I'm seeing the Weirtis girl, Imny."

"Wasn't she the one burned?" asked Righteous. He turned his attention to Delora. "You were burned too, right? You better now?"

Delora's smile faded and she dropped her gaze. "I'm fine."

Sophie could have kicked Righteous for opening his big mouth. She glared at him in the rearview. Righteous realized his mistake right away and changed the subject. "So who's the father? She's only what, sixteen?"

"She's seventeen now and seeing the Adams boy."

"So they gettin' hitched?"

"Umhmm, I guess he'll go to work for the oil refinery like his daddy." Sophie navigated a difficult patch of road. They were going farther along the Bayou Lisse now, and the dirt road had grown deeply rutted with shallow pools of water filling the ruts. Trees interlaced above the car and Delora's curiosity grew. She'd never been so far into the bayou's interior before, and she found the scenery fascinating. It was almost like being on another planet.

Sophie noted Delora's piqued interest and began to forgive Righteous his earlier *faux pas*. "It's amazing, isn't it?"

"Wow," Delora responded. "People really live down here?"

"You'd be surprised."

"Don't you know about these people?" Righteous asked Delora.

"What do you mean?"

"Righteous," Sophie said in a low warning tone.

"What?" Righteous responded. "She needs to know if she's part of your life."

Sophie blushed, feeling Delora's eyes on her.

"What is it, Sophie?"

After a moment of silence, Righteous continued. "The whole bayou is full of people, but no one knows about them. You won't find 'em on the census papers or voting or goin' into town. It's like they don't exist."

"But how do they live?" Delora asked. "I mean, don't they work or buy food? How about school?"

Righteous leaned back and fanned his face with one hand. "It's like tribal or something. They get by 'cause they help each other. They have their own Gypsy laws that have nothing to do with Redstar and they make things to trade with each other for money. I guess you figured out Sophie doctors them and they pay her in food and other stuff. They've lived this way, well, forever."

"Out here?" Delora's eyes were wide.

Sophie jumped in. "It's just a way of life using old customs. It's not so different from what you have in Redstar, it's just not so nine-to-five. The kids, most of them, go to the public schools."

"They party harder, too," Righteous added with a loud laugh.

Sophie bristled. "Just what do you know about it, smartass? You're not even one of us."

"Everyone knows, Miss Sophie," he answered wryly.

Delora laughed. "I didn't know. I've just heard about the healers, off and on most of my life. My foster mother doesn't approve. Says y'all are 'Godless heathens.'"

Sophie grunted. "As far as I'm concerned, living with the bayou puts you a whole lot closer to God than most churches do."

Sophie pulled the car to a halt in front of a small house made mostly of tarred paper and wood scraps. Smoke emanated from the crumbling brick chimney even though it was in the high nineties outside. A large mixed-breed dog circled the car barking with hoarse bursts of sound.

"Will he bite?" asked Righteous as he eyed the dog nervously.

Sophie looked at Delora and they broke into spontaneous laughter.

"What?" Righteous turned to look at them. "I don't like big dogs."

"I do," said Delora as she edged open the door. The dog was there immediately, inserting his nose into the crack and trying to wriggle his way in. Obviously, this dog had never met anyone who wasn't a friend.

"Hi there, big boy," Delora said, opening the door and scrubbing behind the dog's ears. He tried to jump in her lap as big dogs so often do, and Sophie's voice rang out like a gunshot.

"Joe! Sit."

The dog reacted with military precision. He fell away from Delora like rain off a roof, then whined as if in apology. Delora turned and saw Sophie had come around her side of the car, her backpack trailing from one hand.

Delora pondered this new side of Sophie, having never seen her raise her voice. It was a little frightening but also garnered respect. Slowly she swung her legs out of the car until her feet were on the ground. She turned and looked at Righteous who shrugged and opened his own door. Cautiously, Delora extended one hand and rubbed the dog's ear. He did not rise, but his tail swept the ground gleefully. His tongue lolled and he appeared to be smiling. Delora rose and moved past him, and the dog eyed Sophie expectantly. She nodded and, rising calmly, he followed them toward the front porch.

An elderly woman wearing a tattered dress and a grimy white apron answered the door.

"Hello, *púridaia*. I'm here to see *tikni*. Arisel called me."

The woman eyed Righteous and Delora with mistrust.

"They *Geyro, Geyri* are with me and mean no harm to *ken*. No *mumpli, narkri*."

Still eyeing the strangers with cautionary eyes, the woman opened the door wider. Sophie entered first with Delora behind and Righteous last.

"Don't say anything or look at anything too closely," Sophie whispered to them as they passed through. "Please be careful."

Frightened into silence, Delora and Righteous clustered close. They tried not to stare too obviously at the heavily furnished home. Though highly cluttered with belongings, the home was elegant due to the wealth of colorful hangings that draped the walls of the large, one-room home. Beds, situated around three of the walls, were partially recessed and draped with heavy tapestries. A kitchen of sorts had been built as an outcropping on one wall and a large wood cookstove emitted an uncomfortable heat into the room. The smell of spices and an odd smell, reminding Delora of how dry and scentless a cat smells, filled the home.

Two dark-haired children sat on cushions in the center of the floor, surrounded by wooden toys. They looked up expectantly when the trio entered. One child, the smaller of the two, looking to be about three years old, immediately draped one arm across half her face. Her body ducked forward from the waist as she tried to disappear from sight.

Sophie spoke softly to the older child, Lally, who might have been six, her voice a singsong of harsh gutturals and trilling lilts. Lally spoke to the younger and, taking her free hand, led her toward the door. The elderly woman spoke then.

"*Drabéngro, purochikni?*"

"*Dood* better. I must see, *dik dik*, to help the healing. We go to the front for light only, no *dur*."

"*Kushti*," the old woman agreed, nodding. She accompanied them onto the front porch. The small child hesitated coming through the door, and the grandmother and sister urged her onward with soft admonishments.

Delora's eyes were wide as she watched Sophie turn the ravaged child into full sunlight. The child was pretty, with rust-colored skin and hair shining like coal in the afternoon light. She peered shyly at Delora and Righteous with her one good eye. The other, mostly hidden by her arm, was half-buried beneath skin that had melted along one cheek. The burn slashed across her face and onto her neck, and Delora wondered what could have caused such a thing.

"It was a bonfire," Sophie explained as if reading Delora's thoughts. She said it in a singsong voice as she playfully pulled the child's arm from the burned area so she could see. Delora realized that the child didn't understand English as Sophie started singing to her in that language of their people. Romany, was it? They were playing a game in which Sophie would sing a phrase and pull down the child's protective arm. The child would respond with her own lilting phrase and, laughing, cover her face again, peering out at Sophie with her one good eye. Joe, wanting to be involved in the fun, came lumbering onto the porch, almost knocking Delora over. He raced around Sophie and Imny until Lally grabbed his collar and, slapping his haunches, made him sit still.

Reaching into her pack, Sophie brought out a plastic water bottle with no label, but marked with a large black X, and shook it to mix the contents.

"*Lon meski*," she explained to Imny, making sure the grandmother heard. "*Drab, drab, no goodlo, no peeve, wafti peeve, jin Imny? Jin púridaia? Jin borri pen?*"

Sophie eyed the grandmother and sister archly until they nodded with solemn grace. "This is not for drinking. It's medicine," she reiterated in English. Soaking a sterile gauze square with the mixture, she laid it on part of Imny's wound. The small girl stood very still as Sophie added two more gauze squares to cover the burned area and then pressed the girl's hand up to them to hold them in place. "*Desh, desh*. Hold it twenty minutes. *Jin?*"

"*Jin*," Imny replied. With one more bashful look at Delora and Righteous, Imny scurried inside.

Sophie bent and lifted Lally into her arms. They danced around the porch as Sophie hummed, Lally breaking into helpless laughter.

The grandmother looked on with a stoic face. Sophie put Lally down finally and spoke at length to the child, who smiled shyly at Delora and Righteous as she slipped wraith-like through the door and inside.

Delora and Righteous moved down the steps, understanding that the visit was almost over. Delora motioned Joe to her and began scratching him along his back. He chuffed with pleasure.

Digging into her pack, Sophie produced a small squat plastic container. She handed the grandmother the container and the bottle and instructed her in how to apply the salve and made sure she knew how often to apply the salt-tea. She also gave her a stack of sterile gauze squares and promised to come back in a week.

Eyes darting to the strangers, the grandmother spoke low to Sophie, then moved inside. Sophie smiled at Delora and waited, making sure her pack was closed. Moments later the old woman reappeared and handed Sophie a handkerchief tied in a knot. Sophie bowed low and pressed the back of the woman's hand to her cheek. The grandmother smiled slightly and disappeared inside.

In the car the trio were silent for some time, almost until they reached the turn for the Skope place. "Well," Sophie said. "Everybody okay?"

"That poor kid," Righteous said softly. "Will it ever get any better?"

"Oh, sure, as she grows. The medicines I gave her will help keep any infection down and will slough off the top layers of disfigured skin. She'll always have some redness, but it'll be okay."

Her eyes went to Delora. "Lora, you okay?" She was anxious to see her reaction to Imny Weirtis's burns. The sight had rocked Sophie the first time, and she'd waited for this day to bring Delora along. It was a way of reminding Delora that there were others worse off.

"How did it happen?"

"Imny fell during the dancing at the Beltane bonfire. That's this past May. She landed right on a burning log."

"How awful. It must have hurt her so badly."

Sophie sighed. "Yes, it did. She was in pain for a while and so young she couldn't understand why we had to hurt her further to examine her. Grandam came with me the first time because she and the grandmother there knew one another. It made things easier but was still tough. They live by the old ways and would have let the child die."

"No!" Delora exclaimed, one hand covering her mouth.

"She's right, Delora. These old families leave everything to fate, not believing in modern medicine. Imny never went to a hospital, did she, Sophie?"

"Nope. Just me and Grandam."

"I'm glad she lived," Delora exclaimed tentatively.

Sophie parked the car outside a weather-worn Victorian home, and watched Delora closely. "Really? Even though her life will be harder? Her family will have a hard time arranging a mate for her. Many of the clan will think her disfigurement will pass on to the children. They won't know any better."

Delora dropped her head and nodded. "Even so."

Righteous opened the back door of the car and stretched in the hot midday sun.

"Howdy, Mrs. Skope," he called to a dark-haired woman who sat on the front porch, fanning herself with a magazine.

"Who's that with Miss Sophie?" the woman called, coming to her feet.

"It's me, Righteous Michie," he said, moving closer.

"Lawd, will you look," she exclaimed coming slowly down the porch steps and drawing the lanky man close. "As I live and breathe."

She turned to Delora. "I changed this boy's diapers," she crowed.

Sophie came around the side of the car. "I wouldn't admit that, Shirley. It must have been an alarming experience."

Shirley pulled a face and laughed until she was hunched over gasping for air. Sophie watched Delora watching Shirley and felt amusement tickle her. Delora obviously didn't know quite what to make of the bayou people. Shirley wore traditional dress mostly, with the scarf over her dark hair and the vibrantly colored long skirt. Unfortunately, she also defied custom and wore a blue Dallas Cowboys T-shirt. And flip-flops on her bare feet. She was a large woman too, with a good-sized double chin and a wide girth that she carried gracefully.

"Shirley, this is my friend Delora. She's riding with me today. I hope you don't mind."

Shirley grinned. "Shoot no, happy for the company. Got lots of iced tea. Or fresh sweet lemonade if you'd druther. Come on in here and set a spell."

"I can't stay long, Mrs. Skope. You know I'm working over in Goshen now."

"Yes, I heard, Righteous, and I can't say I appreciate you working in such a place. Why don't you come on back here? Redstar's gotta have something for you. The women here are better too." She looked at Delora, her matchmaker's mind obviously whirling. "You just need to find a good woman to settle with."

Sophie jumped to Righteous's rescue. "Now, Shirley, leave the boy be. Where's Firis? Is she feeling okay?"

They had entered into a spacious, well-used kitchen. Plants decorated the windows and cooking supplies littered the countertops. A bowl of lemons rested next to a cutting board covered with cut and squeezed lemon halves. The cold pitcher of lemonade drew Righteous.

"Looks good, Mrs. Skope."

"You help yourself, boy." She scurried to a cabinet and pulled down three glasses. She handed one to Righteous and waited while he poured.

Sophie meandered through the house until she reached a bedroom door that looked as though it belonged to a teen. She knocked and a weak voice called out for her to enter. Inside she found Firis Skope, a somewhat pudgy seventeen-year-old, lying supine with a pillow over her face.

"Hey, Firis, it's me," Sophie said loudly as she entered the room. "Feeling pretty bad, huh?"

Firis turned her head and gestured weakly. "Laws, so sick, Miss Sophie. Feel like I could just lay over and die."

Sophie clucked sympathetically. "Now what good would that do? I promise it'll pass."

She moved to sit on the bed next to the moaning teen. Her probing questions were gentle and kind as one hand pressed coolness into the girl's forehead.

Delora looked after Sophie and felt torn between following her or engaging in the entertaining gossip Shirley was sharing with Righteous. They were like two magpies raucously discussing people Delora didn't know. Delora felt as though she was really missing out on an exciting facet of worldly existence.

Moving gingerly, she sank into the chair Shirley absently pulled out for her. Someone named Lorent Mays had passed on a scorching case of herpes to a gal named Alice Shores and she wasn't the first. Seems Alice found out, after the fact, that dear Lorent had quite a reputation in southern Alabama. Shirley found out all this firsthand, as Alice was a member of the Fun & Fit club in Redstar. Seems Alice was having a good bit of pain every time she went to urinate and she shared this information with the cluster of women in her workout group, hoping for a remedy that worked. Only then did she discover what had been passed to her. She asked for their prayers in one breath and cursed Lorent's heritage in the next. She would certainly never see that snake again.

"But you know she will," declared Shirley, confiding in her audience. "He's charmed her and will again. Some men just do that."

Righteous bit his lip, aghast at the news. "I hear about this sort of thing all the time at the Thirsty Rogue." He shuddered. "Even though people are warned. I just don't understand it."

Delora watched in amazement as the talk moved on to the best recipe for icebox pickles. Righteous shared one from his grandmother and Shirley declared that more lime soak than a little made for a much better pickle.

"I agree," Sophie said as she entered the room and slid into the fourth chair at the table. She helped herself to a glass of iced tea. "Clary always puts two to one even though most recipes call for one to one. Makes a big difference in how crisp the cukes come out."

Her eyes found Delora, gauging her comfort level. Delora glanced back at her, eyes complacent.

Shirley leaned forward. "So, it is, isn't it?"

Sophie nodded. "Looks like January or February. Will she stay with school?"

"Hmmm." Shirley shook her head in the negative. "Probably not. Never been good there."

The four fell silent.

"There's the GED. Make sure she does that. The schools all have a program now. I can help her find out about it if she needs me to. Okay?"

Shirley leaned forward to pat Sophie's hand. "We sure do thank you, Miss Sophie. I'll keep after her and let her know you'll help."

"I'll check back in about a month. Let me know if there's any bleeding or pain."

She lifted her pack to her knees and rummaged through it. "Here's tea for the sickness. May want to make some now. She's having a lot of that and can have the tea whenever she complains. Here's vitamins too, one every night at bedtime. Make sure she drinks juice, orange is best, and try to make her eat good food, like green stuff. These first few months are the most important even though she's not showing yet. The baby's in there, coming together, and it needs the best it can get, okay?"

"Yes, ma'am," Shirley said with a very serious air. She lifted the plastic bag of tea and rose to put the kettle on. She stood by the range reading the directions Sophie had written on the outside of the packet. "She'll be glad to have this, I know."

Delora studied the box of over-the-counter vitamins and wondered how Sophie could afford to supply the people of the bayou when most paid in barter. The fact that the Cofe family had made it work for so long filled Delora with an odd sense of pride. It was no wonder all the bayou families respected the healers as they did. It was magic, pure and simple.

Righteous was telling a story about his grandmother's herb garden and the teas made from it. Delora watched Sophie's interest and envied her intelligence. There appeared to be a whole universe of knowledge that Delora knew nothing about. This herb knowledge...the knowing what a growing baby needed the first few months after conception... the knowing of what to apply to poor Imny's burned skin. Delora's hand crept low and pressed against her abdomen. Without her realizing it, the injury to her own burns had convalesced after Sophie's ministration. Delora felt whole for the first time in a long time.

Firis appeared in the hallway. Her face was flushed and she was unsteady. Without thinking, Delora leapt up to take the girl's arm and guide her to the chair. Firis looked at Delora in surprise but smiled and let herself be led to the table.

"Firis, this is my friend, Delora November." After her initial surprise, Sophie felt a sense of completeness fill her.

"Hi, Firis," Delora said. "I hear congratulations are due. Are you excited?"

Firis settled into Delora's abandoned chair and rested her face in both hands. "Not yet, Miss Delora, just sick so far. Feels like my stomach wants to come out my mouth."

Shirley filled the cup she'd prepared with water from the kettle. "You'll have some of this tea Miss Sophie brought, sweet girl, and I bet it'll make you right in no time."

Sophie stood and patted Firis's shoulder. "You'll be fine, little mama. All new moms go through it and come out okay. You will too. Your mama's got my number and you call if you need anything."

"Yes, ma'am," Firis said, her voice muffled by her hands.

"Thank you much for the refreshment, Mrs. Skope. I was right parched by the heat," Righteous said as he stood and straightened his damp shorts over his thin legs.

"Me too," Delora added. "Thank you for your kindness." She handed her empty glass to Shirley.

"My pleasure, darlin's. Come back again real soon." She set a steaming cup of tea in front of her daughter and moved her bulk around the table. She reached into a worn satchel resting on the counter closest to the hallway door. "Miss Sophie, I'd like to give you a little something for comin' out today."

"Lord, Shirley," Sophie interrupted. "I just stopped in. Didn't do much. There's no need to worry on that account—you don't owe me a thing. I was happy to sit a spell with you."

"Well, you're sweet." She persisted, however, opening her change purse. "You take this little bit of egg money. For the tea and all." She pushed a creased ten-dollar bill toward Sophie and shook it imperiously.

Sophie paused and shook her head. Sighing, she took the money. "I do thank you, Shirley. You're too good to me."

Shirley's satisfied smile beamed as she snapped her coin purse closed.

CHAPTER THIRTY-SIX

The noise level at the Thirsty Rogue had risen during the long evening. Thus Righteous didn't hear the hushed voices that grew around him that moonless August night. In fact, he had no indication at all that he was about to be beaten almost to death. He didn't realize the little blond chickie's boyfriend was behind him until he saw the look of absolute horror spread across the relief bartender's face.

The pain began then, a pain that would follow him in one way or another for the remainder of his life. One minute he'd been happily cooing with the cute towhead preparatory to getting a little action in the back room before he went home. The next minute he was on the floor looking up at colored strobes, his head numb yet throbbing.

A face appeared above him. The head was oddly square and surrounded by a blond bristling of hair. The face twisted in anger and something in the eyes disturbed Righteous. He was filled with a kind of paralyzing fear he'd never experienced before. For some insane reason he felt a sense of release. The jig was up. His life was about to change and change big.

Righteous had fallen into a stereotypical situation; he'd messed with another man's man and been caught. Dime novel stuff at its finest.

He lifted his arms over his head and the beating began in earnest. He got in a few good licks, connecting with jarring satisfaction, but there was just no time to strike. He couldn't draw back to hit because he had to protect himself against the waterfall of blows raining onto him. He didn't stand much of a chance. The guy outweighed him twice over. His last mental image before blackness descended on his burning body was a single, clear picture of Stephen's beautiful face.

Some time later he woke in a new environment. The smell of plastic had replaced the beer and apricot smell of his bar. The lights were too bright and penetrated the skin of his eyelids.

There was a sheet lying across his body, and he knew that if he moved at all, its restriction would make his pain even more unbearable. Still he felt compelled to see where he was, to orient himself. Distant beeping and the smell implied a hospital. Panic set in. He had no health insurance. Stephen had tried to get him on his plan at work, but the company only allowed marriage benefits.

Righteous took a deep breath and felt a sob well in his chest. He was pretty well fucked and not in a nice way.

He soon realized only one eye would open and that only halfway, the other one presumably swelled shut. Lifting his good eyelid made his arms and legs feel like they were going to crack right off his body and splinter on the floor. He let the good eye track along the tubing that led to the IV bag. He saw that he was in a small area surrounded by privacy curtains. Other sounds began to penetrate—telephones buzzing, the rustle of cloth as people passed.

"Corrine said to call when you got settled," a woman's mellow voice said on his right.

"What?" he tried to say, but the word was little more than a hoarse croak.

"Mama said she'd be here right after work too," she continued.

Someone replied with a harsh grunt and a moan of pain.

"I know, I told her you might not be up to it. I told her to come tomorrow to be here after the gallbladder's out, but she wasn't having none of it."

A new silence fell, and Righteous realized finally that he was listening to a conversation from the next cubicle.

Trying to escape sudden claustrophobia, Righteous tried to piece together what had happened.

He remembered examining the towhead's pretty features, wondering what pleasures the night would bring. Had he been

CHAPTER THIRTY-SEVEN

Sometime later—Righteous, dozing, wasn't sure how much—the curtain swept aside and Stephen appeared. Tears filled Righteous's eyes and fled away along his dark cheeks. A sorrowful sob caught in his throat. He choked and fresh blood welled in his mouth. He allowed it to leak from the corner of his mouth. He hated to be so gross but knew he'd choke if the blood remained there. He couldn't open his mouth at all. He blinked his one good eye to try to clear his vision.

Stephen didn't say a word. He stood just inside the curtain-framed portal, his form still. The movement of the nurse's station progressed with surrealistic ease behind him. Stephen looked bad, his hair mussed in back and his eyes puffy with sleep.

"Stephen," Righteous croaked. "Sorry, Stephen."

There was no sympathy in Stephen's eyes. Righteous saw only pain and aloofness. If Stephen turned from him Righteous didn't know what he would do.

Stephen took a deep breath and moved closer to the bed. Veering abruptly, he walked to the end of the bed and picked up Righteous's chart.

"Looks like you've done it this time, buckaroo. Let's see...broken jaw wired shut, broken collarbone, internal bruising and they're going to keep you overnight for observation until you stop peeing red."

Righteous tried to lift his hand to brush the drying blood off his cheek, but the arm shrieked with pain and would not move. Fresh tears fell and he knew he was at a complete nadir. He couldn't get much lower than this.

Stephen was still regarding him with hard eyes. Where had the love gone? Righteous realized suddenly that he, and he alone, had killed Stephen's love for him. The devil on his shoulder tried to interject a good dose of self-pity, but the angel on the other shoulder knew that this was the bed he'd made and, by golly, he was lying in that bed now. He had no one to blame but himself. Bottom line. The buck stopped with him.

If only he could talk, could make new promises, there might be a chance. His infidelities were over. He'd had enough. Sowed all the wild oats he was going to sow. Stephen needed to know this.

"Stephen," he moaned, his voice a rasp of pain and mortification. "Doan' leave ee."

Stephen watched him without touching him. "What?"

Righteous panted and realized it was a futile exercise to try to talk. His jaw plain wouldn't work and the swelling of his cheeks barely allowed his tongue the space to move properly.

Some feeling stirred in Stephen for he moved closer and laid one hand atop Righteous's hand. Righteous's throat threatened to close from the emotion he was feeling.

"Listen. You focus on getting well, okay. Everything else can wait until then."

He leaned over and pressed a kiss to the small square of unbandaged skin on Righteous's forehead. "Just get better."

As Stephen left the area, Righteous felt darkness descend and pain drift away. Escaping the misery of his life, Righteous eagerly sought that peace.

Sophie grabbed Stephen's arm as he passed through the waiting room and pulled him into her embrace. He broke down and sobbed in her arms. She crooned and rubbed the back of his neck like he was a baby, trying to soothe his pain.

"How could this happen, Sophie? My life is over."

Sophie grabbed up a nearby box of tissues and used a handful to mop his face.

"Stop it. What do you mean, over? He'll get better. It takes time. Six weeks and he'll be good as new. I already asked the doctor."

Stephen shook his head. "No, I'm not taking any more, Sophie. This is it for me. Life is too damned short. There're other fish out there. Faithful fish. Safe fish."

Stephen regarded the amazed healer for a long moment, then walked away.

"He's all yours," he called back as the automatic door closed behind him.

"Stephen," Sophie called after him but quickly realized it would be pointless to talk to him right now. Maybe time and some reflection would bring him back to Righteous.

She fished her cell phone from her jeans pocket and dialed.

"Hey," she said a moment later. "It's me. I think Stephen's left Righteous."

Delora, on the other end, replied, "Oh no. Why?"

"Righteous got himself beaten to a pulp last night, well, early this morning, at Thirsty's. Stephen's had enough, I guess."

"Is Righteous okay?"

Delora and Righteous had hit it off right away, and she knew Delora's concern was heartfelt.

"He's broken up pretty bad, but they say he'll be okay. I'm more worried about Stephen's mental health right now."

"He's taking it hard, obviously."

"He said he's had enough and he left."

"What does that mean? Is he really abandoning him now, of all times?"

Sophie grunted hollowly. "I'm not real sure. I hope he'll reconsider as time passes."

"Me too. Listen, I can leave. We're slow as molasses here. How about if I come over there to be with you two? Are you going to be there a while?"

"Sure. I'm still trying to find out if they're keeping him more than one night. He may have some internal bleeding."

"I hope not. I'll be right there. Give me half an hour or so."

"Okay, Delora. I'll see you then." Sophie's voice had grown soft and her tone endearing.

"Okay," Delora said, her own voice going gentle and warm.

CHAPTER THIRTY-EIGHT

Delora's first sight of Righteous would haunt her for some time. The bed barely held his long, narrow form, and his swollen and bandaged head was overlarge and stark white. Sophie'd told her his jaw was wired shut so he wouldn't be able to talk to her. She hadn't warned Delora that his eyes were swollen shut, his nose was sitting on his face like a fat plum and that several cuts where the skin had split had been stitched with a Frankenstein-ish flair.

Marshaling her shock and emotion, Delora moved across the room to his bed. The other bed in his room was unoccupied, and Delora hoped he would continue to have some solitude during his time at the hospital.

"Righteous?" She took his hand. "How are you feeling?"

Righteous stirred and opened one bloodshot eye to regard her. She smiled at him and watched as tears filled the eye and escaped along his cheek.

"Aw, honey, don't do that. I know it hurts, but you'll be right as rain in no time."

She grabbed a tissue from the box next to his bed and carefully wiped the bloody tears away. Something broke loose in her heart, and a fragile freedom filled her. Not sure what to do with these feelings, she started talking. She told Righteous about the maps on her bedroom walls and all the places she would like to go. Settling her small bottom next to him on the bed, she held his free hand in hers.

"We're survivors, you and me, Righteous. Let me tell you what happened to me a few years ago. I was in the hospital just like you are now, only I was there because I had third-degree burns."

She talked on, telling Righteous things she'd never shared before with anyone but Bucky. She found herself telling Righteous all of it. About how it felt when the fire penetrated the oily sheen of lighter fluid and bit into her skin.

She told him about the feelings of betrayal—the understanding that Louie could and would do this to her. How the attempted murder almost became a suicide too when a part of the fire had followed the fluid across the bed to the open can of fluid Louie had left sitting next to it. How the explosion had wiped the satisfied smirk from Louie's face. Clothing ablaze, he'd tried to run, leaving her there to burn. She'd found out later he'd broken an ankle in that mad dash.

Paralyzed at first—from the pain and the previous night's beer—Delora had managed to roll onto her stomach. She told him how the flame had seemed to be a living beast and was unwilling to die beneath her. The fire had leapt up, escaping on either side and finding new tender tissues to punish and the fresh pain had made her scream anew. By then the room had been on fire. Old farmhouses were tinderboxes and theirs had been no exception. Surrounded by fire and choking smoke, Delora had passed through walls of flame to run outside and into the smothering blanket held by a neighbor.

Delora told Righteous about being in this same hospital and then, within a few days, at the burn unit in Mobile. She told him about meeting Bucky Clyde Thorpe and their present relationship. She explained how the days had turned into weeks and weeks into months and how painful the debriding of the dead, burned tissue had been, how the heavy pain medications had become addictive and how it had been a pure act of will to walk away from them.

She told him about the stylized tattoo on her thigh, about the legend of the phoenix, the beautiful bird from ancient Greek mythology, the symbol of resurrection and life after burning. The phoenix's flight from the ashes of his blazing death was said to represent the ability to leave the world and its problems behind, flying toward the sun and clear skies.

She told him how she'd read once that the bird not only represented immortality but also an individual who stands apart from the rest. A creature re-created by fire. Repeatedly studying the phoenix tattoo had given her the power to leave the pain pills behind. It was a reminder that she was forever changed.

She eventually told Righteous about how she felt less than whole. How she could no longer bear children or have sex. How sometimes she felt it had been a huge mistake to live through the fire.

And finally, her voice was hoarse from exertion, she admitted that she still lived with Louie but that he was sleeping with Rosalie.

Righteous drifted in and out of consciousness, but Delora didn't care. She knew the words would comfort him and saying them certainly comforted her.

Sophie, standing just outside the door, with her back to the cold tile wall and her head leaned back, allowed the tears to fall freely as silent sobs shook her. The silence emanating from the room warned her that Delora would soon emerge, and she really didn't want her to see that she'd heard. She didn't want to embarrass Delora or make her feel uncomfortable. As soon as she was able, she shifted forward and, wiping at her streaming eyes, moved toward the waiting area.

CHAPTER THIRTY-NINE

"Hey."

"Hey, yourself," Delora replied. "It's good to hear your voice."

"You didn't call me last night and I got worried. What's going on? Everything all right?"

"Sure. All kinds of stuff going on, though. I met this guy, a friend of Sophie's. His name is Righteous and he's in a relationship with this guy named Stephen. It's really weird. Besides being openly gay, Stephen's white and Righteous is black so that's pretty different for Redstar."

Bucky made a chuckling noise. "I imagine so."

"Anyway, Righteous was beaten up where he works. He was cheating on Stephen and the other boy's boyfriend beat Righteous almost to death."

"Oh no, will he be okay?"

Delora sighed and twirled the broom handle between the five fingers of her right hand. Her left hand, minus the splint but with the pinkie and ring finger still securely taped to each other, held the phone. She'd been sweeping the porch when her cell phone rang. "Yeah, he'll heal. He's staying with Sophie for a while. I was there with them last night until pretty late. That's why I didn't call."

"You don't have to feel beholden to call. I was just worried. Your situation there at Rosalie's is pretty scary. So I worry and won't apologize for it."

"It's not beholden why I call." She took a deep breath and haphazardly swiped at the porch floorboards with the broom. It was a hot night. "I'd go plumb crazy if I didn't have you to talk to. I swear you keep me sane. You're my best friend, Bucky."

"Hmm. Seems like that might be changing, Lora, and if it's so, I can deal with it. I do hope you'll keep calling me, though."

"Nothing will change that. What you and I have been through no one else could really understand." She paused. "Yesterday I was trying to make Righteous feel better so I told him all about what happened and about you."

"What did he say?"

"Nothing. He was in and out of it, you know. Pain meds. I think me talking made him feel better."

"Did it make you feel better?"

Delora smiled. *Bucky, bless his heart.* "Yeah, I think so."

"How's Sophie? Do you love her? Does she love you?"

Alone on the porch, Delora blushed. "Bucky!" She paused. "Yeah. We've got it awful. It's all new for me, you know?"

"Yeah. Must be strange. Are you handling it okay? What about Louie? Are you finally gonna cut the rat bastard loose?"

Delora laughed helplessly. "Rat bastard. That's a new one. I guess so, Bucky. I'm just in wait-and-see mode. Nothing's really happened yet…"

"You're kidding! It's been a while."

Delora sighed. "I know. I just can't seem to get there. Afraid, I guess. When she kisses me, though…well, it's pretty powerful stuff."

"That's probably what scares you. How good it is."

"True. It sure is good." Louie's heavy step sounded from the kitchen adjacent the porch and Delora started guiltily. "Gotta go, Louie's coming. I'll call you tonight."

"What are you doing?" Louie said just on the other side of the screen door. His head was cocked to one side and Delora knew he was using his keen sense of hearing to find out who she was talking with.

"Just Nita May, Louie," Delora responded, her voice sullen.

"Umm hmm. I bet it's that damn Hinchey Barlowe again."

Delora moved the broom with such furious intensity that her taped finger smarted. "Get on with you, Louie. I'm busy."

He stood listening to her for a long time, long enough to make the hair on the back of her sweaty neck crawl. Finally he moved inside and Delora breathed a sigh of relief.

CHAPTER FORTY

"I've been dreaming about leaving Redstar," Hinchey told Delora Wednesday morning.

Blossom's was quiet that morning. Johnny Pellen was there, sullen over coffee and eggs as there was no one to talk to, save Hinchey, and he was at the other end of the counter with Delora.

Hinchey seemed morose as well, lingering over coffee and a half-eaten bear claw pastry.

"Aren't you going to be late for work, Hinchey?" Delora asked. She was filling sugar dispensers in a dreamy mood. Righteous's condition had stabilized and she was thinking about Sophie, about the way her skin looked in the dappled sunlight of the bayou.

"Don't you want to know what the dream was like?"

"Sure. What was it like? Where did you go?"

"Over to Texas. It was different from here. There was lots of open land and almost no trees. I dreamed I was on horseback and you know what?"

She looked up with a questioning glance.

"You were with me. Right there on a horse beside me."

"Oh really." She screwed three caps on, one right after another. "And what were we doing there in Texas?"

"Nothing. Just being together. You and me. We just packed up and took off."

"And what was Louie doing during this little jaunt of ours? What was your mama saying about it?"

"I swear, Delora. There is no romance in your soul." He shook his head and gulped his tepid coffee.

Delora, stung by the remark, moved to refresh his coffee. "My romance deals with reality, Hinchey, that's all. It's a nice fantasy to think about running off somewhere, but you and me both know it ain't gonna happen."

"It could, Delora. If you and me was brave enough. There's nothing we couldn't do together."

Delora fell silent and let her mind play with the idea. It didn't have to be Texas. It could be over in Florida, over on the coast. She could forget about Louie, about Rosalie, but not about Sophie and Clary. She'd miss them. Her mind relived Sophie's hot hands on her skin and she knew she'd never leave her.

"My life is here, Hinchey. I know…"

The harsh jangle of the phone silenced her, and she walked around the corner to answer it. Tommy Jay watched her in silence, his eyes sad and his mouth working a stalk of celery, probably filched from an impromptu bloody Mary he'd mixed in the back. Delora ignored him.

"Delora, Phyllis got sick again, and I need to go be with her. I'm gonna leave Louie off at the park and you need to pick him up."

"Who? Your sister?" She hated the staccato way Rosalie talked to her. She always sounded like a dog barking.

"Yes, how many Phyllis's do you know, Delora?" Her voice dripped sarcasm. "She's sick so you have to fetch Louie home."

"When?"

"Just after the lunch rush. What's that? About one, two?"

"More like two."

"He'll be fine till then. I'm sending him with a packed lunch and plenty of sweet tea. Make sure you fetch his lunch pail and bring it back home with y'all."

"Okay, but I may be…" The phone clicked in her ear; Rosalie had hung up.

"Shit!"

"What's wrong?" Hinchey stood nearby but on the other side of the counter.

"I finally got my car in to Jerry to have the muffler worked on, and I gotta pick Louie up at two today.

"Well, where's it at?"

"Over at Jerry's."

Tommy Jay was still staring, and she had an overwhelming urge to stick out her tongue at him. She didn't but had to turn and face Hinchey to avoid bad behavior.

"Hell, girl, that could take all day. You need a ride to the garage anyway. I'll come by and take you over. If it's not ready, I'll take you to pick him up."

"Not a good idea, Hinchey. You know how he gets."

"I ain't afraid of Louie, never have been. I got the whole day off except for delivering a truck over to the Shermans, something I was supposed to do yesterday. I'd be happy to drop back by here after."

Delora thought it over. It was a nice gesture, but she'd have hell to pay later with Louie's mouth spouting on about it. She started to tell him no but realized suddenly that Louie's wrath would be worse if he was kept waiting until five o'clock. Reluctantly she agreed and thanked him. He left with a smile and she moved to clear away his dishes.

The afternoon moved slow and Delora was glad to see Hinchey's car pull up outside. Marina had come in for the expected lunch rush, but it had proved nonexistent and she was glad to leave the boredom of the diner.

Worried because Hinchey was later than expected, she waved goodbye to Marina and slid onto the seat next to Hinchey. She was glad to see he'd brought the bigger car—a sedan. He obviously realized that Louie might have trouble climbing into the truck.

"Hey, sorry I'm late. The man didn't pick me up when he said after I dropped that truck off."

"That's okay, Hinchey. Louie's just gonna have to understand people can't always jump when he says jump."

Hinchey was watching Delora. His gaze felt like strangler fig.

"What?" she said. "Say what's on your mind, Hinchey."

"Nothin', just wondering how life woulda been different if we'd gotten together in high school. You wouldn't have had to go through what happened. It woulda been nice."

Delora combed her hair with her fingers, a fast, nervous gesture. "Yeah. Water under the bridge, Hinchey." She sighed. "I've kinda stopped thinking that way. I just try to look forward and get on with it. Know what I mean?"

"I do." He nodded.

They approached Manahassanaugh Park. Louie was waiting for them, pacing angrily back and forth in front of the concrete bathrooms.

He lumbered along, pivoting on his cane. There was no goodwill in his scarred face.

"Uh-oh," Delora muttered as she hurried from the car.

"Delora!" Louie said as she approached.

"Yes, Louie. It's me. Come on and let's get you home." She tried to offer her arm.

"Where the fuck have you been?" His voice rumbled like faraway thunder. "It's like an oven out here."

Delora cringed. "I was working, Louie. Come on now."

Hinchey approached. "It's my fault, Lou. I was held up delivering a truck over in Goshen."

Louie's head tilted when he heard Hinchey's voice. "Oh ho, so that's the way of it. You sorry dog. I shoulda known you'd be hittin' that thing if you got a chance."

"No, Lou, you got it all wrong. I just gave Delora a ride. Her car's over at Jerry's. That's all."

Louie leaned his head back and jutted his chin at Hinchey. "She's damaged goods, you know. Burned."

"Yeah, I know, Louie. Maybe we should…"

Louie crowed, victorious. "You know? Fuck, *you know*. Rose says you can't see nothin' outside her clothes, so just how is it 'you know'?"

"Louie, you are getting on my last nerve. Here this man is, doin' you a favor and you act all stupid to him. You know that ain't right."

Louie's head tilted toward Delora. "You know better than to sass me, woman. Don't get me riled."

Delora sighed loudly and offered her arm by touching his so he'd know where to hold. "Let's go home, Louie, get you some cold tea and some dinner. I'm sorry we were late, but it happens sometimes."

Louie took her arm and squeezed it.

Delora grimaced and fell to her knees.

"Whoa, hold up now, Lou. Delora ain't done nothing, I told you it was my fault." Hinchey took one step closer, arm extended helplessly.

Louie took advantage of Delora's lowered position and twisted her arm up and behind her, mercilessly. She gasped in pain even as anger swelled in her.

"Don't worry, Hinchey," she spat out. "He can't help himself. Once an asshole, always an asshole."

Louie, as easy as breathing, lifted one booted foot and slammed it into Delora's flank. She flew to one side, landing on the soft grass outside the concrete flooring.

"No!" Hinchey roared as he charged Louie. Delora raised up in time to see Hinchey tackle Louie in a takedown as pretty as his high school football heyday. Louie's breath expelled in a loud whoosh as Hinchey's smaller body hit him dead center. Both men went down in a heap of flying limbs.

Delora saw then that Louie wasn't moving. Hinchey realized it too and lifted himself. Both understood in that instant that Louie's head had slammed into the heavy concrete and iron waste bin that the city had installed next to the bathrooms.

"Lou?" Hinchey queried.

Delora scrambled to her feet and made her way painfully across the concrete. "Louie? You okay?"

There was an eerie silence as Delora and Hinchey both unconsciously held their breath. There was no movement from Louie's twisted form. His back was not rising and falling.

"He's just winded," Hinchey said finally, his voice quavering. "Come on, Lou." He nudged him with his foot. His body rocked but did not move.

It was then Delora noticed the unnatural angle of his head. The harsh smell of urine rose to their nostrils as his bladder released.

"No," Delora said, horror washing across her. "Hinchey, I think he's dead."

She moved to touch his neck along the side, searching for a pulse. There was none and she could see one open eye staring toward the sky. She backed away.

"Delora, he's okay, right?"

Delora shook her head from side to side. "No. He's not all right. He must have died right away."

Hinchey crossed his arms across his chest, a protective gesture. One low wail escaped him.

CHAPTER FORTY-ONE

They stared at the body in silence. Delora's thoughts turned slow but came out in a rush. Who had seen? She glanced about, first wildly, then more furtively as she saw no one. She stood still, mouth agape.

"Delora? Lora? You with me?" Hinchey moved closer and took her arm in a firm grasp. "I didn't mean to hurt him, I swear. It just...just... happened. I don't know how."

"I...I know, Hinchey. I know. Wait just a minute and let me see what to do now."

What did someone do in a situation like this? Did one call the police as advised in every movie she'd seen or...?

Louie lay motionless, his body twisted abnormally. Blood was pooling about the one ear pressed into the tan concrete. Oddly enough, she felt no sorrow at his death, no pity for the blow he'd suffered. A great well of release swelled low in her belly and an unbidden sigh brought the relief into being. Horrified at her reaction, she whirled away from the body and strode purposefully toward Hinchey's car. Hinchey ran after her.

"Lora? Lora? What are you gonna do? I swear I didn't mean it."

Reaching the car, Delora clambered into the driver's seat and sat very still, the only movement the muscles in her jaw as she gnawed the skin around her thumbnail. Hinchey slid into the passenger seat and waited, his breathing harsh and fast. They watched Louie's body through the windshield.

"I guess I'd better turn myself in," he said finally, hanging his head in shame and sorrow.

She thought a good while before speaking. Life at its simplest is a series of images. She would never forget Hinchey's stunned face; the image of him standing there watching Louie's prone body had been burned into her memory forever.

"I guess you could, Hinchey, but what would be the use? Louie would still be dead and then your life'd be ruined too. Louie brought this on himself by never acting right and kind." She was studying the scene with intense interest.

Hinchey wrapped his arms about his waist, a self-comforting hug. He rocked back and forth, keening softly under his breath. "But someone's gotta pay. I killed him dead, Delora. Plain and simple. The law's gotta know."

Delora sat a little straighter and took her hands from her mouth. She twisted the key and the big car purred to life. She backed it out like a crazy woman, spinning and spewing gravel onto the grass. The car swerved and heaved into alignment and then she pressed the gas hard, leaping forward onto the asphalt of Appletree Road. Once there she jerked the car into park and turned to Hinchey.

"I'm going to be a gambling woman today, Hinchey." She took her eyes from his mystified face and studied the road in both directions. "I'm gambling that you can pull this off. We found him like that, you hear me. It looks like he fell and hit his head and that's what we'll let nature tell the authorities. You and me just found him that way when we come to pick him up. That's all. Can you make it this way? In your mind, I mean?"

Hinchey thought a moment, forehead wrinkled as if in pain. "Yeah, I guess I can, but..."

"And I'm gambling that there was no one else there in the park today. That by the time the law gets involved there won't be any evidence of the fight and that the people who know me, know Louie, will find no loss in his passing."

She paused and took a deep breath. "It's a chance, I know, but I also know there's nothing fair in you going to jail for helping put an old, mean-spirited dog out of his misery."

Hinchey sighed and stared at the countryside rolling away on the other side of the boundary fence. Delora got out of the car.

"Now, get over here and drive out to the road where you can get a signal. You just call an ambulance and tell them Louie November is hurt at Manahassanaugh Park. Just call an ambulance, no one else. Hear me?"

Hinchey slid across until he sat behind the wheel, his eyes, almost hopeful, met Delora's steady gaze. "I'm sorry, Lora. I never meant to cause you any grief."

"Then do this one thing right." She leaned in and pressed one palm to his cheek. "You know, no one has ever stood up for me before. That's special and I'll never forget it. No matter what happens with this, I'll always know you did that for me."

Hinchey felt his heart constrict with love for this woman but realized with keen loss that there would never be anything more. Within seconds, he had accepted this fact and resigned himself to it.

Delora patted the side of the car. "Go on then, and hurry. Say he's hurt and they need to come quick."

After Hinchey spun away, Delora walked back to Louie. She studied the angle of the waste can and Louie's head and decided that yes, it could have happened that way. He could have been walking along, lost his balance, fallen. Using the toe of her sneaker, she nudged his cane into a more believable position, then fell to her knees beside the body. Bracing herself, she turned him over fully, shuddering as his half-bloodied face turned to the sky. His burned eyes, now relaxed in death, didn't seem so mocking and she was glad for that. If his gaze had continued to mock her even after death, she would have had them carry her away in a straitjacket. Thoughts filled her head then. It was a type of wake, a remembrance of her life with Louie. She saw no joy there and felt only sorrow for two wasted lives. By the time the ambulance lumbered in with flashing red and yellow lights, tears were bathing her cheeks. Tears not for the loss of Louie, but for the loss of her youth.

CHAPTER FORTY-TWO

Rosalie was still with her sister so the house was unusually silent when Delora entered later that evening. Nevertheless, she moved quickly. In her bedroom, she gathered everything she owned into a pile in the middle of the bed then into two huge garbage bags she fetched from underneath the kitchen sink. Everything fit nicely into the two bags—her whole life. She left the cooler in the bottom of the closet. She left the vodka too.

There was no sadness in leaving this house. She'd had few good times here. Now that her duty—no, bondage—to Louie was through, there was nothing to hold her here. Dropping her bags beside the front door, she moved back through the long dark hallway and into the sunlit kitchen. It looked so normal, for goodness' sake, as if Louie wasn't dead and Delora leaving and Rosalie alone again. It would see breakfast again, dinner tonight. Delora shuddered and moved to the laundry room door. It took mere minutes for her to shift the moveable panel of plywood and see the huge jars filled with money on shelves behind it.

Conscience stayed her hand. This was stealing, pure and simple. Obviously, this money was important to Rosalie or she wouldn't be hoarding it.

Then Delora thought of working three jobs, of turning over Louie's disability check every month. *I've earned this*, she thought harshly. Shutting down her nagging conscience, she hefted one of the gallon-plus-sized pickle jars, then lifted a second. Fetching two more garbage bags from under the sink, she carefully placed a jar in each. Dragging one in each hand, she moved through the eerily silent house and out the front door. Hinchey sat behind the wheel of the idling car as she'd asked. She didn't want him seeing this. For some odd reason, she knew it would embarrass her if he saw how she and Louie had lived. She put the jars in the open trunk and turned back to the house.

An onslaught of exhaustion washed across her as she mounted the porch steps, making her dizzy. She grasped the handrail to steady herself until the faintness eased but realized her reserves were dangerously low. Quickly she hefted the other two bags and hurried back to the car. After a moment of thought she made one more trip back inside.

In the laundry room, she moved jars around until she was sure it would take some time before Rosalie realized Delora had taken some of them. Fighting a new ambush of guilt, she lifted one more dusty jar, from a bottom far corner. She hoped this one held some of the Social Security payments from her parents' death. She looked at it a long time, her breathing shallow and measured. The faded currency inside gave no clue, but Delora was convinced this money was her legacy from them. Closing the wall panel and making sure all was as it had been before, she walked from Rosalie's house for the final time. She knew, no matter what happened to her, she'd never willingly return here. Too much had changed. She had changed.

The car waited, trunk gaping, as she made her way to it. Having such a small life meant she could easily re-create it, mold it to whatever she wanted it to be. This thought was exhilarating; she felt young and expectant once again. She turned and looked at the house one final time. She felt some sadness for Louie's passing but more relief that Sheriff Jonas had believed their story.

There'd been no doubt in his blue eyes. He'd listened to Delora's account as the rescue crew bundled up Louie's brawny form. He'd nodded, gaze sad as he told her that the state might need an autopsy, but he'd have to check the law book on that. He'd patted Delora on the back, shaken Hinchey's hand and expressed real sorrow for the loss. Then he was gone and Hinchey had driven Delora here.

Stowing the last jar of money in with her bags of clothing, Delora allowed the trunk lid to close and scrambled into the passenger seat next to Hinchey.

CHAPTER FORTY-THREE

"Bucky? Louie's dead."

Bucky didn't say anything for a long moment.

"He's dead? What do you mean? What happened?"

"Well," she sighed heavily. "Hinchey gave me a ride over to the park to pick him up. They got into a fight—they've always hated one another—and Louie fell."

"Fell?"

"Yeah, and hit his head. There was this concrete trash can…"

"So he's really dead? He's gone?"

Delora knew Bucky was trying hard to gauge her feelings. To see whether he should express the elation he was feeling or whether he should grieve as he supported her during this loss.

"Yeah. At last he's out of my life."

Bucky took a deep breath of relief. "Are you okay? Are you sad?"

"Not sad. Scared. I can't imagine life on my own. I've been… dealing with him for so long…"

"Where are you? What are you going to do now?"

Delora looked around the parking lot of the Clarence Road Shopping Center next door to where she'd had her car serviced. She studied the busy women hurrying into the line of intriguing stores. It was a given that she would never be like them. Her life experiences had changed her into something far different. "I don't know, Bucky. Guess I'm in limbo right now."

"How are things with Sophie?"

The mention of Sophie's name stirred something good deep inside. Then alarm. "I'm not so sure about that."

"Whoa. What's going on?"

"She can't want me. Not how I am." She sighed as tears welled.

"Self-pity. Never thought it connected with you."

It took her a good while to discern his meaning. Then she bristled. "It's a fact, Bucky."

"Oh, she told you this. That must have hurt."

"Well…"

"Right. Why don't you stop trying to think for her."

She had to smile. There was no bullshit with Bucky. "Okay, point taken. I'm afraid though, Buck. I'm afraid Hinchey will get in trouble with the police…"

"Could he?"

"Sure. They could say he pushed him. I'm not so sure he didn't. I mean, he was defending me and jumped on him. I think Louie lost his footing and that's what I'll tell them if they ever ask. It all happened so fast."

"Did anyone else see?"

"No. We were alone. Hinchey wanted to tell the police everything, but I told him not to. I told him to lie and say we found him that way. Was that wrong?"

Bucky was quiet.

"I mean, I don't *feel* it was wrong, but I know it should be, you know?"

"Let it go, Delora. Hinchey sounds like a good old boy who wouldn't hurt a fly. Why let Louie's death ruin his life?"

"Yeah."

"What else is bothering you?"

"I'm afraid Sophie won't want me, that Rosalie is going to give me a lot of grief, that I can't take care of myself. That I'll be alone again…" Her voice broke as a sob escaped. She was perilously close to tears.

"Self-pity." He sighed. "Such a waste. Just stop and put one foot in front of the other. Look at what you've come through. The burning. The healing. The meds. Do you really think there's anything you can't overcome. That you can't deal with?"

Delora thought about his words. About the truth there. Damn Bucky. Her hand crept down to pinch at the phoenix tattoo hidden beneath her jeans.

"I'm keeping my jobs," she said as if beginning a list. "My friend Annie owns some houses, so I'll see if she has one I can rent. I took money from Rosalie's so I should be okay for a while."

"Ah, the money in the wall. How much?"

"I don't know. I haven't even counted it. I will. I'm sure it's enough. I left her plenty too."

"And Sophie?" he interjected.

Delora laughed softly. "I guess I'll see how she feels."

"Good answer."

Silence fell.

"Are you sad about Louie at all?"

"I don't feel much about him," she replied thoughtfully. "All I can think about is Sophie and about helping the people here. They're so cool, Bucky. You have no idea. They have no money and their houses are just shit but they…they're so cool. It's like they keep getting in their own way, though. They have no money, no education, but they get by. Day after day. It's amazing. And what Sophie does…I can't believe what she knows and what she can do. It kills me to watch her."

"She must be awesome."

Delora sighed, eyes welling with tears. "I'm gonna say this one more self-pitying thing and then I'll stop."

"Okay," he replied softly.

"Why now, Buck? After the burns? Why couldn't I have met her before? I've got to be repulsive to her and she's so…" a new sob tore through her, "so incredible."

"Listen." His voice was soothing in its no-nonsense delivery. "Maybe you weren't ready then. You've told me what your life was like. Didn't sound too healthy. Maybe that's what would have put her off."

Delora had never thought of this aspect. "Maybe you're right," she admitted.

"Can I come see you?"

Delora realized suddenly that Bucky Clyde could visit now that Louie was gone. In the past, she'd always discouraged the possibility because she knew Louie would not have understood their friendship. He wouldn't have understood the closeness. The idea of Bucky Clyde visiting filled her with excitement.

"Could you? I mean…"

"Absolutely. I can't come right away because I'm in contract negotiations with Frank and tied down. Two weeks, though. Would that be okay? I can suspend this new round of therapy and come down for a long visit."

"Oh, Bucky. That would be perfect. It would allow things to settle down a little, and I should be in my own place by then."

"Good. Will the people there be okay with me?"

"Does it really matter?"

Bucky chuckled softly. "Touché."

Delora felt oddly pleased. "It'll be fine. I can't wait."

CHAPTER FORTY-FOUR

The Red Roof Inn outside downtown Redstar wasn't fancy, but it was quiet, secluded and certainly fit Delora's need to reflect on her life and her future. Going back to Rosalie's would be like entering the mouth of a volcano. No way.

Once settled into the room, she took a long, very hot shower and allowed her mind to empty of everything. Rational thinking was the first to go, and she found herself thinking insanely of a nursery rhyme her mother had sung often. *Lambs eat oats and mares eat oats* rambled repeatedly through her mind until she began to wonder if this behavior heralded her descent into the loony bin. The idle thought was comforting. Emotion left her next, and her being centered around the wet heat of the shower and the sensory experience of the soft rain of water sluicing across her skin.

She touched her scarred abdomen, reveling in the numbness there as she never had before. A New-Agey aspect of herself declared that she loved this infirm part of her body. For more than two years, she had hated it. Though not admitting it openly, she blamed the wounded area as harshly as she blamed Louie for what had happened to her. After all, the wounds would keep her from love and life just as effectively as Louie's actions that hateful morning. She knew now that this attitude was wrong and against nature. Sophie had taught her this.

Sophie.

Delora smiled when she thought of her new companion. Sophie had become the love of her life. She knew that now too.

She dried slowly, pressing the hotel towel with patient care against all exposed expanses of skin. The towel felt good against her cheeks, and she thought of Sophie's lips there the night on the bayou. She remembered the way Sophie's hands felt against her back as she held her. The thoughts made old longings reappear and Delora sighed in frustration. What was she to do?

Rational thought reappeared. There was so much to do. She dressed slowly in loose cotton trousers and a short pink T-shirt as her mind listed possibilities.

First, she needed to decide where she was going to live. Her time with Rosalie was done, and she needed to move on.

She turned and looked at the jars of money. There had to be thousands of dollars inside, and she was glad about that. She needed to count it and take stock of her situation, but she didn't feel like dealing with it just now.

She sighed and curled up in the room's only armchair with the little notebook she carried in her backpack.

"Look for apartment or house," she wrote. Then above that phrase, she wrote in bigger letters, "Get newspaper tomorrow morning." That was better, one step at a time.

Under "look for apartment," she wrote, "Call Sophie and tell her what happened."

As far as income, she knew she'd keep all three jobs for a while, just until she had some money saved, a security blanket. So she wouldn't have to worry. She needed a bank account, something she'd never bothered with before. Adding "Go to bank" to her list, she sighed. So much to do.

She looked around the neat, bare hotel room. It was a shame she couldn't live here. She liked this room. It was controlled and felt safe.

She wondered what twists and turns Louie's death was going to bring to her life. She was glad he was gone. What repercussions did a death bring? Her parents' deaths had brought her a different life and a tattered pack of old photos and mementos from a more idyllic time.

The physical assets from Louie would be slim, and she felt as though she had gotten everything from Rosalie's house that she wanted. What about legalities, though? She supposed she would have to make herself available to Bud Corman, her family's lawyer. She had a bad case of the "I don't wannas" about that. What she wanted was to disappear for a while until she had regained her bearings.

"Call Bud," she wrote reluctantly.

She also knew she'd have to face Rosalie at some point. What was she going to tell her? Lies. Would Rosalie know she was lying? She had always been able to tell before. What did it matter anymore, really? Delora was no longer a teenager trying to get away with drinking with the older college kids. This was a little more serious, though, and because of that, even less of a problem. An event this big swept away all the foolishness that had gone before. Delora knew that Louie was gone; nothing could be done to change that. Her only duty now was to protect Hinchey as best she could so Louie wouldn't destroy his life as he had hers. And this she would do, whether to Rosalie, an army of policemen or simply to herself. She knew that when she woke tomorrow morning the truth would be gone, hidden under the story she and Hinchey had crafted. They found Louie that way when they went to pick him up.

Maybe Hinchey would move away. Life for Delora would go on. Only this time it would be under her terms and her terms only. She felt fully free for the first time since her parents' deaths.

She leaned her head back and studied the ceiling. What did she want for her life? She knew one thing—being with Sophie, working alongside her, felt like an answer to prayer. Would Sophie train her? She laughed, feeling stupid and coy. She didn't want Sophie that way. Maybe Sophie would teach her more secrets of woman love, teach her about that ravishing ache she felt after an evening of Sophie's kisses. Delora felt like Sophie's kisses brought her to life. No man had ever moved her that way. She walked across virgin soil and for some odd reason, even though she was burned and was what many would call disfigured, she felt okay, even learning to welcome the changes her life was moving toward.

Afraid to hope too fiercely, Delora laid aside her list and rose from the chair. She moved to the bed and folded down the thick coverlet. She slid from her clothing and crawled into the coolness of the sheets. She debated watching television, half-afraid she'd see Louie's death on the local broadcast. Instead, she switched off the light and lay in darkness. Light from a streetlight peeked from around the window curtain. Delora watched the penetrating glow, wishing the window would open so she could hear the sounds from the night outside. She would find that soothing. A sudden shadow passed by her window, a figure moving outside on the balcony, momentarily blocking the light from the window. It passed on and hesitantly returned. A knock sounded.

CHAPTER FORTY-FIVE

Delora rose as if on greased wheels. She shrugged into her robe. Sophie's body was dark against the streetlamp's glow.

"Delora, are you okay?" she asked. "I heard what happened."

Delora moved back, effectively inviting Sophie inside.

"You are okay, aren't you?" she persisted as she pressed the door closed.

"I'm okay," Delora agreed softly. She studied Sophie in the dimness a long time, as if examining her for possibilities. How did she always manage to find her?

Sophie's eyes found Delora's, and the younger woman felt herself moving forward into a new expanding dimension. Little else mattered except keeping Sophie's gaze on her in the dimness.

"Sophie, I…"

Sophie waited expectantly. "What? Tell me."

"You know I'm burned."

"Yes. Technically, you were burned, now you're healed."

Delora had to smile. "True, but the scars…they're pretty bad."

Sophie nodded. "I know. I've seen worse, honey."

"I know…but…really?"

Sophie nodded again. "Ummhmm."

Delora's consciousness shifted just a little. "Hmm. Well, I just want you to know things between us are…I understand if you don't want to…you know."

Sophie smiled, her eyes going all hard and dark. "Oh, I want to. No doubt about that."

A thrill sped along Delora's nerves, leaving her breath ragged and her body aroused. Goose bumps circled along her breasts, bringing her nipples to delicious erection. Her shy eyes lifted to Sophie and the look there made that strange plummeting sensation begin in her stomach and groin again.

"Oh," Delora said.

"What?" Sophie replied. "Are you all right?"

"Yes." Delora's voice was low and breathy.

Sophie leaned in and took Delora's hands in hers. "I knew as soon as I met you that we were a special pair and meant to be together," she explained. "Love began to grow—that minute. Everything about you that I've seen since has just reinforced that love. I'm not one to play games, really. Never have been. What you see in me is what you get and I'm telling you now straight out. I love you and I hope one day, a hope helped by what I see in your eyes, that you will grow to love me as much. It's not such an outlandish hope, although I know this isn't the best time to point out that you're a free woman."

Delora said. "It's okay. There wasn't anything there anyway."

"I understand if you're holding out for another man, but I hope it's not because you feel like you can't love a woman?"

Mulling this over, Delora fiddled with the collar of her robe. Her feelings were so confused; she didn't know what to think. The voices of her physicians echoed in her mind. She wanted to be sure that she didn't fall into a relationship with a woman just because she couldn't have a relationship with a man.

"Sophie, I don't know," she said finally. "You don't understand. The doctors at the burn unit told me I'd never be able to have sex again. They managed to rebuild my vagina, but the skin inside there is really thin. They said it can't be penetrated with any force so I figured it was all over. That was a little more than two years ago and I haven't thought seriously about sex since. It was a nonissue. Then I meet you and I start having all these feelings."

She lowered her head. "You make me feel all squirmy inside and I start wanting you. I've never been with a woman, though, and don't know what to expect. I feel…I care about you, I do. I'm just not sure I can love you physically. I'm not sure it would work," she finished sorrowfully.

Sophie was silent a long time. So long that Delora considered opening the door to usher her out.

"Delora, women can love one another in a lot of different ways. My body craves closeness with yours and it sounds like you crave me too. Maybe the physical will work out, maybe it won't, but I don't think you and I should agonize over it. Most of the time things have a way of working out on their own without a whole lot of intervention from us. Even though we like to think we're in control of our lives." She paused. "You can say no to me and send me on my way. Or you can open your arms to me. Life will go on if you say no, but think what we may miss if you send me away."

She leaned closer. "I feel what we have. I feel it big. I don't want to go away. I want to see what will happen, what adventures we can have together."

Delora was tired of warnings, tired of thinking. She moved toward Sophie. Sophie moved to meet her. The kiss lasted an eternity; lips parted and met time and again, each instance of meeting deepening and lasting longer. Their tongues met and mated, then came back for more.

Delora abandoned herself to the rapture that kissing Sophie engendered in her and felt the desire growing in her body. She began to feel a sense of languor move across her. Limbs became heavy and the mind sluggish. She transformed into a creature of pure sensation. Her pelvis swelled anew and the craving for release led her to press herself against Sophie. Sophie's hand moved low, cupped her sex, and moved it with subtle pressures. Delora forgot her scars and responded with pushes of her own. The attention there felt so good, so necessary. Abruptly it stopped as Sophie moved away. Delora had a moment of panic. Suppose Sophie didn't want her after all? Sophie's eyes told a different tale as she reached to slowly untie Delora's robe, allowing it to slip with sensuous weight along her back and to the floor.

Delora stood naked and in shadow, and Sophie paused to study her slimness. Delora had the body of a boy except for the small bulge of breast. The nipples were high with a heavy swell of breast underneath. Cuppable breasts. Sophie moved close to hold one in each palm.

Sophie unbuttoned her own shirt and slipped it from her shoulders. She unfastened her jeans and let them drop. Clad only in an undershirt and panties, she led Delora into the bathroom.

"I need to shower. And it'll be easier for you there." Allowing the bathroom to stay dark, save for a nearby streetlight shining through the frosted window, Sophie turned the knobs of the shower until the spray hovered two notches up from warm. She shed the rest of her clothing and stepped inside, pulling silent, obedient Delora in after her. The water cocooned them in warmth as Sophie held her close, hands caressing her back and neck. Delora felt loved absolutely in this hot, womb-like environment, and when Sophie's lips found hers again, she sought them eagerly until both were swooning from sensation.

"Wait," Sophie said hoarsely as she stepped from the spray. "Let's take our time."

Using the soap, Sophie lathered herself, then reached for Delora. Sliding the bar of soap across skin, she followed the path of the soap with her hand, further lathering Delora's skin until slick foam covered them both.

The sensation was new to Delora, and she reveled in it. Sophie's hands were hot and sensual, so soft, gliding across her skin. The warmth penetrated through and a new throbbing sensation awoke in her. It felt like her breathing had been constricted since the fire and now she could, finally, take a full, deep breath.

The hand moved lower, and Sophie's hand was between her legs, sleek movement across the engorged nub of nerve buried under the scar tissue. Sensation assaulted Delora and she began to move her hips against Sophie's firm pressure. A feeling grew in her and she knew if she continued her world would explode into stardust again.

Sophie moved her hand away and Delora cried out in an automatic wail of loss.

"It's okay, baby. I'm here." She pressed the soap into Delora's hand. "Now me. Do me."

Delora rubbed the soap between her hands, then laid the soap and her soapy hand on Sophie's shoulder, rubbing the sleekness along her arm. Emboldened by Sophie's shadowed gaze, she moved her hands to Sophie's small breasts and felt entranced by the firm weight of them. The skin was so soft there and the tawny peaks so hard, such a dichotomy of sensation under her palms. Sophie's eyes closed and her breathing came heavy and fast.

Was Delora's touch arousing Sophie as she had aroused Delora? Growing in confidence, Delora slid her hand lower to Sophie's slim waist, moving around to soap her back. The heat of their bodies connecting was delicious. Delora's right hand, with the soap, moved lower to lather the heavy mat of hair at the apex of Sophie's legs. Her fingers reveled in the marvelous feel of short, soapy hair. She moved lower, slipping easily between Sophie's legs. Sophie moaned and Delora started with surprise. She was in complete control of Sophie's pleasure and this realization filled Delora with power. She welcomed it and slipped the soap through Sophie's thighs, catching it in her left hand on the other side. Her right hand remained, however, and her fingers fell into Sophie's dark softness. Delora's exploratory hand moved deep into Sophie's body. She fell back against the shower wall, pushing her lower body hard onto Delora's hands.

"*So this is it*," thought Delora as she moved her hand in the way she imagined she would like to be touched. Sophie's moans and gasps grew stronger as she rocked against Delora's palm and fingers.

"Press there," she said, pulling the heel of Delora's palm hard against the swell of her sex. Delora's other arm pulled Sophie's body tight against her, the left hand soaping deep into the split of Sophie's backside. She felt as though she held the entire essence of the older woman between her two forearms.

"There, baby, there, baby. That's right," Sophie was muttering as Delora manipulated her body. Delora could feel the swelling of Sophie's nipples against her arm as Sophie passed into orgasm. Sophie keened softly as she shuddered against Delora and her arms reached to pull Delora tighter. Her slimness heaved and Delora could feel the rhythmic clenching of muscles inside Sophie as they closed on her hand. She felt she might faint from her own sudden, sharp arousal. Gently she allowed her touch to slip from Sophie.

Sophie, instead of being sated, became rougher with Delora. She clamped her mouth onto Delora with white-hot energy, tongue plundering. Delora felt passion transforming her, and she responded as ardently. Hands on Sophie's breasts, she pressed the nipples between her fingers until Sophie moaned, then she cupped them in her hands. Sophie found the soap and used it to lubricate between Delora's thighs. The soap fell with a clatter as Sophie's hand gently, lightly penetrated Delora. Delora gasped, certain she'd never experienced such pleasure before. Sophie was pressing upward with firm yet gentle strokes and Delora exploded into her own climax as Sophie sucked at her breasts one after the other. Spent and exhausted, Delora fell back against the shower wall, her world spinning.

Gently slipping her hand from Delora, Sophie continued to caress and kiss her until Delora could see again.

Delora moaned as her body throbbed and spun in a dervish dance of sparking passion. "It's never been like that before," she admitted in a breathy voice.

Sophie had fallen against Delora, sheltering her from the spray, their sensitive, soapy bodies sliding together easily. She shifted herself and placed a forearm on either side of Delora's head. She stared deeply into Delora's eyes. "So does this mean you might like to do it again sometime?" she asked, her eyes twinkling with merriment.

Delora ran her hands along Sophie's hips. "Hmm, not sure. Kiss me again and let's see."

CHAPTER FORTY-SIX

Beulah lay supine on her bed, head whirling with thought.

She'd known the time was nigh for days—no, months really—since the death beetle had clicked her awake one morning at the beginning of summer. She had no problem with it—her life had been long and full. She'd loved well. The long line of men she'd loved or simply dallied with passed through her mind. She wondered which of them she'd loved the most. Oddly enough, she believed it to be perpetual playboy, Syria Boost, with his cocky good humor and playful lovemaking. Her coupling with him had been far too brief but more sensual than all the rest. She relived for a moment the sleek feel of his hands on her skin. He'd been one of the few to know how to really please a woman. He knew how to say all the right things to make a woman feel a certain way. He'd panted over her, working her body like a warm piece of clay, molding her into pleasurable pain and ecstasy.

Lying still, the sounds of the bayou cocooning her, Beulah experienced the thrill again, allowing it to pass from her as easily as she'd allowed Syria to pass on to his next woman. A man like that, who made loving his life, his talent, wouldn't stay; she'd known this the first time setting eyes on him.

She thought of Faye and how she was drawn to those type of men, willing to sacrifice stability for that all-consuming thrill. Would

Sophie follow that path? There'd been no indication of it; Sophie was as dependable as one season following the next. This comforted her as she knew her people would be cared for after her passing.

Delora's sweet face rested on her mind's eye. She would be good for Sophie. Beulah knew this. She sensed trouble coming but didn't bother long with that thought. She'd once thought Sophie destined to be alone forever but saw then that the coming of the young woman would foretell the time of her passing. She was to be a comfort to Sophie.

Beulah remembered the pain of childbirth, how Keene's birth had split her rudely into motherhood. She remembered the smell of Keene's neck and how bringing him forth had seemed so right. She remembered the caul that had covered Faye's face and how she had harbored such great expectations for the two of them, she and Faye as companion healers. Then granddaughter Sophie, born with the same golden hair as Faye and being more to Beulah than Faye could ever have been.

Pain, sweet and intense, flooded her mind as her brain suffered the assault of misplaced blood. A feeling of restful peace followed, suffusing her from fingertip to toe. She felt the Others approach, slowly surrounding her as they came to welcome her to Their side.

Beulah thought of all those she'd hated and felt relief to know she'd never fostered anger but moved on to more positive thinking. Her scorecard was good. Even the many lives she'd taken were held as mercy or forwarding the rightful order of things. Right and proper. Her acceptance by the Others was complete.

"I see you there," she crooned, her voice barely audible. "I'm 'bout ready."

She thought of all that she'd miss. The language of the bayou, Sophie's smile, the smell of sweaty babies as she rocked them, the heat of sun on worn wooden floorboards, the prestige of helping the Manu Lisse and their gratitude, leaf lettuce fresh from the garden on a cool morning and the smell of new cigarette smoke after nightfall. Simple things she realized, but important to her. She hoped there would be touching on the other side. And good smells. And smiles.

The Others were closer and, as if reassuring her, she could feel them against the skin of her arms. Though ritual dictated otherwise, she was grateful that Clary and Sophie were about their own business and not tending to hers.

"Good," she said. "Good."

She drifted on.

CHAPTER FORTY-SEVEN

It hit Sophie when she pulled into the yard. An important light had gone out. She was filled with sudden loss, her breath rattling through her chest on its way to the outside.

"No," she muttered in disbelief. "I should have been here."

Racing from her car, she leapt onto the porch and slammed through the kitchen door. She paused only when she reached the opening to Grandam's bedroom. The body was there, lying calmly in the bed, but Grandam had gone. Acute loneliness beset Sophie; a keening of loss welled in her throat and escaped. Sitting on the edge of her grandmother's bed, Sophie propelled her upper body to and fro, a low wail echoing in the room. She covered her face with both hands as tears fell freely.

Intellectually, Sophie knew it was time for her grandmother to leave, yet emotionally she was a small child abandoned by her only real parent and the pain was unbearable. Sensible, level-headed Sophie, who had known this parting was imminent, was nevertheless devastated.

Turning, she took the cold, brittle hand in hers and felt paltry that her hands could not heal this. Too late, too late. And she hadn't been able to say goodbye.

"I'm sorry I wasn't here with you," she whispered to the room. "*Atchava. Atchava. Rove. Misto. Danners rat méripen tard gilo púridaia múlladipóov. Non Tacha.*"

After a time of silence, she added, "You shouldn't have been alone."

She pulled Grandam's hands together and tucked them neatly on her abdomen, as she'd done for dozens of others. The time-marked face was slack, mouth and eyes partially opened. Sophie's hands caressed the cool, aged cheeks, and she was able finally to turn away.

Staggering into the kitchen, she spread her arms, bracing her body in the doorway to outside. She sought solace from the bayou. How would she survive without Grandam's daily guidance?

A warm blanket of sensation slid across Sophie. Surprised, she looked up to see if a sudden shaft of sunlight had appeared. Nothing was different yet the heat persisted even though she stood mostly in shadow. Peace followed the heat, and she knew that Grandam hadn't gone anywhere. She was able to smile then, and she wrapped her arms around her own body in a fierce hug.

She sighed and hung her head. Next step. Move forward. Keep moving forward, that was the key and is what Grandam would say.

Moving mechanically, Sophie reached for the phone.

"Clary? It's Sophie."

"Hold on a minute, Miss Sophie. Clare's here." Salty, who usually took a good half hour to say anything, must have sensed Sophie's urgency.

"Sophie? What you need, honey?"

"Grandam's gone on. Can you come?"

Clary fell silent as she sensed the truth of Sophie's words. Still unwilling to believe she said, "What do you mean, gone on?"

"It was her time, Clary. I'm gonna call Brother Kinder and then Womack. We'll have to do things the outsider way because so many of her people were, but I'll need your help to get her back after."

"Okay," Clary said in a low voice. "Twenty minutes. Are you okay?"

"I think so."

"Wait there at the house until I get there, okay?"

"I will."

Sophie replaced the handset and paused. Brother Kinder's number, a number that she had dialed by memory most of her life, eluded her.

CHAPTER FORTY-EIGHT

An ominous silence fell at the French Club. Sensing it, Delora lifted her head and saw Rosalie approaching the bar. She was a formidable sight, a frigate on high seas, four hundred pounds of moving flesh. She'd taken the time to comb her short black hair into an orderly cap and to add to her already abundant cosmetic base. Her heavily mascaraed eyes studied Delora with more than the usual disdain.

"Hello, Rosalie," Delora said evenly, although her heart felt as though it was going to pound out of her chest.

"Delora. I'm here to see what you have to say for yourself."

"What do you mean?" Delora asked. "What did I do?"

Rosalie insinuated her bulk sideways between two barstools and glared at her foster daughter. "You and Louie didn't come home last night. You didn't answer my calls. Then I get a call from Brother Kinder, find out your husband lies dead and you stay out all night like some common trollop. Where were you?" Her voice was a harsh whisper as she leaned closer to Delora.

"I was at the hotel is all, Mama, with the phone off. I'm not coming back." Her chin lifted just a little. She heard Esther's sudden indrawn breath behind her.

"What do you mean, not coming back? This is your home we're talking about."

Delora sighed and moved to light a cigarette with trembling hands. Hinchey cowered over to her left, his big hands curled paw-like around a beer bottle. His head hung low and she felt a sudden ache of pity for him. She knew he blamed himself for all that had happened even though not one iota of it was his fault.

She turned back to Rosalie. "Listen, I appreciate all you did for me, taking me in after my folks died and all, but I have to say life with you hasn't been a warm, fuzzy experience."

She drew on her cigarette as she watched Rosalie's face change from amazement to outrage in the space of seconds.

"Well, excuse me for not being Miss Hoity-Toity June Cleaver. I gave you everything you needed. There's no denyin' that."

Delora nodded. "True. But here lately, I been paying for it, seems like."

The other woman grew indignant, her form wriggling for better vantage against the bar. "What are you saying?"

"I'm saying, I work two jobs to pay you rent and utilities and a third so I'll have some pocket money for myself. You also cash Louie's disability checks for groceries just as fast as they cross my palm."

Rosalie smiled a sickly sweet smile. "You're an adult, Delora, and back at home under my roof. There's nothing wrong in you helping with the rent and food and electric. Everyone at the church says so."

Delora shook her head, a grim smile on her lips. Her cigarette had burned halfway down and a length of ash was resting on her work-weary hand. She looked down at it. "Louie's disability covers all that. Why do you need so much more from me? Speaking of Louie's check, I guess that'll stop now, won't it? I wonder if I'm gonna get widow's benefits. Could that be why you're in such a hurry to get me home again?"

Rosalie flushed a deep burgundy and had the grace to look sheepish. "I'm not worried about that, Delora, and I can't believe you are. Your husband is dead. By the way, I have a lot of questions about how that happened."

Refusing to acknowledge Hinchey's panicked grimace or her memory of how Louie died, Delora replied with simple grace. "It was his time. You should just let it go at that, Rosalie." She paused a long moment. "We don't need to be stirring up any shit. Why don't we just let the dead rest in peace?"

Delora expertly mixed a rum and Coke for Lem Staton and took it down the bar to him as Rosalie studied her.

"That's your limit, Lem," she said to the tottering older man as she placed the glass on the bar in front of him.

"Aww, come on, Lora, Don't cut me off just yet. The night is young." His eyes drifted curiously to Rosalie, who still stood sentinel at the bar.

Delora grinned at him. "Yeah, but you ain't. It's getting late and you need to sober up for about an hour or so before I can let you out of here."

"That's right, Lem," Esther added, appearing at Delora's elbow. "I spoke to Mary the other day and she told me to keep tabs on you."

Lem shrugged and took a deep swallow of his fresh drink.

"You know better than to listen to her, Esther. Just cuz we married she thinks she can tell me what to do."

Delora laughed hollowly. "And it's a damn good thing. If she wasn't looking out for you, no telling where you'd be today."

Lem's friends laughed and slapped his back good-naturedly.

Delora turned back to Rosalie, who started in on her right away. "All I know is if you'd been leading him proper he'd be alive today."

"I did all I could to bring him back. Hinchey, too. He was already about dead when we got there." Her voice trembled, and she hoped Rosalie wouldn't notice. She'd always had a suspicious nature when it came to Delora.

"That may be, but I think I'll have a word with Sheriff Jonas and tell him he ought to have another look into what happened that day."

"Esther, watch the bar," Delora snapped as she exited through the saloon-style doors. Her face grim, she motioned for Rosalie to follow her. Once Rosalie had extricated herself from the barstools they moved to the vestibule outside the bathrooms. Delora moved forward and placed her face right up next to Rosalie's. "If you say one thing about Louie, I swear I will tell everyone I work with what you and Louie been doin' while I'm out workin' three jobs to support everyone."

Rosalie's jaw dropped. Delora felt powerful, ready finally to shed the meekness that had plagued her since her parents' deaths. Her newfound relationship with Sophie had made her strong.

"What are you saying? No one's going to believe your pack of lies. Just who in the hell do you think you are?"

"I'm a woman who's tired of bullshit—yours and everyone else's. Leave it be."

"But…"

"Louie's gone and that's it. Leave it be, Rose. I'm willing to if you will. I'm not coming back under your roof and that's the way of that. You'll just have to get on without me, okay?"

Rosalie sneered and moved away from her foster daughter.

"You'll be back. How do you think you're going to make it on your own?"

"Probably by working three jobs like I been doing. Slaving for your place or for my own place couldn't be but so different."

Delora turned from Rosalie and walked back to the bar and the expectant, curious faces of her friends. She knew that another chapter of her life had closed and it felt good.

CHAPTER FORTY-NINE

The house on the bayou had not changed in the five years since Faye had last passed through. It still seemed like it had been birthed entire from the depths of the swamp. Spanish moss-draped trees hugged close as if huge protective lares. She remembered hearing the branches scrape against the thin walls of her bedroom. The sound had terrified her as a child. Her mama had been good about it, however, finding no fault in her troubled daughter.

Faye sighed. She still couldn't believe she would not see her mother framed in the door of Salamander House. If truth be told, she was a little angry about the whole thing. Without thinking about it too hard, Faye had somehow expected her mother to live on forever the same. The thought of her death, even as frail as she had appeared on Faye's last visit, had never bothered Faye. And now her mother was gone. Like her brother Keene, taken by cancer four years ago.

Wearily, Faye opened the car door and stood next to the dark blue Buick. "Wake up, Johnny."

Johnny Macht, who was snoring gently from his slumped position in the passenger seat, stirred and peered about through sleep-thickened eyes.

Faye strode toward the house as Johnny extricated himself from the car.

"Well, hello. How was the trip, darlin'?"

Faye flew across the deck and caught the skinny black woman in her arms. The large, heavy pocketbook she carried swung to one side and knocked them both off balance.

"Lord, what do you have in there?" Clary asked once their embarrassed laughter had subsided.

"Just some doodads for y'all." Faye tucked in an escaped strand of her shiny blond hair. "Where's Sophie?"

"Had a baby to catch. Said she'd be on as quick as she could. Was the drive okay?"

Faye moved into the house, past the screen door that Clary held wide. "What do you think ten hours in a car with a man would be like?" She turned back, suddenly realizing that her husband wasn't with her. "Now, where is he?"

Clary looked behind and watched Johnny struggling to remove bags from the trunk of the car. "He'll be on, I expect," she answered absently.

"So anyway, I'm glad to be in one place for a while. Just sorry it has to be under such circumstances. Has Sophie started the burial yet? I hear Mama was alone when she died."

Clary hung her head, ashamed her lust for Salty had caused her to leave Beulah's side. "Yes. It was a bad thing. But there's been no anger here. I think she's at peace."

Faye dropped her bag on the sofa and lit a cigarette thoughtfully. "Doesn't seem like the same place…" She looked around the living room, eyes sorrowful and a little afraid.

Clary moved to give the woman a one-armed squeeze. "It'll be okay, Miss Faye. Don't you worry. Sophie and me are still here. Guess we always will be."

Faye smiled up at her. "Thank goodness for that." She pressed a kiss to Clary's cheek then extricated herself to go to the door and check on Johnny.

"Mama!" Sophie called as she burst through the screen door, her arms laden with luggage. She dropped the bags to one side, then grabbed her mother in a slow hug, lifting Faye so high that her high-heeled pumps left the floorboards.

"Sophia Rene Cofe! Put me down." Faye tried to sound stern, but she was smiling helplessly.

"But it's so good to see you." She put her mother down, then held her cheeks and turned her face from side to side, examining her. "You look good. Healthy."

"Now why wouldn't I be? I'm not old yet."

Johnny moved through the door and carefully placed his load of luggage next to the load Sophie had brought in. He eyed Clary nervously.

"Johnny, there you are," Faye said.

"Johnny, this is Clary, my best friend since we was practically babies." She took Clary's arm and pressed their bodies together side to side.

"Clary," Johnny said, nodding. "Good to meet you."

Clary took Johnny's extended hand and pulled him toward the kitchen. "I know y'all are starving after that trip. Come on in here and let's have us a sandwich."

Sophie followed the group silently, her arms folded across her chest.

"We just had something a little while ago, Clary, really," Faye protested.

"You know better than that, Mama," Sophie chided softly. She pulled out one of the kitchen chairs and motioned Johnny into it. She slid into the one next to him.

"So, who had a baby?" Faye asked as she took a seat. She glanced once at Grandam's conspicuously empty chair.

"Birdy Lawhorne. Her fifth."

"Oh no," Faye gasped.

"Birdy?" Johnny asked.

"Her fifth, you say?" Faye asked.

"She's Mama's friend from school. They're the same age," Sophie explained to Johnny. "Yes, Mama, three boys and two girls now."

"Damn," Faye muttered. "Who woulda believed that?"

Johnny Macht showed a little personality finally, a devilish grin spreading slowly across his face. "Now, see there, darling, you coulda had all kinds of young 'uns by now."

Faye slapped playfully at him as she lit another cigarette. "No, thank you. I made my contribution."

Her eyes found Sophie and turned soft. "The world got the best I have to give right here. Anything else would be a waste." She held Sophie's hand. "I'm sorry about your grandma, honey. Are you holding up okay?"

Sophie nodded. "I'm just upset I wasn't here, Mama. I should have been with her."

Faye fell silent, thoughtfully drawing on her cigarette. "I thought you people know when each other is moving on, Sophie, honey. Why didn't you know? Where were you?"

Clary, busily moving cold cuts and vegetables from the refrigerator, stilled and the air in the kitchen rapidly grew rarefied as all awaited Sophie's response.

Sophie colored slightly. "I was with Delora, Mama. Her husband had just died and she was going through a rough patch. I spent the night with her. I didn't know Grandam was gone until the next morning when I got home. And as for knowin', I guess I was distracted." Sorrow weighted her voice.

Faye's eyes sought Clary's. "Delora who? Do I know her?"

Sophie shook her head, and Clary placed food on the table in front of them. Bereavement dishes had been appearing since Grandam's death—funeral casserole, green bean casserole, pimiento cheese, deviled eggs, squash, pickles, huge platters of cold cuts and sliced cheese. The Cofe refrigerator had never been so full. Johnny's eyes grew wide at the offerings Clary placed on the table.

"You'll meet her, Mama," Sophie said, helping Clary steady a platter. "She's a Clark who married a November."

"Clarks. Sherman and Rita's girl?"

Sophie nodded.

"Good people, honey, and a little far from the bayou. How in the world did y'all meet?"

Sophie gave her mother a wry look and then told her about Delora's first late-night visit and a little about her injury.

Faye listened intently, her hands busying themselves with making Johnny a sandwich. "Why, that's just awful, Sophie. Poor gal, losing her parents in that squall, then this happening. I guess she's just ready to roll over and die."

Clary smiled broadly and shoved a piece of ham into her mouth. "Not anymore, she ain't," she interjected as she chewed exuberantly.

Faye slid the sandwich plate in front of Johnny and paused. "What does she mean, Soph?"

Sophie chuckled and hung her head. "Nothin', Mama. We're just keeping company is all."

Faye seemed to be pondering this new information. She glanced at Clary and saw the truth confirmed. "Sophie, honey, I thought you'd given up that foolishness," she offered gently.

Sophie's back stiffened just a little, not enough to be noticed unless you were looking for it. Clary noted it right away, knowing this was old ground they trod.

"Mama," Sophie sighed.

"What is it?" Johnny asked, one moistened finger lifting bread crumbs from his plate.

"Nothing," Faye and Sophie said in unison.

"You need to find you a husband, Sophia. Someone who'll take care of you, that you can love proper."

Sophie slapped her thighs and stood. "Well, I gotta run. There's a place I gotta be this evening. I'm gonna take Grandam up the tributary later tonight, Mama, if you want to see her first. I'll be back in just a little while."

"Is everything ready?" Clary studied Sophie's face, seeking signs of discontent. "Can I do anything?"

Sophie tilted her head and regarded her dearest friend. "It's all done. She's in the shed. Maybe y'all can go by and say goodbye while I'm gone."

"I'll do that," Clary said. "We'll do that," she added, looking pointedly at Faye.

CHAPTER FIFTY

The people of Rosalie's church were confused. They knew condolences for Louie November's death were necessary, but they didn't know at which house to pay them. The rumor mill took the Rosalie-Delora altercation and ran with it. As a result of this confusion, a wealth of casseroles, fresh baked bread and cold salads piled up on tables at the Glorious Hour Funeral Home on Mangrove Row in Redstar.

"But Miss November, we can't have it," said Womack Remsan in a harsh, frightened whisper. "We're not licensed to serve food here. Not even on family night."

Delora studied his broad, pained face and wanted to laugh. Stifling the unacceptable urge, she realized suddenly that Remsan was one of Sophie's people. Why hadn't she noticed before? She'd known this man most of her life and had never put the pieces together. She'd never really thought much about the people of the bayou back then. It was like they never existed in the world she lived in. Meeting Sophie had opened her eyes to this new world and now she felt she could spot the bayou folk in any crowd.

"I'm so, so sorry, Mr. Remsan. Really. I never agreed to this and I don't know how it happened." She watched as yet another dowager placed a dish on the polished bureau of the anteroom.

"Well, someone's got to do something. We simply can't have it here. My staff will be glad to carry it out to your car and stop any more coming in, but you have to tell them which is your vehicle."

Delora sighed. "Wait. Let me see if Rosalie—Mrs. James—can take it in her car."

Dreading the encounter, Delora entered the main viewing room where the ponderous casket rested. She had asked that the coffin be closed. The fall hadn't improved Louie's face one whit, and she thought a closed coffin would thwart the prurient among the visitors. The coffin, ominous nevertheless, drew her eye immediately. She pulled her gaze away, half expecting Louie to rise up and accuse her of killing him.

Rosalie and her two sisters were on the left side in the front row. The two sisters were trying to comfort Rosalie, who was weeping copiously.

"Mama, there's a problem with the food," Delora began. All three heads snapped up, and Delora could see the contempt roiling in them.

Refusing to be intimidated, Delora greeted them. "Hello, Aunt Phyllis, Aunt Grace." She'd been in the back attending to last-minute paperwork, and this was the first time she'd seen the trio since Louie's death.

Rosalie made a huffing sound but not one word fell back in greeting.

"Well," Delora continued, "Mr. Remsan says the food has to be taken somewhere else because of licensing. Can I get his people to put it in your car? So you can take it home after?"

"I guess you can't take it because you don't need a home," Phyllis replied.

Delora ignored her.

"Is it unlocked, Mama?"

Rosalie nodded, shook a wet tissue at Delora and broke into fresh tears. Delora moved away, wishing she could feel some sympathy in her heart for her foster mother. It simply didn't exist anymore.

After showing the funeral director which car was Rosalie's, Delora was surprised and relieved to see Sophie standing in the entryway. She immediately went to her.

"You're so good to come, Sophie. I know with what's weighing on you it must have been a real task to come out tonight." Her eyes searched Sophie's dear face, seeking comfort and solace. The eyes were shuttered tonight, however, and weren't lit with their usual deep light. Sadness has her, thought Delora, feeling her heart tug in her chest. She wished she could comfort Sophie somehow, could hold her and make it better. She felt so helpless.

"The coffin is closed. Do you need to go in?"

"It doesn't matter, Lora. I'm here for you. I figured it must be a tough time."

"You don't know how tough," Delora replied and went on to tell Sophie about the altercation with Rosalie the day before. "She's in there with her sisters now and they're not really talking to me 'cept to talk trash." She paused and studied Sophie. "When will Grandam be laid to rest?"

Sophie tamed her hair with both palms. She looked dressier than usual tonight, having taken great pains with her appearance. She wore a sedate black cotton suit with a white button-down blouse. Polished black shoes peeked from the bottoms of her long trousers and a thick silver ring adorned each hand. Silver earrings caressed earlobes framed by a corona of braided hair. "I guess day after tomorrow. Can you come?"

"Absolutely. I'll call for directions." Delora looked around at the milling, socializing crowd and suddenly felt claustrophobic. "Hey, can we go outside a minute?"

Without a moment's hesitation, Sophie pushed open the glass door and ushered Delora through.

"I don't know what to make of this," Delora said as soon as they had moved around the side of the building. "I know I should be upset he's gone, but I just can't be. I don't think that sorrow is even anywhere in me. Am I that horrible?"

"He killed whatever love y'all had a long time ago, hon. It's that simple."

"I hate it that I'm that way," Delora commented, chewing the skin around her thumbnail. "Some wife I was."

Sophie's gaze grew warm, her voice low. "You'd be a good wife to me."

Delora lowered her hand and smiled, thrilling Sophie. "Wife. I like that. I'd enjoy taking care of you."

"Working alongside me," Sophie corrected.

"Do you think I could, Sophie? Work with you, I mean. Help people?"

Sophie was thoughtful, her eyes taking in the night sky. Delora enjoyed watching her. It was as if Sophie spoke the same language as the night. It was as if her time among humans was almost an annoyance. Though she seemed comfortable no matter where she was, Delora knew her real place was out here, among nature.

"You'd be good, Delora," she said finally. "I saw you with Firis, how you helped her. That's all we do."

"Right," Delora muttered with some sarcasm. She leaned against the brick wall of the funeral home, hoping no salamanders were crushed by the move. She studied Sophie again, disturbed by her sadness. "I know you miss Grandam."

Sophie nodded. "I do." She took a deep breath and shifted her weight. "Listen, honey, tonight I…"

A shrill call fractured the night, momentarily silencing the normal evening song. Alarmed, Delora fished frantically in her pocket and pulled out her cell phone. Abruptly silencing a second peal of noise, she flipped it open and answered.

"No, Aunt Freda, there's no need to come. I know you've been feeling poorly. Yes, a tragic accident." Her eyes found Sophie and she mimed helplessly.

Sophie could tell this was going to be an involved call so she leaned in to give Delora a quick kiss on the lips. "I gotta go," she whispered.

Humming in agreement with her aunt, Delora trailed her finger along Sophie's arm and their hands brushed in a gentle farewell. Their eyes met and lingered fondly.

CHAPTER FIFTY-ONE

Louie's interment was a dismal affair. Hinchey was there, his demeanor glum and guilty. Rosalie was still angry, but Delora didn't much care. As a stolid counterpoint to Rosalie's loud grief, Delora remained silent and held her head high during the twenty-minute graveside service.

Surprisingly, several of Louie's park cronies attended, even the one she called Hard Eyes. His gaze crawled across her, and she felt soiled by his thoughts. Each of the three men had made a concerted effort to spruce up for the event, but the suits were ill-fitting and threadbare in places.

Louie's friends, Delora thought sadly, as she studied the small gathering. He sure hadn't gone out of his way to make friends. He'd been a brute and Delora couldn't help trying to analyze the reasons behind his angry, irascible personality. He was intolerant, bigoted, misogynistic and brutal. Losing his mother could have contributed, but if that was so, why wasn't Delora more like Louie? She'd lost both mother and father at once.

Perhaps Louie's father had been more abusive than she realized. Delora had only met the late Bob November three times during their marriage and each time at a large family gathering. She'd had little one-on-one with the man. She realized suddenly that she hadn't really known Mister November at all. He'd been a distant voice on the phone, calling to get Louie to check something at his home while he was away hauling freight. He may have beaten Louie as a child, but Louie had never discussed it with Delora.

Louie's death troubled Delora. She'd wanted him gone from her life for so long. Then to have him die in this tragic way and Delora lie about it. It would surely have some repercussions, perhaps even on her soul for allowing the lie to take root and grow. No matter how she shook the issue, however, she just couldn't see the good in allowing Hinchey to take the blame for something that really went directly sideways of being his fault. By rights, he should never have been any part of Louie and Delora's sick relationship.

She sighed and shifted her weight from one foot to the other. She'd be glad to get back to the quiet of her hotel room. Unfortunately, there was still the gathering at Rosalie's house, which could take several hours. Several hours of feigning sadness for Louie's absence in her life. Several hours of making small talk with people she knew only in passing. She'd never connected with any of these people. They were Rosalie's friends, Louie's friends or long-ago friends of her parents. They had little to do with Delora and her life, and she bore some resentment that she was forced, by society's dictates, to make nice-nice with these well-meaning but mostly just curious townsfolk.

The service ended and Reverend Lorenz handed Delora a long-stemmed white carnation from a nearby arrangement. A prolonged silence fell and Delora realized that she was supposed to make some profound gesture. Frowning, she stepped forward and laid the flower atop the polished wood of the casket. Reverend Lorenz gestured and the crowd began to disperse. Behind them, the casket began to lurch downward. Delora looked back once as the primary source of her life's discontent moved below the ground. She stopped walking, startled and afraid. Oh God, what if she still wasn't happy?

She lowered her chin to her chest and stubbornly plodded toward the waiting car. She thought of Sophie. Dear Sophie. The thought of Sophie sustained Delora as she shook the hands and accepted the condolences of well-wishers.

At some point, she found herself in the sleek black family car sitting across from Rosalie. She was staring out the window, her mind blank. It was a nice thing that she could think as much as she wanted and everyone believed she was lost in grief over her husband's death. In actuality, she was pondering the new direction of her life. The goal that had sustained her for so long, now that it was so close to realization, had abruptly dissipated. Delora knew the reason lay in her newfound love for Sophie. There was no reason now for her to escape Redstar. Louie was gone and she was free—even when bound to Sophie. This was Sophie's home and would continue to be Delora's. It had a good feeling.

In this frame of mind, she was delighted to see Sophie's car parked outside Rosalie's house. And worried. Surely the townsfolk would be able to see the extent of the two women's feelings if they were observed together. Delora still felt unsure of how others would react to the idea of two women in love. It was best ignored as long as possible. A hard task, feeling the way she did about Sophie.

Yet seeing Sophie's lean form in the kitchen doorway set her mind at ease. Breath entered and filled a chest she hadn't realized was empty. The pathway to Sophie was filled with condolences, however, and it was some time before Delora made her way to the kitchen. The range was hidden by the bulk of flesh that was Rosalie's younger sister, Phyllis. Clary washed serving utensils at the sink, and Sophie was uncovering casseroles. Clary looked up when Delora entered. Drying her hands, she moved to pull the younger woman into a loving, compassionate embrace.

"I'm sorry for your loss, honey," she whispered into Delora's ear.

Peace washed across Delora and a type of sorrow. She would not cry. Would not break down under this kindness. Phyllis turned and watched with keen interest as Sophie approached Delora and held her, murmuring soothing words. Delora, uncomfortable under Phyllis's relentless interest, gave Sophie the most cursory of hugs and did not meet her eyes.

Delora could tell Sophie sensed her hesitancy, and, to her credit, she followed Delora's lead, backing away almost immediately and casting her gaze downward.

"I'm so sorry, Delora. About your loss. I know the hereafter will greet him with welcoming arms."

Sophie raised her eyes for one sweet moment before she turned back to the task at hand. Delora remained rooted, feeling superfluous and lost with all the activity around her.

Sophie must have sensed Delora's distress because as was her way, she silently pressed used plastic wrap into Delora's hands, which

had, without anyone's knowledge, prepared and gathered together all that she would need to be carried properly to the next world. She had patiently braided summer woodbine into long ropes—ropes that would be used to bind her coffin—and laid them in thick coils atop her wardrobe.

The coffin itself would be made of smooth willow splits, which Grandam had no doubt purchased from the hardware store and had stacked inside the shed lean-to out back of the house. Herbs and imported spices had been set aside, hidden under the head of her bed. Her shroud, sewn by her own hands, was intricately embroidered with the symbols of a prosperous, happy afterlife.

Sophie found the folded shroud in the press in Grandam's bedroom. She found the coils of woodbine and the herb pouches easily and piled them, alongside the shroud, on the top cover of Grandam's bed. She took the toiletries from the bureau and added them, her touch lingering on the heavy hairbrush used to untangle the long gray strands each evening before retiring.

Sophie sighed. Life would never be the same.

Bringing up the four corners of Grandam's coverlet, Sophie lifted the items and carried them through the house, the family turning their backs to her as she passed. She went through the kitchen, out the door and across the lawn to the sloping bank of the bayou. After resting the bundle against one of the dock posts, she made her way to the shed, sure she would find the coffin splits there under a heavy tarpaulin.

During the next hour, as she wove the long splits and the woodbine rope into a flat mat, Sophie relived the highlights of her life with Beulah Cofe. She remembered their eyes meeting in relief after the difficult but successful birth. Their time together reciting and reasoning out the ailments of the community. The sweet smiles of triumph when Sophie had remembered the ingredients of a difficult potion. Sophie's eyes moved to the lean-to where her grandmother lay waiting.

People not of the bayou didn't take kindly to the bayou ways of death and dying so preparing the body was always done after dark. The herbs Sophie would use to prepare Grandam's body had all been carefully labeled and the use of each had been just as carefully passed from grandmother to granddaughter. There were ones for the mouth, nose and ears and others for between the legs. Some went beneath the arms and others at the soles of the feet. Each placement was accompanied by a specific chant. Sophie ran them through her mind as she carried each of the four twenty-pound lead balls from their neat stack beneath the ancient oak tree at the northernmost point of Cofe land. One of the kith had already brought the burial flatboat and two poles and left them at the water's edge so she placed the four balls against the side of the boat. They would be added last, when the coffin was bound tight.

After the back and forth trips, which when combined amounted to several miles, Sophie rested and watched as dusk settled onto the bayou. Her stomach rumbled and she welcomed the grounding that reminded her she was still alive. It was tradition that the nearest family member fast the day of the bayou funeral. Otherwise it would have been too easy to complacently follow the dead into their watery grave.

Wearily she rose, fetched items from Grandam's coverlet and entered the lean-to. She smelled Grandam's familiar rosemary scent, now enhanced by the hours lying dead in the hot shed. Womack hadn't touched her beyond checking to make sure she was truly dead, so she looked peaceful even though her face and body had begun to stiffen. Steeling herself, Sophie touched her grandmother's icy arm, once more getting used to the oddly sub-zero dead weight of a body. Each time she prepared a body for burial, it was a shock. Trying not to think about who the person had been, she respectfully removed the clothing, bathed her with clean bayou water, then brushed the long, unbound hair one final time. She applied the herbs with the appropriate prayers and chants. The entire process took almost two hours, and by the time she was finished, she felt as though she'd lost a part of herself to iron will. Gaunt with misery, she wrapped her grandmother in the embroidered shroud and lifted her.

The warm bayou air felt good as she strode from the shed, Beulah an awkward weight in her arms. Earlier she had laid the newly woven coffin across the boat. Now she tenderly placed her grandmother in the center and touched her cheek one last time before placing the weights evenly next to the body. She covered Grandam with the quilt from her bed, as if simply tucking her in for the night, and lovingly placed her favorite possessions around her. Pulling the coffin sides close, she began weaving the edges together with woodbine cord.

She looked up through the dimness and saw her mother and Clary standing on the slope toward Salamander House. Johnny stood behind them. Clary had offered to help and Sophie knew she had taken Sophie's refusal as an insult. Perhaps one day she would come to realize that Sophie just couldn't share this last task her grandmother had requested of her. Even if Faye had offered to help, Sophie would have said no. It was Sophie's place and hers alone.

"Okay, Grandam," Sophie said. "You're ready."

She stepped off the boat and glanced once more at her watching family before sliding the boat into the water. Yes, only one person was allowed on Grandam's final voyage and Sophie had been chosen. Some would fault Beulah for not choosing Faye, but no one, Faye included, had been as close to Grandam as Sophie. If Beulah's son Keene had still been alive, Grandam might have requested he pole the boat and that would have been fine by Sophie.

As Sophie leapt onboard and pushed the boat from the bank, she looked back and saw Faye collapse into Clary's arms. She was glad Clary was there to comfort her mother. Faye had suffered a great loss too, for her sense of home had been ripped away.

Turning her eyes forward, Sophie faced the sultry humidity of the inner bayou. A chain of lights along both shores gave her pause. She immediately thought of the fairy lights she often saw beneath the water and for a few seconds thought the lights had risen from the depths. Then she realized it was the people of the bayou; they had gathered along the shore to say goodbye. Holding lanterns, candles, rushes and flashlights, they bore silent witness to Grandam's final journey into the bayou. She could see the faces of a few of the mourners, had treated most of them. Most had their heads bowed, hands over their hearts in gestures of respect. Those who met Sophie's gaze nodded their encouragement as she passed.

Standing on the boat with Grandam lying next to her, Sophie felt infused with a sense of power and oneness with the bayou. A cool wind caught her and wispy curls stirred around her face.

"I sure will miss having you with me every day, Grandam. I don't know why good people can't live forever. I know the ways of nature and that it's a necessity that all things pass on, but it still rankles that you have to leave us."

She paused a long beat as she maneuvered the boat around a bend. "I sure hope you'll come be with me when I tend the sick. I still need you."

The wind caressed her once more and her thoughts left Grandam and moved on to Delora. Images of her flitted through Sophie's mind like film frames filing through a projector. Delora listening to her, eyes curious. Delora smiling at children. Delora lying below her, eyes darkened by passion.

Guilt beset her. Burying her grandmother was no time to be filled with thoughts of Delora. She still couldn't deal with the fact she'd been with Delora when Grandam had died. It broke her heart to realize that Beulah had died alone. She knew it would trouble her for some time to come.

Poling the boat along, she passed familiar landmarks. The lore passed along the bayou was so specific she had known exactly where she was during her first trek along this path at the age of twelve. Her first journey upbayou had been to take a stillborn baby, Lithin Sirois, to his final rest. Sophie had learned a lot about herself during that first journey.

Just ahead, on her left, was the triangle-shaped rock outcropping. Ten minutes farther on there were three red rocks lined up along the west bank. The tree of enchantment loomed ahead. Over the decades it had been festooned with colorful ribbons creating a rainbow of movement in the gentle wind that continued to blow. Bearing right at the ribbon tree, Sophie found herself in a very old, very dark area of Bayou Lisse. Here there was no sound. The bayou water lapping at the banks was even strangely muted. The only sound was the intrusive insertion of Sophie's pole as it penetrated the water and the soft susurrus of the boat's passage.

Suddenly it felt as though Grandam quickened at Sophie's feet, as if her body eagerly sought its new home. It was disconcerting, but Sophie had felt it before. It seemed the dead know their abode. Within minutes, she reached the point where the rocky bank made an inverted V, creating a large cul-de-sac. Sophie slowed, allowing the current to maneuver the small flat boat into the mouth of the hidden area. The boat was almost too large, and Sophie stumbled when the sides of the boat encountered land on two sides. Regaining her equilibrium with a determined two-step, she glanced down through the dimness to make sure she had enough of an area to place Grandam.

Her imagination ran rampant, or perhaps it was her sensitive nature, but she could feel the souls of all those buried here beneath the water. She knew some had gone away, scattered helter-skelter by hurricane fury. A storm came along every few years and washed the remains away, back to the vastness of the bayou. Others, more recent burials, rested below in woven wooden coffins, silently. Peacefully. Small fish and crustaceans fed here and carried parts back into nature's extensive web of life.

Sighing, Sophie pulled her pole free and stowed it in the lock. She crouched and lay both palms on the polished wood splits, her fingers grasping hold.

"My love and faith to you, Grandmother. Care for your new companions and they will care for you. From one world to the next, only that endures," she said softly, then she repeated it in the old language for those below who wouldn't have understood.

Tears filled her eyes. She paused then and slid a heavy necklace of hematite beads from around her neck. She fastened it securely to the edge of the coffin.

"Goodbye, Beulah Rene Fox Cofe. May your rest be peaceful and your next life filled with joy."

Moving to the back, she slid Grandam down the specially designed ramp of the boat. She stood, hands clasped and watched as the bayou water crept inside and claimed Grandam's body. She stood a long time, here in this place of the dead, until the bubbles stopped rising and Grandam had settled herself among the sleeping ones below. Warmth suffused Sophie and she felt comforted.

CHAPTER FIFTY-THREE

Light of Holiness Church was overflowing with bodies, color and sound. Beulah's family wore their finest to mark her passing. All knew the elaborate coffin, closed as traditional with the Manu Lisse, lay empty at the front of the church, but it didn't matter; this social event would serve to celebrate the life of the bayou's beloved healer. The *gange* people of Redstar would have been horrified to discover that Beulah wasn't inside, but it was a cherished secret knowledge only among the Manu.

Sophie supposed every person they'd ever helped had come to pay their last respects. The people spilled from the church, completely filling the expansive green outside. Her heart swelled to think her grandmother's memory beat in so many hearts. Grandam would be pleased. A few seemed to be just this side of the veil themselves, no doubt thinking they would soon reunite with Beulah.

As was their way, while Brother Kinder spoke about the importance of Beulah Cofe's life, the women keened softly, slow petitions to entreat the Others to guard her well and make her life a welcome asset to them. The sound formed a bridge of transfer as this life gave up the well-loved woman to the Other Side.

Sophie moved in a cloud of numbness, the grief from Grandam's real funeral lingering. It may have been simple fatigue that deadened her; she had not rested a moment since Grandam had passed. There had been so much to do, taking care of loose ends and orchestrating all the necessary ritual. Dying creates a whole new set of chores for those left behind. The tasks were winding down now, however, and soon life would return to something resembling normalcy. She knew this, deep in her soul; today however, she was plain tuckered out.

Also troubling was Delora's notable absence. She'd not returned any of Sophie's hurried messages and hadn't spoken to her since Louie's funeral. It pained her heart to think Delora didn't care.

Then the service was over and Sophie accepted the hugs and handshakes of those who had loved or known her grandmother. Their faces passed in a familiar blur. They presented a daily diary of their healing career. Her grandmother had once presented her to each of them, proud that Sophie was following her life as a healer.

Sophie sighed as she accepted the condolences of Reggie Platte. She smiled and held his hand as he told her an endless story about his time with Beulah. After he moved on, she allowed her gaze to roam the room, searching for that one familiar face.

And there she was. She stood to Sophie's left, over at the end of the church, where the pews ended. Sophie's heart skipped a beat and joy warmed her. Delora's smile was sweet and sad when their eyes met. Her eyes appeared red and Sophie wondered at this.

Distracted by another well-wisher, Sophie pulled her gaze away and moments later Delora approached her.

"Sophie, I'm so sorry I didn't call. Things have been nuts with Rosalie and finding a place to live. Can you forgive me?"

Sophie's eyes let her know all was okay. "I'm glad you're here," she said, taking Delora's hand in both of hers. "Can you stay after?"

"Of course," Delora replied. "As long as you need me."

She moved away into the crowd and Sophie felt the void.

"Is that your little girl? The one Clary told me about?" Faye appeared at Sophie's side.

"Yeah, her name's Delora. I'll introduce you later."

"She's pretty." Her eyes followed Delora as the small woman approached Stephen.

"Yes, she is," Sophie agreed. The crowd had finally begun to disperse and she felt relieved. "Her husband just died."

"I thought you said that. When?"

"Almost a week ago. He was a monster and she's well shed of him."

"How will she get on?" Faye examined one of her perfectly polished fingernails.

Sophie's face screwed in irritation as she regarded her mother. "She works harder than anyone I know. She'll be fine."

"Still. Does she have family?"

"Yes, Mama," Sophie said, taking in a deep breath as she moved away. She was eager to bid Faye farewell. Life was so much easier without her at Salamander House. "We need to go speak to Brother Kinder, then let's get on back home. I'm tired."

"Sure, honey, sure." Faye watched her daughter with a concerned expression.

"So what are the chances of this happening? Louie dying and you losing your grandma at about the same time?" Delora had pulled her knees to her chest and was resting her chin on them. Her mien was thoughtful.

"Slim," Sophie replied quietly.

They were sitting side-by-side on the wooden steps of the shed behind Salamander House. Most of the visitors had left, but a wealth of family remained inside.

"I mean, it's just too weird."

"It is," Sophie agreed.

Delora glanced at the house and saw Faye in the kitchen holding court.

"Your mom is something, isn't she?"

"Yeah," Sophie laughed softly. "She is that."

Delora took Sophie's hand and pressed it into the dress fabric stretched across her knee. The hand was tanned and strong and Delora loved the feel of the knuckles as she pressed them with her palm.

"Will you be okay? I know how dear she was to you. To everyone."

Sophie sighed and squeezed Delora's hand once quickly. She pulled the hand away and seemed to collapse into herself. Delora noted the phenomenon right away.

"I buried her, you know."

"I know, baby. I was there."

"No." Sophie shook her head. "She wasn't there today. I buried her last night. In the bayou, in the old ways of our people."

"You did what?" Delora turned her head, cheek on her knees, and studied Sophie.

"Up the river, where all our family lay."

"So who was in the coffin?" Delora was trying to understand Sophie's words.

"No one." The phrase was a sigh, sad and low. "I took her there alone, up the water to the grotto. She'll rest there." She said it with conviction, as if trying to convince herself. "It was really beautiful, Lora. All the Manu were there on the banks with lanterns and candles. Even flashlights. They were there to light her journey to the Others."

"The Others? Sophie, honey, I don't understand. Where is your grandmother?"

Sophie rose abruptly and paced to and fro with unusual urgency. "Never mind. I shouldn't be telling you this anyway. I'm breaking all the rules for you—a *gange* who can't possibly understand the importance of the issue of dying alone with no family to ease your passage. It's just not done and I really feel like I've let the family down."

"But Sophie, I don't know..."

The other woman turned away and folded her arms protectively. "And I shouldn't expect you to, Delora. I'm just feeling guilty. My place was here that night."

Delora felt a spark of anger stir, righteous, yet sorrowful. "Here. Not in Redstar."

Sophie, her face twisted with pain, hung her head sadly. Moving quickly, she stepped away in through the screen door. The sound of voices talking swallowed her and she was gone.

Delora sat stunned for several moments, then found her footing and moved rapidly toward her car.

CHAPTER FIFTY-FOUR

The house was small, but that suited Delora. The close walls gave her a secure feeling. There was one good-sized bedroom, a smaller bedroom the size of a large closet, and a bathroom with a handheld shower above a clawfoot tub. The living room held a worn sofa, one chair and a battered TV set.

"I'll take it," she said to Annie. "It's perfect."

Annie shrugged and leaned toward the wall, resting her weight on one shoulder. "Well, not perfect, certainly. But comfortable and it's a month to month. Sorry it's so far from town."

"It's about the same as I was driving before. Just from a different direction." She moved to the kitchen window and peered through. A view of the bayou greeted her. Sun touched the water, the rays dancing atop the moving current like tiny whirling stars.

"Has Rose gotten over you moving?"

"No," Delora sighed and looked in one of the spacious kitchen cabinets. "But ask me if I care. I'm so pissed at her for treating me so mean all those years."

Annie sighed. "That just ain't right, Delora. You don't mistreat family. Not really. Even if they're not your blood."

"Right and that there's a point, isn't it. Shows what she thought of me."

"Are you gonna be all right here? Sure?" Annie's eyes filled with concern as she regarded her new tenant.

Delora smiled bravely. "Tough as nails. Don't you worry."

"I do worry, but I'm glad you're living here where it's pretty safe. Watch out for moccasins and gators though. The baby gators come up in the yard sometimes and eat pet food or scrap food if you leave it out."

Delora's mouth fell open as she followed Annie to the door. "Wow."

Annie laughed and opened her car door. "Well, back to the bookkeeping. You call me you need anything, hear?"

Delora nodded and waved until Annie had pulled out of the drive.

Once the sound of Annie's car faded, the sound of the swamp inundated Delora. It amazed her with its growing noise. Squinting her eyes, she stepped off the low porch and moseyed back to her car and the belongings it held. The grass in her yard was nowhere near as pretty as that at Salamander House, and she felt a sudden urge to call Sophie and ask her what she did to make it so green. She shook her head as she hoisted two garbage bags from the trunk and carried them into the house. Not a good idea.

The thought of never talking to Sophie again nagged at her but was held at bay by the anger she harbored toward her. No one had a right to talk to her that way. No right to wrongly blame her for something.

But Sophie. This was Sophie. So precious. So good. It rankled on one end that the woman she loved was angry with her. And about what? For making love? It rankled another way that it was Sophie, the finest, sweetest woman she knew. This rejection hurt worse than the rejection of her love. Obviously Sophie thought she was just a bad person all the way around. That smarted because Delora wanted so badly to *be* good, to please Sophie. She really had thought the two of them had created something worthy of cherishing and fostering. Now here she was alone. Again. With her guilt.

After fetching a large cardboard box from the backseat, Delora stood in the middle of the haphazardly furnished living room and surveyed her possessions. The box held new household items purchased from Mannings Grocery. Once she took full stock of what she'd need, she'd make a trip to Goshen. The Walmart there had everything.

As she pulled rolled maps from one of the bags, she felt a tremulous smile creep out and touch upon her lips. This was her new home.

She no longer needed to be quiet when she came in from work. She no longer had to deal with Louie's abusive comments or Rosalie's disdain. Home. Her eyes scanned the walls, seeking the best place for the transportation department map. She found a likely spot and climbed onto the sofa. She allowed the map to roll open along her legs as she held it up to the wall. Sudden sadness washed across her. She no longer wanted to leave Redstar. She wanted to stay here. Here with Sophie. Dropping to sit on the sofa, she tossed the map onto the floor and wept silent, bitter tears.

CHAPTER FIFTY-FIVE

They stopped in front of the Cape Cod where Hinchey lived with his mother. Hinchey glanced with nervous eyes toward the blank living room windows.

"I sure don't know what to tell her," he said quietly. "There's no way she's gonna understand my leaving."

"Do you have to leave?" Delora studied her hands on the steering wheel to avoid looking at Hinchey. "I mean, I think we've been through the worst of it."

Hinchey looked at Delora, hope flaring in his heart. Did she really want him to stay? Watching her closely, he noticed she was nervous—walking a fine line, not wanting him to see too much. He knew that if she really wanted more from him, he would know.

"No, it's past time I leave Redstar."

They fell silent as sorrow writhed in Hinchey's heart. He turned his attention toward his mother and looked again toward the house. Resigned, he sighed and moved from the vehicle.

"Wait here."

Delora nodded and leaned back in the driver's seat.

The television droned a news patois as Hinchey quietly entered. A gentle snore greeted him and he saw his mother was sleeping in the recliner. Grateful, he crept to the stairway and mounted quietly, still unsure what he would say about why he was leaving so suddenly. He wasn't sure he knew why himself. Delora had certainly covered the truth about Louie. No one knew what really happened, he was sure of that. Upstairs he could hear the television in his mother's room as well, though tuned to a different station. Jay Leno's tenor laugh sounded regularly.

His bedroom waited quietly as if it knew nothing about the life-changing events that had transpired during the past few weeks. It no longer fit him, however, appearing suddenly too small and foreign. Uncomfortable, he rushed to pack the suitcase he had used on his one and only trip—to Las Vegas to visit his Aunt Corrine during the week his mom had her hysterectomy. He hadn't much liked Vegas. The constant noise and bustle of the gambling community grated on his nerves. No one ever slept in Vegas, even on the outskirts where Corrine and Arthur lived with their spoiled son, Robert. The flight had been fun, though, with pretty flight attendants doting on the twelve-year-old flying alone halfway across the country.

He filled the suitcase with essentials, sadly bidding farewell to his extensive video collection and his 19-inch TV. Could he manage without them? His dreams for a better life had been so wrapped up in these visions crafted by others.

He caught a glimpse of his face in the bureau mirror and slowly smiled at himself. Maybe it was time—to the devil with fear and hesitation—for him to make dreams come true. His favorite clothes went into the suitcase, stacking nicely due to his mother's talent for precise folding. He managed to fit in two pair of shoes, one dress pair and his slippers. He gathered his toiletries from the bathroom and tucked them into a small case that he slid into a corner of the larger bag. There was little else he needed. Looking around the room, he saw nothing he couldn't do without. Fetching the CDs and DVDs from his desk, he tossed them into the case and zipped it closed. He wrapped his laptop securely in its cord and stuffed it into its carrying case. He stood a long moment, composing himself, before he scrawled a brief note telling his mother he would call her with an explanation.

Heart beating in his chest like a jackhammer, he descended the stairs and paused at the living room door. His mother slept on, oblivious to the massive change occurring in her life. He almost woke her but reconsidered. He watched her a moment but not long enough for his presence to penetrate the haze of her slumber. He placed the note on the kitchen table.

"Everything okay?" Delora asked as he settled himself into the car. Hinchey tried to shake off burgeoning feelings of sadness.

"There's one more thing," Delora said, her mouth in a firm line as she pulled her bag closer.

"What?"

"Wait, what's this?" Hinchey asked when she handed him the stack of money that she pulled from her bag.

"Money."

"But…"

"Just shut up, Hinchey. Wait while I get through this traffic."

"Delora, I can't keep this," Hinchey exclaimed as he counted it. "There's like a thousand dollars here."

Delora glanced at him and laughed. He resembled a modern-day Midas, covered with green lucre and clutching bills in his left hand.

"Do you see this?" he exclaimed.

"I want you to have it. To start your new life. I don't want to hear any more about it."

"But Delora…"

"Hinchey," she replied in a menacing tone.

They pulled onto Main Street and found themselves in unusually heavy traffic for a hot night in August. A chain of bright lights unrolled past them.

"Damn. Who opened the gate?" muttered Hinchey. He still held the money spread in his lap.

Delora looked at him. "You'd better put that away or pack it up somehow."

Hinchey complied, rolling bundles of bills and stuffing them into his computer bag.

"So, what did you do with your truck?" Delora asked as they neared the bus station.

"I left it with Larry at the dealership. He's gonna sell it and give the money to Mama."

"Can I do anything for you?"

"I'd give it to you if we weren't trying to keep ourselves separate. It would just look too suspicious. Larry'll just sell it is all."

"Oh no, I agree that's best. She'll need the money without your income." Delora winced, hoping she hadn't touched on a sore topic.

Surprisingly he replied in a positive vein. "Mama'll be all right. She's tough as nails. Now she'll have a chance to prove it."

CHAPTER FIFTY-SIX

"I don't know why you're dragging me down here," Stephen complained in a whisper as they entered the Tyson County Public Library.

The building was relatively new, and its clean, sweeping architectural lines screamed modern. Sophie liked it, though, and came here often to do research. A healer was only as good as her knowledge, and Grandam always said knowledge must be fed as often as the body.

"What? Am I keeping you away from Conrad? How is he by the way?"

"We're not seeing each other anymore. He's a drama queen and a player." His tone was peevish.

"And you're not? A drama queen, I mean." They approached the reference stacks.

"Lay off, Sophie." He paused and studied the ranks of multicolored spines. "So what are we looking for?"

"You find the *PDR* and I'll look up dermatology. I've seen a new rash I'm not sure about."

He favored Sophie with a quizzical stare. "The PD what?"

Sophie, already engrossed in a thick nursing book, answered absently. "*Physician's Desk Reference*. It's a big red book, says *PDR*."

"Here you go, Stephen," said a familiar voice.

Sophie looked up, her mouth falling open.

Righteous looked good. His smooth face would always bear the dark, rough scars of his beating, but his eyes were serene. He was dressed well too, more conservative than before, in dark slacks and a dark green oxford shirt.

"This is the most recent," he continued, pulling the book from the shelf and handing it to Stephen.

Stephen's hands moved to automatically take the book. He turned his head toward Sophie, his eyes never leaving Righteous's face. "Sophie, did you...?"

"I swear, I didn't know," Sophie replied quietly as she took the *PDR* from Stephen and beat a hasty retreat, taking a seat at one of the reading tables in the middle of the open area.

"How are you, Stephen?" Righteous's voice was low and gentle.

"I'm good, Righteous. You? You look good."

Righteous laughed and Stephen could see two new silver teeth, probably crowning teeth damaged in the beating. "Sure do ache sometimes."

"Yeah, getting old is hell, ain't it?" Stephen smiled in return.

Righteous sobered. "I work here now. I put the books back on the shelves and help borrowers with online stuff. It's a good job."

Stephen watched Righteous as if mesmerized. He had magically morphed into all that Stephen had wanted him to be.

"How about you? Still at Backslant?"

"Yeah. Still there."

A pause fell, pregnant and enticing.

"Why are you looking at me like that?" Righteous's eyes grew doubtful.

"I'm wondering what time you get off and if you'll have dinner with me."

Righteous dropped his gaze and lowered his head. "Are you sure you want that?"

"Yeah, I do. Why wouldn't I?"

Righteous didn't answer right away. He shifted his weight from one foot to the other. He sighed loudly. "Stephen, I'm not the same person I used to be. I'm reminded of that every time I look in the mirror. I want you to know that. I've changed my life, my job, the people I see, my way of thinking."

Stephen cocked his head to one side, studying Righteous closely. "For the better?"

"I think so. I know so."

"Good. That's good then."

Capturing his full lower lip in silver teeth, Righteous seemed hesitant to express his thoughts. Stephen waited patiently. He longed to touch Righteous but knew the road back there would be a long one after what he'd done. After what Righteous had done. Although Righteous turned his head away, his words found Stephen and lodged in his heart.

"Even dinner would mean a lot to me. Too much. Maybe it would be better if..."

Frowning, Stephen sought Sophie with his eyes in order to stall for time and allow him to think. She sat at the table engrossed in a book, not seeming to feel his gaze. He took his time, wanting to make sure his next words were as precise as possible.

"What? Maybe it would be better if we pretend we didn't see one another? Pretend what we have between us—what we still have between us—doesn't exist? I can't do that. I won't."

Righteous's surprised eyes found Stephen. "Still? After all I've put you through?"

Stephen only laughed ruefully, allowing his eyes to speak his feelings.

Righteous grinned, round cheeks darkening with pleasure. "Five. I get off at five."

Moments later Stephen plopped into the hard wooden chair across from Sophie.

"Well, that's that," he said.

Sophie gave him her full attention. "What did you do?"

"We're going to dinner tonight."

"Well, I'm impressed. That was fast."

"Hmmm," he agreed. "Strange, isn't it. All I have to do is see him and all the feelings come back, no matter what."

Sophie craned her neck so she could see Righteous. He was helping an elderly woman, one of the Bennets, use the computer. "He looks good. Better than last time you saw him."

"I feel bad about that, about running out on him. That wasn't fair."

Sophie shrugged. "You'd been through a lot. Don't beat yourself up about it."

Stephen crossed his legs, resting the ankle of one on the knee of the other. His fingers plucked at the hem of his jeans. "I'm past all that. The question is, do you think he still loves me?"

"He's not seeing anyone. Hasn't since the beating. I'm not sure he ever stopped loving you."

"Even after I left him that way?"

Sophie was losing patience. Dealing with the loss of Beulah, her mother's presence and the problems with Delora were wearing on her. "It looks to me like you're about even finally. He cheated until he got beat almost to death. You ran out on him and had your fling with Conrad…"

She felt a sudden rush of her natural compassion and reached to press his hand. "Give it a chance. It'll all work out."

She didn't want to tell him that Righteous never said a bad word about Stephen and the abandonment during his lengthy recovery. Each time Sophie visited him at his cousin Leon's house, his eyes would ask an unspoken question. The first few times Sophie had obliged by telling him local gossip, including an update on Stephen, that he was still working, still living in the trailer. She did not tell him when Stephen took up with Conrad, and when she stopped mentioning him, the unasked questions had stopped.

Stephen lowered his leg and leaned forward. "How are you doing, Soph? I think about you every day since Miss Beulah passed."

"Fair," Sophie replied with a shaky breath. "I miss her all the time."

"What's going on with you and Delora? You haven't seen her, have you?"

"No." She glanced away, eyes searching the library as she organized her thoughts. "I was with her when Grandam passed. I'm having trouble with that."

"Why?"

"I should have been with Grandam."

Stephen's mind raced with this information. He knew something about the Manus's belief that a person should never die alone because it sets up a situation of anger in the next world. Makes the spirits restless.

"Sophie, this is Beulah we're talkin' about, come on."

"I know and it's not her, it's Mama and Clary and the other people I work with. I see it in their eyes. Some don't know where I was, they don't care, but they know I wasn't there, with her. I didn't find her 'til the next morning, and it was a night that Clary wasn't there. We didn't usually leave her alone since the strokes. And then this time… it means that Grandam," her voice broke, but she continued on, "that she was alone in the house when she passed. No loved person should die alone."

They fell silent. Sophie's palm rubbed obsessively against the smooth texture of the paper bound into the book she'd been reading.

"I just have this to say, Sophie. You've been treating me for every cold and scrape for years and one of the most important things I've learned from you is the power of believing. You always tell me I have to believe myself well, that my mindset is what determines my life. See, I have been listening to you." He smiled to engage her full attention.

"Now I see you losing your faith in yourself, in your own power to shape your life the way that's right for you. You need to move forward. You can't change the past, but you can shape the future. This little Delora gal made you as happy as I've ever seen you. I can't see you shutting her out."

Sophie's mouth formed a twist as she mentally chewed his words. "You're a wise man, Stephen. Too wise. Go find something to read until I'm finished here."

"So you'll call her?"

"Go. Read." Her tone was firm.

He rose and moved away, muttering. "Try to reason with some people..."

CHAPTER FIFTY-SEVEN

Blossom's was unusually quiet, which was a relief. Delora was troubled, though. Mostly by the shark of a man sitting at the end of the bar. It was Louie's friend, Hard Eyes. She would never forget his face and the way he looked at her. He was looking at her the same way now.

He lifted his coffee cup to her, his eyes fastening on her hips, her breasts, her hair—anywhere but where they were supposed to look.

"You holdin' up okay, darlin'?" he asked as Delora leaned over to fill his cup.

"I'm good. And you?"

He sighed and reared back, flicking his cigarette ashes into the ashtray on the counter. "I miss my jawin' buddy, but I bet you're missin' a whole lot more, sleepin' alone at night."

Delora pressed her lips together and turned away, carrying the carafe back to the machine. He watched her as she lit a cigarette of her own. She hoped he couldn't see her hands shaking. Out of the corner of her eye, she saw his head swivel as he took in the empty diner before speaking again.

"I have a little story to tell if you're interested in hearin' it."

Delora wanted to interrupt, but he gave her no opportunity to speak.

"Bud Carey useta sit with us too, you know. Good man but drinks more than a little. I saw him just the other day, and we was talkin' about the funeral and so on, and you know what he tells me?"

Delora waited, wishing she had the courage to be outright rude to a customer.

"He says that you killed old Lou. You and some feller out at the park."

Delora felt as if she'd been doused with ice water. Every hair on her body was standing on end, and she could not find her voice. She did not look at him as she tried to compose herself.

"Now why would I kill him? And who is this fellow he's talking about?" she asked after some time had passed.

Hard Eyes sighed. "Don't know who the feller is, but I think I might just have to find out. That is, unless you and me can come to some sort of understandin'."

Delora cringed. "What is it you want from me?"

"Well, I know you must've got a good payoff, otherwise, why bother doin' him in? I just want a piece of that is all."

"What are you talking about?"

He glanced around the diner once more to make sure they were alone. "Money, is what. You give me a little to get me by. I don't need much. Not much at all."

His eyes roamed across her like kudzu in a stand of young trees.

Delora felt her own eyes grow hard. "What makes you think I have money?"

He drew on his cigarette until the ash end reflected bright on his cheeks and fingers as he removed it from his lips. Smoke followed the cigarette, a looping tail of exhaust. Everything seemed to be moving way too slow. Delora could not believe this was happening. She should have known better. What was she thinking, actually believing she could have a life free from the burden of Louie? It must be her karma or something because now here was Mister Hard Eyes stepping right in to take old Louie's place.

"From what I see, you had it pretty soft there for a while. You had Lou's check comin' regular. Lived with your ma who took care of everythin'. There plain weren't no reason to kill him unless there was some life insurance money out there."

Delora took her time crushing out her cigarette. She leaned back against the cash register and studied Hard Eyes. He was a weasel. A big weasel with swarthy features and greasy hair. He was good looking, in a foreign way, but he sure sickened her. "You are one crazy motherfucker, you know that? Louie fell before I even got there."

"Naw." Hard Eyes shook his head in the negative and closed his eyes. He chuckled deep in his throat. "Naw, that ain't how Bud says it. Says y'all had a fight and that boy of yourn' pushed Louie into the concrete and kilt him."

Delora felt her breath stop. She was straight on dying right here in front of this blackmailing son-of-a-bitch. Anger swelled in her until she could breathe again. It was everything she could do not to crawl across the bar and rip his Adam's apple right out of his sorry throat. He was watching her for some reaction, making him victorious, but she would die before she'd give him the satisfaction of seeing he'd riled her.

"Well, Bud's had just one snort too many is all I can tell you," she said finally, her voice shaky. "You tell him to mind his own business."

Hard Eyes sighed and pushed his cigarette butt hard into the ashtray. "Well, he and the sheriff will just have to talk about how much Bud had that day, won't they?"

Delora ignored him, checking the level of the ice bin and straightening the rail booze behind her. She knew he was studying her in the mirror.

"Look," she said finally. "I ain't got nothin' for you. You need to just get on with yourself."

The heavy outside door squealed and with relief Delora saw Marina enter. Her eyes left Marina and snapped to Hard Eyes to see what he would do. He gathered his cigarettes and lighter, his eyes undressing her. "You meet me Friday, here, when your shift ends. We'll talk this out."

He nodded to Marina as he passed her on his way out.

CHAPTER FIFTY-EIGHT

"I want you to come to Florida with me and Johnny. There's nothing for you here now."

Sophie's head snapped up and Clary turned from the sink in a slow roll of motion.

"You want what?" Clary's voice was incredulous. "You can't take her from..."

"Hold on, honey, hold on," Sophie interrupted. "What are you talkin' about, Mama?"

Faye paused doubtfully and shrugged. "I just think that now Mama's gone, you might want to have a change. You could go to college, maybe meet someone to settle down with. I don't know. I just think it's a good idea is all." Her long, crimson nails fiddled with the cloth placemat on the table in front of her.

Johnny, pausing in his consumption of rhubarb pie, cleared his throat. "You'd be welcome, Sophie, no doubt about that. We've got plenty of room and even a swimming pool. You might want to think about it."

Sophie chewed the idea and found it tasty. She was sore, sick and tired of just about everything at this moment. She'd been looking after the same people with the same ailments for more than twenty years. The thought of carrying on without Grandam was not a pleasant one.

"Johnny does all right, honey. We've got a big house. Gulf Coast College and the University of Florida are both close. Loving books the way you do, I bet you'd do good at school."

Clary was glaring at Sophie and the gaze felt hot on her skin. "I don't know, Mama. It sounds nice, but who'd look after all the folks here?"

Clary relaxed a little.

"Let them go to a regular doctor just like everyone else," Faye said in a scornful voice. "They get such a free ride with you looking after them. You end up paying for everything."

Sophie sighed. It was true, to a degree.

"Faye, you leave her be. You know Sophie's place is here with her people. Your place is here too, if you'd admit it to yourself." Clary dried a glass dish so enthusiastically Sophie worried she'd break it.

"Clare, stay out of this," Faye warned. She leaned back and lit a cigarette. "This is Sophie's call. Why should she feel like she has to waste herself here in the bayou? There's a big world out there and with someone as bright as she is, there's no end to what she can do. I think she deserves that chance. You would to, if you really cared about her."

"Cared about her? Shit, Faye, you've gone loony." Clary slammed the dish on the counter. "All that damned money you got now must have addled your brain."

Faye watched Clary with jaundiced eyes. "Don't go there, Clary. I can still whip your ass if I have to."

Clary's mouth fell open. Johnny turned wide eyes to his wife.

"Stop it, you two. Mama, I appreciate the offer, I really do." She thought of Delora and pain ripped her heart anew. "Maybe I could come stay a little while. Maybe before all the kids start school again and they start up with colds and all."

"I can't be party to this shit," Clary said, gathering up her handbag and car keys. "Go home, Faye, go back to your life. You left here a long time ago. You made that choice and Soph made hers. Deal with it. I love you and you're my dearest friend, but go home and leave this girl alone." She turned to Sophie. "Sophia Cofe, when you come to your senses, you call me."

Sophie stared at the empty space Clary had occupied for a long time. "Well," she said finally.

CHAPTER FIFTY-NINE

She didn't call beforehand, although she could have. She wasn't sure what prompted the need for secrecy, but it was as if she had to feel Delora's presence before seeing her again. Standing outside the small cottage, Sophie felt energized and comforted by the other woman's proximity and the heat of the sun on her shoulders. She watched a long time, the better part of an hour. She studied Delora's small car, the bare, sandy patch of lawn, how the blue storm shutters attached perfectly to each front window and how the newly planted oleander bushes added to the beauty of the home.

"Sophie?" Delora had either seen or felt her.

Sophie smiled and moved toward the partially opened screen door. Her eyes met Delora's and she knew everything was going to be okay. Better than okay.

"What are you doing out in the heat?" Delora asked as she pulled Sophie inside. Box fans peppered the two small rooms and a surprisingly cool movement of air circled the two of them. "Why didn't you come on in?"

Sophie stood just inside the door, hesitant and curious. "I wasn't sure…"

Delora nodded as she moved toward the kitchen area. "I know," she said quietly as she poured sweet tea. "I'm having a hard time with it too."

She passed a glass to Sophie and indicated they should sit. Side by side on the sofa, they fell silent as they sipped coolness. The drone of the fans was peaceful and they stayed that way a good while.

"Mama wants me to move to Florida with her," Sophie said finally.

"No. Don't leave us, Sophie. Don't leave me, I couldn't bear it." Delora spoke to her glass, eyes downcast, but Sophie felt each syllable as it crawled along her spine and gripped her heart. The joy of heaven's divine light filled her and a dizzying wave of giddiness rocked her.

"Whew," she said.

Delora turned a tremulous but loving gaze on Sophie, and they fell together like butter on hot toast. Their glasses of iced tea barely made it to the coffee table, and it felt as though they choked on each other's gasps of delight. The kisses were everlasting and encompassing and both women spun dizzily in a swirling dance of free joy and passion. Delora's body ached from the compass arrow of desire that was pointing toward Sophie. Sophie felt as though she had become water, a stream that flowed across Delora and settled possessively into every crevice.

Sophie lifted Delora's T-shirt and pressed her lips to the salty expanse of skin below her breasts. She spread her large, strong hands wide and splayed them across Delora's moist skin. The heady lemon scent of Delora, the feel of her small body so close, brought tears of relief to her eyes. She pressed her cheek against Delora's flank and breathed a harsh sigh of relief. How could she ever think of leaving this love of her life? "I love you, Lora, so much."

Delora pulled Sophie's face close to hers. "Don't leave me, Sophie. Don't leave."

"No," Sophie whispered against Delora's lips. "I'm wherever you are, sweetheart."

Filled with joyful passion, Delora snaked Sophie's shirt over her shoulders and threw it to one side. Her small hands roamed the sleek expanse of Sophie's broad shoulders.

"You're so beautiful," she whispered, her eyes finding Sophie's. She pressed her lips to the swell of Sophie's breast and unknowingly lit a fire. Sophie's breathing stopped as Delora's hands moved lower, gently cupping the breasts, her fingers tantalizing the sensitive nipples. When Delora looked up, Sophie saw that Delora's eyes had deepened in color and sharpened with passion. The sight, so desired yet unexpected, caused a low moan to rip from Sophie. She felt paralyzed suddenly by the depth of her own need. The swollen cleft that represented her womanhood lurched in desperate longing and she felt faint.

Delora showed no mercy. Her kisses on Sophie's body lingered, her tongue drawing tribal symbols until Sophie wanted to scream. Her senses were torn between intense pleasure and a need for time to react. Both needs were unbearable, yet she felt powerless to move away or toward, held in some devilish hinterland, every sensation heightened to unimagined heights.

"Delora," she gasped, confused and not sure what she wanted to say.

Delora's hand slid along Sophie's hip. She muttered an acknowledgment, but when Sophie didn't respond, she reclined farther and insinuated one leg between Sophie's thighs, pulling her closer. The pressure caused Sophie to orgasm, harshly and powerfully. Gasping, Sophie shuddered as Delora held her close, raining soft kisses along her face and neck.

Sophie fought to recover. Limp, she pressed her mouth onto Delora's. She pushed her tongue inside and felt Delora's indrawn breath. Heat radiated from Delora and, bathed in this, Sophie regained her energy and sense of self. Renewed passion ignited and Sophie undressed her lover, their gazes locked. She leaned in to press a forceful, fucking kiss into her, then leaned back to see what new blaze had erupted. She did this time and again as their clothes burned away and their hands gently frolicked in heated wet ponds and stroked bundles of mounting tension. Hours passed and, blending their bodies, the two women found each other anew while rekindling everything that had come before.

CHAPTER SIXTY

"I need to tell you something."

Sophie swam out of a welcome doze so she could pay attention to what Delora was saying.

"What is it, honey?" she muttered.

"Hinchey killed Louie."

Sophie rolled over, readjusting the sheet that covered them. She was fully awake.

"What?"

Delora sighed and chewed on her thumbnail. She was propped against the headboard and looked adorable with her blond hair mussed from lovemaking. "Not on purpose, of course. He was just protecting me. He tackled Louie and Louie hit his head on one of those concrete trash cans at the park. It was an accident."

Sophie thought about this for a long minute. "Is Hinchey okay? You need to tell him it's okay. It was just Louie's time to go."

"He's struggling some. He left Redstar last week. Went to Arizona, New Mexico…somewhere like that. He met this gal on the Internet and she lives there. I think he'll be okay. The problem is, someone, some drunk, saw, and now this no-account bastard is trying to blackmail me about it. Wants me to pay him a little each month to keep quiet."

Silence grew sharp in the room, and Delora could sense Sophie's anger swell.

"Who is he, Delora?" Sophie asked, her voice tight.

Delora watched Sophie, marveling at her tightly controlled anger. "I...I don't know, Sophie. I never got his name."

Sophie rose into a sitting position and, though naked, her anger gave her a presence and command that no three-piece power suit could have imparted. "You need to tell me everything you remember about him."

Delora recoiled slightly. Subconsciously, she had sensed the other woman's incredible authority over life and nature, but it was not something she could put into words. Now, in this moment, she was seeing it and it was daunting. She knew, horribly, that Sophie could and would do whatever was necessary to further the good in life. Delora's mind raced. She didn't know whether to be alarmed or intrigued. The hard part of her, the part that had dealt with the burns, with Louie and Rosalie, with losing her family and overcoming the addiction to pain medication...that part found some comfort in Sophie's wrath. It wrapped about her and let her know that, at last, someone cared when no one had for such a long time. She slowly began talking and told Sophie everything she could remember, beginning with the day she'd first seen Hard Eyes.

Sophie listened, her head cocked thoughtfully to one side, even long after Delora quieted. When she spoke, her words sent a chill down Delora's spine, even as they comforted her. "Thank you, sweetheart. I want you to forget about this man. I'll meet with him tomorrow, so don't you worry. You did nothing wrong." She captured Delora's face between her two palms so she would be forced to look into Sophie's eyes. "Do you believe me?"

Delora did believe her and a sense of relief coursed across her. Speechless, she pulled free and buried her face in the curve of Sophie's neck. Sophie held her close.

CHAPTER SIXTY-ONE

He walked into Blossom's right at two p.m. Marina had come to relieve Delora, and she studied him with curious eyes.

"I don't like the look of him," she whispered to Delora as they passed behind the counter. "Why he all of a sudden hangin' around here?" She eyed her co-worker accusingly. "You ain't foolin' with him, are you?"

"God, no," Delora said. "You know me better than that."

Marina's eyes grew fond. "I thought I did," she agreed.

Sophie entered the diner, and her gaze fell on Hard Eyes right away. She looked to Delora and a silent signal passed between them. Fear rattled inside as she watched Sophie slide into the booth across from the blackmailer. They knew one another, she could tell, and she wasn't sure how she should feel about that.

"That's your Sophie. What's she doing?" Marina said behind Delora.

Delora glanced back. "My Sophie? What do you mean?"

Marina bestowed Delora with a knowing smirk as she rearranged napkin holders on the counter. "Don't be silly," she answered.

Delora blushed, wondering who else in Redstar knew they were a couple. She realized suddenly that it no longer mattered. If they were going to make their home here, everyone would know soon enough.

"I don't know what she's doing," she mused, watching as the two sat in the booth and conversed. She was surprised to see them laugh together.

Sophie stood and motioned for Delora to follow her as she left Blossom's.

Delora told Marina goodbye and turned toward the kitchen. She leaned to hang her apron on the hook just inside the door and Hard Eyes seemed to materialize next to her.

"I didn't know you was Miss Sophie's girl," he began haltingly. "I just wanted to apologize is all. I didn't mean no harm."

Delora watched him calmly, though hatred still churned in her heart like a timid rodent. She tried to rise above it. "No harm done," she said, pushing past him and out the back door.

Marina stepped in to replace her, lifting one slim, tanned arm to block the kitchen entryway. "I'm sorry, sir. Customers are not allowed inside," she said smugly.

CHAPTER SIXTY-TWO

"I don't know how to do this," Delora muttered, eyes darting to Sophie.

Mary, even in the midst of the contraction, heard the remark and tried to reassure her. Ever the mother, she boasted Delora's capabilities between every gasp of the next contraction.

"It'll be all right, honey. You go ahead and try—we've been down this road a number of times before and Lady Sophie's right here. She borned my other three."

Her knobbed hands tightened on her stomach as she paused to let pain stomp across her.

"She's probably just tired of seein' what I can push out. Must be your turn."

Hot water poured from Mary's body and bathed Delora's knees even though she jumped aside to avoid the bulk of it. The baby's crown appeared, dark hair matted and wet, looking weirdly like a button fastening together the opening of Mary's body.

"You loosen the baby like this," Sophie guided, her gloved fingers smoothing the outer rim of the baby's skull and gently stretching the opening, pushing the taut labia to either side. The baby's head protruded suddenly amid more avid fonts of blood-tinged water.

Delora instinctively reached to prevent the imminent fall, palms and fingers curved with perfect capture round that warm globe of soft flesh and hair. The feeling was incredible, and she stroked presses of flesh one against the other. Another contraction sent a sluice of water across her forearms.

Remembering Sophie's instruction, she turned the baby as best she could and the face was there—little pruned-up features right there in her face. She held the baby as Sophie suctioned out the nose and mouth and he was crying. Not even out of the birth canal and this baby was spouting off. *I bet it's a boy*, Delora thought with much merriment.

Then the baby was slippery in her hands, hot and wet and heavy, all the while feeling like a bag of bones and snot and she just knew she was going to drop it and Mary would hate her and Sophie would turn from her. Somehow she held on, then Sophie was there with a warm blanket, and she took the baby into the safety of the blanket, reminding Delora to tie off the cord. The baby was crying, his swollen testicles bobbing with every yell he expressed. Kicking his feet, he almost threw himself off the blanket and Sophie had to steady him while Delora tied surgical twine on two places along the umbilical cord.

Then, with a snip, Cody Ramp Staton became a separate being— attached to his mother with bonds of love and trust only. The thought touched Delora's heart, and she held the scissors a long time, totally still amid the frantic activity of cleaning and wrapping the infant.

Sophie, after a preliminary examination, left the infant to Mary's two sisters and moved to massage the fundus of Mary's uterus. She studied Delora with gentle pride. "She did well, didn't she, Mary?"

Mary raised her head and looked at Delora with tired, puffy eyes. "Good job, young 'un. I think you've got the healer in you."

Embarrassed, Delora dipped her head and set about tidying the glorious mess of childbirth. Later, studying the life she'd helped bring into the world, she felt suffused with something. A type of wellness, of healing, stole across her. Life meanings clicked into place and, for the very first time in her life, almost everything made sense in a wonderful nonsensical way.

CHAPTER SIXTY-THREE

"This is it," Delora said quietly as she held the passenger door open for Bucky.

Bucky pulled himself from the car and accepted the leg harness she handed him.

The unique new contraption Bucky was wearing when he disembarked the plane had amazed Delora. Normal crutches and prostheses were a hard fit for Bucky Clyde as he was missing his entire left arm and left leg and so had no good anchor. Using his game developing software, as he had explained on the drive into Redstar, Bucky had designed the leather and rigid plastic harness that belted across his body like a corset. Extending from this, from a beautifully articulated steel joint over his shoulder, was a polished steel framework arm ending in three soft, rubber-tipped metal fingers. Although robotic in appearance, it was a marvel of useful engineering and served him well.

The bottom of the corset held a secondary wraparound molded plastic harness that cupped his lower body and held a similar steel cage leg. The only difference, which was downright strange, was that Bucky had opted for an alien design that in no way resembled a human limb. The bottom of the leg was a bent spade of semi-rigid metal that buoyed him along better than any natural appendage. Seeing him lope almost gracefully across the airport terminal had brought hot tears to her eyes. She hadn't known Bucky before the crash that had changed him, but for the first time Delora had an inkling of who he used to be.

"This place is great," Bucky said as he leaned against the car and strapped on his lower harness.

Delora, fetching his bag from the trunk, smiled at him. "It is. I can't imagine living anywhere else now. I used to have a little cottage a couple miles down the road but gave it up when Sophie and me started working together. It just made sense."

"I bet," he said, his one good eye mocking her. "Speak of the devil. Is that her?"

Delora turned and saw that Sophie had come out of Salamander House and was leaning over the porch railing watching them. An irresistible smile found Delora's lips as she gazed upon the source of her newfound happiness. Sophie smiled back and beckoned them toward the house.

"That's her," Delora responded.

"I see," Bucky said, amusement flavoring his voice.

"Stop it," Delora said, laughing. "Come on, let's go in."

Delora allowed Bucky to go first so she could follow at his pace. She needn't have bothered. Bucky made it across the lawn and up the porch steps surprisingly quickly with no trouble.

"I have to say, it's finally good to meet you, Bucky Clyde. Lora talks about you all the time, every day," Sophie told him. "You've been a good friend to her."

"And her to me," he responded, watching Sophie carefully as if wondering how much of his sentence she would get and how repulsed she would be by his appearance.

"That's our Delora," Sophie responded with a smile, taking his words and appearance in stride, chattering on about the construction of the house. When Delora gained the porch, Sophie comfortably wrapped one arm about her waist, pulling her close as they made small talk.

"So this is him," Clary stated as she stepped through the screen door. She studied Bucky, standing with her hands on her hips, a damp dishtowel trailing from one hand. She was wearing her usual jeans with a sleeveless pink shirt and her tightly curled hair was pinned into a cheerful mop atop her head. Her smooth brown face tried for severity but failed. "Shoot. You said he was missing some parts, Delora. Looks to me, he's got more than enough and can get around better than we can."

She moved forward and impulsively touched his metal and plastic shoulder. Bucky smiled and postured for her.

"Designed it myself," he said proudly.

"What?"

Delora started to interpret, but Clary gestured her to silence. "He can tell me," she said.

Sophie laughed softly. "They're a pair, those two," she said to Delora.

"I designed them." He took his time, enunciating as clearly as possible.

"No shit! You did a fine job." She allowed her fingers and eyes to admire the intricate workings for another moment before linking her arm through his prosthesis and leading him inside. "I just know you're hungry," she said, her voice trailing back to Sophie and Delora.

Sophie looked at Delora when Bucky tried to protest. "Don't even try, Bucky," she called.

Delora and Sophie laughed like two fools.

CHAPTER SIXTY-FOUR

Late that evening, with Bucky settled into Grandam's bedroom, Clary came into Sophie and Delora's bedroom to say goodnight.

"I'm off to my cubbyhole," she said, entering the room and climbing onto the bed to sit tailor-style between the two women.

"You're staying the night then?" Sophie asked. She was lying against a mass of pillows, her head pillowed against her folded arm. Delora was next to her, lying on her side facing Sophie. She appeared to be asleep.

"Yeah, thought I would so I could fix a proper breakfast for y'all. Toaster tarts and cereal are not a breakfast, especially for a guest."

"See, Salty gives you a ring and you feel just that secure that you can step out for a night," Sophie said, laughing.

"She's got a point, Clary." Delora's comment was muffled, but she couldn't hide the giggle that followed.

Clary, instead of taking offense at the ribbing, merely admired the platinum and diamond engagement ring Salty had presented to her several weeks past. "It is beautiful, isn't it?"

"And to think we were all worried about what he was up to," Sophie muttered.

"Working is what. He wouldn't buy it on credit like most people do."

"Smart man," said Delora, rolling onto her back.

"So when are you guys getting hitched?" Sophie asked.

"We were thinking about next spring." She paused and studied the two women. "I'd appreciate it if both of you would stand with me."

Sophie and Delora looked at one another. "Of course we will, Clary. You're family," Sophie said.

"No, I mean, really stand with me. Get hitched. Not legal, of course, and I know y'all say you're already married in spirit, but let's do it up right, with a big party."

"Marry me, Delora?" Sophie asked, gazing at Delora with loving eyes.

Delora gazed back just as lovingly. "Of course, Sophie. Anytime, anyplace."

Bella Books, Inc.

Women. Books. Even Better Together.

P.O. Box 10543
Tallahassee, FL 32302

Phone: 800-729-4992
www.bellabooks.com

Printed in the USA
CPSIA information can be obtained
at www.ICGtesting.com
JSHW082155140824
68134JS00014B/252